Gun Ball Hill

Other Books by Ellen Cooney

Small Town Girl
All the Way Home
The Old Ballerina
The White Palazzo

Hardscrabble Books—Fiction of New England

G. F. Michelsen, *Hard Bottom*

Don Mitchell, *The Nature Notebooks*

Anne Whitney Pierce, *Rain Line*

Kit Reed, *J. Eden*

Rowland E. Robinson (David Budbill, ed.), *Danvis Tales: Selected Stories*

Roxana Robinson, *Summer Light*

Rebecca Rule, *The Best Revenge: Short Stories*

Catharine Maria Sedgwick (Maria Karafilis, ed.), *The Linwoods: or, "Sixty Years Since" in America*

R. D. Skillings, *How Many Die*

R. D. Skillings, *Where the Times Goes*

Lynn Stegner, *Pipers at the Gates of Dawn: A Triptych*

Theodore Weesner, *Novemberfest*

W. D. Wetherell, *The Wisest Man in America*

Edith Wharton (Barbara A. White, ed.), *Wharton's New England: Seven Stories and* Ethan frome

Thomas Williams, *The Hair of Harold Roux*

Suzi Wizowaty, *The Round Barn*

GUN BALL HILL

A novel by

ELLEN COONEY

University Press of New England

HANOVER AND LONDON

Published by University Press of New England,
One Court Street, Lebanon, NH 03766
www.upne.com
© 2004 by Ellen Cooney
Printed in the United States of America

5 4 3 2 1

Library of Congress Cataloging-in-Publication Data

Cooney, Ellen.
Gun Ball Hill : a novel / by Ellen Cooney.
    p.   cm. — (Hardscrabble books)
ISBN 1–58465–356–6 (cloth : alk. paper)
    1. Maine—History—Colonial period, ca. 1600–1775—Fiction.   I. Title.
II. Series.
PS3553.O5788G86 2004
813'.54—dc22   2004007938

To Noah Lukeman, for being there
and to my dad, Will Cooney, for his inspiration

Gun Ball Hill

ᴄMASSACRE

T HEY WANTED A PILOT to steer them up the Kennebec, stopping at forts along the way. They weren't novices, but they
knew what they were in for if they tried it on their own, without a
local. So they came out of the woods and threw a coat on his head.

This was fourteen years ago. They had lumber, furs, rum, corn,
guns, dried cod, taken from Maine and bound for English troops
in Canada. The war against the French was looking like it wouldn't
be over soon. The Mowlans held on to the illusion that it did not
concern them.

Lavinia thought he'd come back in just a couple of weeks. It did
not occur to her that the English would harm a colonist. Every day
that was not the day he came back became one more day when she
told herself, "He'll come back tomorrow."

She never imagined he might have been killed. She felt sure she
would have known it, without being told. After they took him, the
child she was pregnant with did not survive.

It was one thing for them to think they could say, "Pay our bills
for us," or, "We own you," and try to take American money. It was
one thing to suddenly put taxes on what the colonists read, what
they drank, what they imported, what went on in their courts as
legal documents. But it was something else to jump out of the
trees and take a man.

Fourteen years ago, it would have seemed unbelievable that
Massachusetts and, by extension, its colony of the Province of
Maine, would exist in a state of martial law. But the signs had been
there all along. It used to feel normal for people in the towns and

villages to think of England as "home," in a dewy-eyed, sentimental, envious way, like modern-day great-grandchildren of an Adam and Eve, who knew they'd never go to Paradise themselves, but it was nice to yearn for it anyway.

"The English have a genius for prisons," he would tell her.

They took him at 4:00 in the afternoon. A summer day. August 19.

Lavinia was with him. They were coming up the road from the village on foot. There was an inn in Grilleyville, which wasn't really a town, as it only had five houses and a blockhouse, and the tavern. They'd had lunch there. Their own town, Tibbetston, was mostly farms, but it had a blacksmith—their friend, Jacques Wabanaki. It also had a small mill for grinding corn, and the docks, a boatyard, and a tannery.

The date the town was first settled was 1619. Perhaps because of Jacques, who was half Indian (and not Wabanaki specifically, that he knew of, although he called himself by the name of that tribe), the town was never attacked in the raids, like most of the others. The Mowlans had been trading with Wabanakis for years, and William had called himself "brother" to three Indians his own age. But that was in the past. It had been a long time since the Mowlans had Indians for neighbors.

William was born here. Lavinia had come up from the town of York to what felt, at first, like an overwhelming nightmare of wilderness, with too much water and sky. She had not felt overwhelmed for long. She and William had been married for a little over a year when they took him.

She had stopped on the way up the hill to pick blueberries. To one side, in the calmness, in the pale yellow sunlight, the bay shimmered flatly, like dark, perfect glass. On the other side was the Kennebec River, as huge and strong as a watery, tidal, salty god.

It was said there'd been many dispatches to London that tried to explain what this river in Maine was really like, but no one, except those who came and saw it for themselves, believed the descriptions were accurate.

William had gone ahead of his wife, mindlessly, stretching his legs and widening his step. Some of the berries Lavinia picked were overripe, and stained her fingers. It had been a good year for berries.

When they took him, she was licking berry juice off her thumb. The last thing she saw him doing that day on his own was walking, just walking ahead of her toward home, as springy and sure of himself as a boy. He would never do that again.

Someone must have told them about him, that there was no river pilot, who was a white man, who knew the river as he did. "A Tibbetston farmer and boatman of unusual height, with the two barns and the biggest fish shed, and with a wife that reads and writes like a man, on the hill that doesn't have a name, where Surrey Road goes up between the bay and the river."

Or maybe it was simpler. "Who you want is a man named William Mowlan."

William Mowlan. The initials of his name were the stars of the constellation Cassiopeia, which was sometimes a W, and sometimes an M. It felt good to Lavinia to have a husband whose name was in the sky.

For the time he was gone, she did not look up at night in clear weather, not even once. She would only look up at fog, at storm clouds. She really had thought there was a God. She had thought that the proof of an actual, fair God was right over her head at night, in the stars and changeable planets, and the wide, white carpet of the Milky Way, which swirled in the sky so close to the top of the hill, she used to feel she might hold up her hand and touch it.

She would never have believed it was possible for one human being to love another the way she loved her husband. She was six months pregnant when they took him. He had wanted to name the child, if a girl, for her. Sometimes he called her by her childhood nickname: Vinna. Sometimes he said her name in three syllables, like everyone else did: La-vin-ya. But it was best when he said it in four. La-vin-ee-ah. The child she was pregnant with was a girl. She didn't give her a name.

They came out of the woods on the bay side. They must have been in hiding, waiting. There were six of them. One of them had taken off his coat, and had slung it on his shoulder, and it seemed for a moment that they were lost. They were not armed. They were very young, maybe eighteen or twenty. Lavinia's first thought was that the soldier might have taken off the coat because of the heat.

Even as William turned to meet them, they threw the coat on his head and tied the sleeves behind him. They had a litter, dragging behind them, which Lavinia hadn't noticed until they were putting him on it. The litter was made with a five-feet-long strip of canvas, which must have been part of a sail. It was attached to two poles. They also had rope. It took them no more than half a minute to secure him. They were shipmen, they'd crossed an ocean, they knew how to tie knots.

They looked as if they'd done this kind of thing before. Four of them carried the litter. Two of them held on to his legs, which were far too long for the canvas. Lavinia knew exactly how long it was by the length of his legs that didn't fit.

They ran with him into the woods on the other side of the road, toward the river. They had horses waiting for them, tied to trees. They left the poles of the litter behind, but took the canvas.

If she hadn't been pregnant, she could have run after them faster. She was tall herself; when she stood beside her husband, the top of her head was level with his shoulder. But running after them faster would not have helped.

The Englishmen disappeared very quickly with him. She would never remember that she'd been screaming and calling. For the rest of her life, she would only be able to speak in a voice barely louder than a whisper. People who met her for the first time thought she did this because she was flower-like, shy.

She didn't go hungry. People from the town were always coming by. Jacques Wabanaki and his wife, Naomi, looked after her, and considered her a part of their family. Her brother, Patrick, and her sister, Josephine, who was always called Jossey, came to stay with her for a while, and didn't push her to go back to town life.

Her mother had died long ago in childbirth—of another child who hadn't lived. She had never stopped missing her mother. Her father, Robert Rouse, ran a sawmill near York: he was a hearty, good man, and he'd made sure his children were educated, even though he was not. This especially applied to Lavinia, the first-born. "Lavinia got the brains, Patrick got the good looks, charm, and imagination, and Jossey got the spunk, the wit, and good nerves," he would say of them, as if, altogether, his three children made up a perfect person. He bought Lavinia all the books she wanted, with money that couldn't really be spared, and never complained of the expense. Almost everything Lavinia read in her youth came from England.

She would wish she had a different language. When William had been missing for almost a year, Robert Rouse took sick. Pneumonia. His lungs were clogged with sawdust. Lavinia did not go down the coast to him, not even when she knew he was dying. Patrick was with him, and so was Jossey. Lavinia didn't dare leave the farm. On the day she learned her father was dead, she went out to the woods and stripped bark off a hemlock and pressed her face against the damp, strong, pungent wood. The smell of it was the same as her father's skin and hair and clothes.

The sawmill was closed, then sold. Jossey married John Avens and went to Boston. Patrick took to the sea, and soon captained his own boat. He went to Canada twice to try to find William, and failed.

William was gone for seventeen months. Like his wife, he had hoped for the best. He had thought that they'd release him as soon as he got them up the river, as if they had only borrowed him, temporarily.

In the seventeen months he was with them, he was never off their ship. He navigated for them as well as if he were doing it for himself, and even when he was alone at the helm, and could have caused them all to be destroyed, he didn't. He didn't even think of it.

When they seized him, when the coat was thrown on his head and he found himself trapped, he didn't panic. He accepted the fact that sooner or later, like a storm, this would pass. For him there was no other option.

He might have stayed alive because his brain would not admit the possibility of anything else. On the ship, some part of him was almost always roped, and he felt lucky that they had not had iron chains. When they finally let him go, they said simply, "We've beaten the French, we've beaten the Indians, and now, as we know what we're doing, go home, we don't need you anymore."

When he came back, he had one foot. He felt lucky that they had not taken both, and that the place above his ankle healed so well. When they'd cut off his right foot, a surgeon was on the ship who had trained at the Royal College.

William kept looking for things to say he was lucky about. He was a fair-minded man, lean and spare, and slow to raise his temper. He'd never change the way he accepted the things that happened to him—quietly, almost passively, without question, without rage. The workings of human beings were the same to him as the weather. Maybe it was because, unlike his wife, he had not grown up in a town. Maybe it was a little more complicated. He was fully a man of the coast, of the woods, of the river, of the tides, of immensity. He was the bravest person Lavinia had ever known, and the best.

But Lavinia was not the same as he was. She knew that you didn't always have to accept everything the same way. There was a difference, she knew, between a thunderstorm, or an ice storm in winter, or a sudden, terrible, blinding fog, and the heart of a man who would pick up a sword and cut off the foot of another, because he didn't want him to run away, and you don't need feet to drive a warship. It was the difference between something in the world that was natural, which you couldn't do anything about, and something that was evil, which you could.

To William they were both the same thing. Not to his wife, and it wasn't only abstractly.

She managed the farm in his absence. She let some of the fields go, but maintained the corn and potatoes and apple trees. She fished in the bay. She went down to the clam flats and learned to be at home in the muck; she learned to live with pain in her back and her legs from digging.

Most of all, she held her ground against Samuel Leyson, her nearest neighbor, a loyalist, who owned four merchant ships—lumber, rum, and people. He'd made a fortune in the trade with the West Indies. He was a pig-eyed little man who refused to call where he lived a farm. He called it his estate. He wore English clothes instead of homespun, and rode his horse in the English way, and considered the well-kept acres of the Mowlans' farm with open greed. He came over with gifts, which Lavinia never accepted. After William had been gone just a month, Leyson had the idea that Lavinia should start calling herself a widow.

There were somewhere between ten and twenty people on his farm who worked for him, Africans, whom he'd bought the way he'd buy a plow or a horse. He was the only one in all the coastal towns who kept slaves, and he was not outside the law to do this. It was the law that all subjects of the crown of England had the right. Samuel Leyson believed this right had come from God. Lavinia hated him.

She did not conceal her feelings in any way. She felt that a thick, invisible, stony shell must have formed itself down the length of her body, covering everything. "Lavinia's growing hard without William," people said. She learned how to handle a gun.

The day William came back did not cancel out the hardness; it just changed it. He laughed when Lavinia told him that Leyson had been sniffling around like a skunk, courting her. He laughed even harder when she described the last time he showed up at the door, with his hair powdered, in his best English frock-coat: and he found himself staring down the barrel of an excellent rifle from Pennsylvania.

William threw away the crutches he'd got from some nuns in Quebec. He made himself new ones, of oak, and soon trained himself to walk with only one. Lavinia asked him, only once, around the time he let her near him again, "What did they do to you?"

She didn't mean the sword that took his right foot, or the scars on his buttocks and back, or the teeth in his mouth that were missing, or the stomach that took months to accept the full eating of a meal. She meant, "What did they do to you that's worse than the scars and wounds I can see?"

And he answered, and would never speak of it again, "The English have a genius for prisons."

He did not let her touch him, really touch him, for almost as many months as he'd been gone.

But then came children. They felt they were lucky, lucky people. Nothing, they felt, would harm them again, because the worst of what could be done had happened already. William had come back. They made a family.

Robert was first: he was ten now, his mother's eldest sweet boy. He took after his father, and was solemn and responsible, and took no feeling lightly, but weighed everything carefully. A shy, proud boy, he always made sure no one else was around when he went to his mother, in a moment of grief or uncertainty, to put his head on her shoulder, and be patted. "He would be the one to take on the farm, after us," his parents said of him.

Then came Seth, eight now, a lean little noisy, never-tired boy, who never followed his brother about, but would be absolutely his own person, with the spunky, funny nature of a chipmunk, and the natural agility of an otter or mink. They were always comparing him to animals. "Seth would be a woodsman, perhaps a lumber-man, and must marry a very patient, very tolerant woman, who may perhaps calm him down," they had said.

And then Nathaniel, who was seven, and fair and quiet and dreamy. He took after his mother's family; he was a Rouse, through and through. He resembled in features Lavinia's mother and sister, and would not be Natty (as everyone tried to call him). He wanted his whole name pronounced, in four syllables, drawn out slowly, with love and special attention, the way he liked to hear his father say "La-vin-ee-ah." He was the smart one. "He should be someone who must perhaps be sent away to college," they said of him.

After all those boys—and the three of them often felt like a dozen—came the girls. Mary was four now. If her parents had expectations that a daughter would be any less trouble than a boy, they were profoundly wrong. Dark-eyed, black-haired Mary was born thinking of herself as a creature who belonged with the river—not near it, or on it, but *in* it. No one ever actually taught her to swim; she just knew. Well-meaning neighbors mentioned to William and Lavinia that perhaps it was not a good idea to let a child her age venture into the river, with those currents. Her parents would answer, "She knows what she is doing." "I want to be a seal when I grow up," she often said. Everyone pretty much agreed. "Mary will be as good at fishing as a seal," they felt. "And God will have to find her a husband who can cook and clean and keep house, and be civilized, for she may never do so, or be so, herself."

And then came the baby, Margaret, almost three now, who favored her father in looks, but had the largest set of lungs ever put into a human baby's chest. It was never that she was whiny, or cried too much. It was just that, when she started to talk, with all the rest of them around her, all larger and older, she did not engage in talking, but in shouting. She defied her baby-ness as soon as she was able. She was tiny in physical size: she was a fairy-child. It was still too soon to make predictions for her, but her parents felt she'd grow up to be musical, and would sing. Or perhaps she'd be in charge of something large and complicated, like a sawmill, and follow in the footsteps of her grandfather Rouse. Margaret was only just now starting to walk. They had feared that something was wrong with her, but she'd been waiting for someone to give her an oak branch her own size, with a shoulder-rest, so she could stick it under her arm and move about like her father. It was her brother Nathaniel who had thought of this, having put himself, in his own words, into his sister's clever mind.

William's parents had been dead for years; he had been an only child, and had no other kin. He made up for that. It often felt that everything he'd gone through, even the worst of it, had been compensated for. "I would cut off my other foot if God wanted it for the price of my wife and my children," he would say.

As for Lavinia, it often happened to her that she wished she had a God to pray to, just to be able to say, "Thank you for what I have."

But all the same, the fact that her husband came back alive from Canada was not enough. The fourteen years between now, and the time they had taken him, were, for her, fourteen years of waiting. Waiting for the time when she'd finally find a way to answer back to them for what they had done.

Because she was a woman she was barred from town meetings. William went to them because she couldn't.

He went down to Falmouth, and to York, and in spite of himself, he spoke up, to please her. He raised his voice to agree with the votes saying there could be no taxation levied on Maine by any government but their own: the government of Massachusetts. But he was convinced that the militias forming all over Maine were unnecessary, were just so much hot air.

He believed, in spite of what they'd done to him, that the English would prove to be reasonable, as if a message would come from Parliament any day, saying, "You are correct to say we are treating you Americans wrongly, and now we'll go away and leave you be."

It wasn't that he was optimistic. He was waiting for the troubles to blow away, for every new law or restriction to be lifted. He'd been a prisoner, he'd been tied in a watery hell, he had survived, he'd come home, he had his family and, by extension, Patrick and the Avenses in Boston, and the Wabanakis, and the rest of their friends, who loved him. He had the farm, he had the land, he had the woods, he had the sky. Why should he agitate himself about laws and taxes?

But Lavinia would say, "We are not English. We should pay no English taxes." To William—and in a way, she envied his reasoning— the demand for money, along with all the new rules, was the same as if a thief came banging on the door, crying out, "Here I am to rob you! Invite me in!" If that happened, William would open the door and talk to him, while his wife would be fetching the gun.

He'd been gone when the English ship arrived at Falmouth with the first batch of new stamps—stamps that were meant to be purchased by colonists, with the money going to London. The new laws were saying that without these stamps, no legal document could be legal, no newspaper could be sold, no degree could be given by a college: to him, coming home from a hell on earth, it was comical that anyone in England would suppose they could actually get away with this.

He thought it was childish that when that stamp-ship had anchored, it was boarded by Maine men, mob-like, thug-like, and the trunk of stamps was seized and hidden. He said, "They should have just ignored it."

Sometimes Lavinia caught him looking at her a certain way, at odd moments, as she cooked, or patted one of the children, or cut fish, or sat at the table reading, and she knew that he was afraid of her. He was afraid of what she might do, as if the things that had happened fourteen years ago were all contained in a pocket, deep inside her, like a pouch of gunpowder, waiting for a flint.

He didn't know what to make of it when their brother-in-law

from Boston—John Avens, Jossey's husband—came up with the idea that Lavinia should write articles for a newspaper where he had friends.

For over a week now, she'd been writing the first article, by the hearth in the big main room. Lavinia was thirty-six years old, but she felt she needed to call her age "thirty-four-and-a-half." She felt she should deduct from her life the seventeen months he'd been gone.

"Write for the newspaper the same way you write us letters," was John Avens's plan.

She wouldn't use her name, and it wasn't because she was a woman. Hardly anyone used names. Except for the leaders like Samuel Adams, most people who wrote for the paper had an alias. "Letters from A Mouth of the Province of Maine," it would be called.

And the fourteen years of waiting for something to do became, almost instantly, a sort of power, like a sail on a mast that was waiting for wind.

Now it was morning. Autumn. It was early October, 1774.

There was much to be done. Lavinia lit the fire in the hearth in the big main room, and left a pot of cooked apples and a plate of corn cakes on the table for everyone's breakfast. It was just after dawn, and everyone else was still asleep, even the baby.

She dressed quickly, and left quietly, and headed down to the bigger of the two barns, where the animals were. The cold, watery air felt wonderful on her face. There was a light fog through the fields, making everything ghostly and lovely.

The older of the two oxen needed shoeing, and she was going to take it herself down the hill to Jacques Wabanaki. Without shoes, the ox would never manage to pull a sledge through the woods—a sledge full of logs, bound for Boston.

John Avens was planning to come up here next week, alone, to arrange for the logs to be brought out of Maine. He considered himself a likely choice for this task: so far in Boston and up the coast, the English didn't know that preachers like John were turning themselves into radicals. They thought that all ministers of all the New England churches were Tory.

The logs would be taken to Boston as firewood, along with every sort of provision they could muster: corn, apples, dried berries, dried fish, hay for horses from down in the salt marshes, squash, pumpkins, smoked turkey.

Some of the trees in the woods had been marked last year, by British surveyors, with the broad painted arrow of the king, as if the towering white pines of Maine had one natural purpose: to be masts for enemy ships. It was a criminal act to take anything an agent of the king had marked "Ours." The Tibbetston men no longer cared; they'd cut them down.

Then this: "You will buy your tea from only us, and we are going to tax you on it."

In December, colonials—disguised, anonymous—dumped 340 chests of East India tea, from three English ships, into the harbor of Boston: the tea was nearly 90,000 pounds in weight, and was worth 9,000 pounds of English money.

The government was suspended. Governor Hutchinson was gone in disgrace to London and the new governor, General Thomas Gage, was setting up a new capital in Salem.

The weight of royal might was hitting hard. The Port of Boston had been closed since June. By English law, nothing was allowed to come and go. Boston was supposed to be isolated, like a patient with smallpox, who must not infect anyone else, and who'd eventually turn over and sigh, one last time, and be still.

But that was not what was happening. From all over—New York, Baltimore, Charleston, Richmond, and now Maine, food and guns and supplies were being arranged for. Provisions were being smuggled in daily. It must have amazed the British that they could not make the sort of prison they'd imagined.

For the first time, the colonies were saying that they were not simply colonies, each one intact on its own. Like fish, they were finding out that it's a better idea to school together: maybe it was temporary, to cope with a crisis; but maybe it was something that would last. John Avens told his parishioners he'd be away next week in Maine to simply visit his wife's family.

To Lavinia, in his last letter, John had promised to tell her everything of what it was like on the Night of the Tea. That was what they called it.

All Lavinia knew so far were facts. He'd only planned to watch, but could not. He had rubbed ashes on his face, and wrapped himself in a blanket instead of a coat, and borrowed a hatchet from a neighbor and rebelled—against the Tea Act, against those taxes, against England. He had first smeared his face with oil from the supper pan, so that the ashes would stick. Many of the others were dressed as Mohawks.

"They were playing, like boys," was William's feeling. And, "It's really just trouble with quarreling, money-hungry merchants, and does not concern us."

He was right to point out, too, that the tax was a small one, and people in Maine prefer cider, and the tea from England was even cheaper than the Dutch tea smuggled in all along. And restitution would sooner or later have to be paid for the destruction of property.

But he was wrong, Lavinia felt, to think it didn't matter. He had no special questions to put to John Avens. He wanted John to keep quiet about the tea—about everything—in front of the children, as if they were too young to understand such things, as if they weren't wild with excitement already. All week, in anticipation of their uncle, they'd been down at the river, all five of them, pretending that the Kennebec was the sheltered, quiet water of Boston. Screaming with joy, they pretended that the sticks in their hands were tomahawks, and the big stones were crates of tea, which they were breaking open and dumping out.

Lavinia had wanted to know more than just facts. She had wanted to know what it was like that night, as clearly as if she'd been there herself. She wanted to know what it felt like to cross the line between thinking, feeling, and knowing, and taking a sort of power into one's own hands, and doing something. She'd decided that, if John held back on her, and didn't describe things fully, she would have told him, "Then you can't take our logs and all that food."

Lavinia knew from her sister that John didn't want his parishioners to know what he'd been up to. He had trained to be a minister at Harvard College, and was now fully ordained. But Lavinia had the feeling that John's ideas on God might have changed, and might be fairly well close to her own.

The day the English established their blockade to seal Boston, bells of every church, including John's, had tolled, all sad and heavy and resentful, as if a hundred funerals were taking place at once. Now there were 3,000 English soldiers in and around Boston. But they weren't in Boston only.

Here in the bay, near Grilleyville, there were three warships. Foraging parties had been spotted last week in Augusta and Dresden, and it was now being said that 400 hungry Englishmen—maybe more—were on their way from Canada to lower Massachusetts, and would stop in Maine for as long as they liked, looking to be sheltered and fed.

It wasn't as if the English had barracks in Maine. It wasn't as if there were inns enough—inns belonging to loyalists—to garrison them. By law, English law, a colonist who refused the access of his house, barns, and land to an officer was a colonist who was committing a criminal act.

Just yesterday, one of the Mowlans' farmhands had been haying in the lower twenty acres when two soldiers appeared in the road on horseback: officers, with pistols. The farmhand had found them well-rested, well-fed; he'd recognized the horses, which belonged to Samuel Leyson. The direction they'd come from was Leyson's place. One of them asked, as if stopping in a neighborly way, "How much cod was dried for your fish shed this autumn?"

"No English," the farmhand replied, haltingly, as if he were talking about language. In fact he was Irish. He was one of the founders of the Tibbetston militia. He was ready to go up to the field where William was working—to get him, and get others as well—but the officers turned and rode away.

That was all Lavinia had been told. But she suspected there was more to it. William came in late for supper last night, and wouldn't say where he'd been, except, "There was a small piece of business near the fort."

What business? The militia had been talking about adapting their rifles to be fitted with bayonets; there was talk, too, of seizing the Grilleyville fort, somehow.

Lavinia felt she had a right to know whatever the men did. Wasn't she directly involved now, as a newspaper writer, and shouldn't the

"Mouth of the Province of Maine" be informed of whatever secrets they were keeping?

William, not surprisingly, was stubborn. "With several other men, I had a small conversation last night with an officer."

What officer? From one of the warships?

"It was not a thing of significance. The officer we spoke to was only looking for food. This is Maine. The war with the French and the Indians is over. Nothing else is going to go badly for us," he said.

His eyes looked untroubled. If he were looking at storm clouds forming blackly over the river, he'd say, "Might rain, though it'll be sure to pass us over."

But he'd already ordered padlocks from Connecticut to secure the two barns, the corn shed, the cider shed, and the fish shed. The padlocks hadn't arrived. Except for the late apples and pumpkins and potatoes and beets, the harvest was in.

"From a Mouth of the Province of Maine, for the Boston Gazette & Country Journal," Lavinia had written.

She felt confident one minute about what she was doing, and unbearably nervous the next. The news had circulated widely that she would write for the paper, and the last time she'd been down into town, she realized that probably everyone from Augusta to York knew about it: the first-ever Maine-to-Boston correspondent, speaking her mind in print—and their minds, too.

Plenty of people were happy to offer her their thoughts, feelings, and particular phrases. The feeling she'd get was something like the way her body felt when she was just about to make love, although she never said so to William. Sometimes when they were together that way, it could be nothing but an act of necessity, with no more tenderness or pleasure than couplings of horses, dogs. But sometimes they were slow about it, and elegant, too, with all their clothes off.

But still, it always seemed to happen to her that the anticipation of making love with her husband was keener, deeper, and more wonderful, than anything they actually did. Maybe it was those seventeen months without him that had done this to her. She'd got used to the power of desire. She had wondered if, like a writer, she'd really be able to transform this desire into the right sort of words.

She couldn't stop thinking about the newspaper. She wondered how often they'd expect her to produce articles. She wondered if people would read her words just in Boston, or in New York as well, and Philadelphia, where they were holding a Congress.

"Continental Congress," they called it. It had started last month, on September 5. The only news to have reached Maine so far was that the representatives of the colonies—Massachusetts, Delaware, New Hampshire, Rhode Island, New Jersey, Pennsylvania, Maryland, Virginia, and North and South Carolina—might draw up, formally, some sort of Declaration of Rights. Would her first article be printed in time to reach the Congress?

She'd been reading the *Gazette* for years; Jossey and John always sent it to her. Would her article be printed near an article by Samuel Adams and if so, how was that going to feel?

And that masthead! It was designed from an engraving by Paul Revere. It was a picture of a fierce, stern, strong Minerva, the Roman goddess of wisdom and force, and the only goddess Lavinia knew of who was always shown in armor, with a breastplate, which no earthly thing could pierce.

Paul Revere had made a marvelous depiction. In Minerva's left hand she held a spear and, with her right hand, she opened the door of a cage to free a bird. On the point of the spear, as if hung there, as on a hook, was a hat. Everyone knew what it was. The "Liberty Cap," it was called.

Lavinia knew that John Avens would not tell the newspaper that the writer of the new articles was a woman, and she didn't mind. She had wondered what sort of solicitations would be printed in columns near her words. She hoped they'd be appropriate. In the most recent copy of the newspaper, among advertisements for potash, clocks, soap, wines, cheese, were things, she felt, that *should not be.*

It was one thing to see notices like, "A woman of Boston with a choice young Breast of milk, would be glad to go into a Gentleman's Family, to Suckle." That was something to feel sorry for.

It was something else to see, "Ran away from me, a Negro, 5 feet 9 inches high. Had on when he went away, a striped cotton shirt, plush breeches, black stockings, and Plated Buckles. Whoever returns him shall have 2 Dollars Reward."

And, "To be sold: A Likely Negro Lad, 17 Years, Speaks English, with Infant age 3 mos. to be given."

There'd been dozens of these notices, in every issue of the paper. How many people in Boston were just like Samuel Leyson? How could a newspaper that called itself the voice of fairness and justice allow for this sort of thing?

The Night of the Tea had been arranged in the offices of the editor of the *Gazette*. Maybe they didn't extend their ideas of what was just and fair to all persons.

People were saying the new Congress was going to abolish all holding of slaves. Lavinia had wondered, should that be put into her first article, something about slaves? The answer she gave herself was "yes."

And now, in the morning quiet, happy to be alone, she was getting the ox, to bring down the hill to Jacques. He wouldn't take money, but Lavinia planned to pay for the iron and the shoeing in barter, with fish the two older boys would bring in.

Robert and Seth had planned to go out on the river today, later on, when the air would be warmer. The two of them maintained their own boat. (Nathaniel didn't care for water, and Mary could not be allowed on a boat, as she would only jump overboard.) William had taught them to fish by explaining what to do, not by showing them. William never once left dry land, not since he'd come back.

Lavinia had always loved dawn silence, especially with a light, salty fog. The dogs, for a change, weren't leaping around at her heels: the spaniel and two hounds were sleeping in the house, against Lavinia's better judgment. This would not be allowed to become a habit, she felt, as much as the children always begged.

But the spaniel had gotten into trouble in the woods with something bigger than itself, and more vicious—a badger or a fox. The wounds on its back were far from healed. William had put it in the lean-to at the back of the house, and the two hounds wouldn't think of being excluded; it was the grandest possible holiday to them. Whole nights behind the hearth! With the children!

Maybe, Lavinia thought, she'd find a way in her second or third article to compare the rights of a farm dog with the rights of a colonist. People liked to read parables.

Her head kept flooding with words, but at last her first article was finished. She'd promised John she'd have it ready when he came for the logs and provisions. "Our town of Tibbetston . . . ," it began.

"Our town of Tibbetston, at the Kennebec River, by the Bay we call Glenmarry, has for population, since the time of the Indian Peace, a hundred seventy-one souls, counting all above eleven years in age. Excepting one neighbor, with hard little eyes to reflect the size of his Brain, who pledges himself as English, yet never once stepped foot abroad, we hold no slaves. We await news of the Congress wherein slavery in these Colonies is abolished.

"We are not English. Of the hundred seventy-one of us, a hundred seventy-one, for a birthplace, have this Province of Maine. A hundred seventy-one have for parents either those born the same, or those of diverse colonies, or from the French in Quebec, or from Scotland. Not a soul of us, not even our False-Lordly Neighbor, can look at this mighty River, or these Forests, and rightly know England as Home. London stays as strange to our mind as an Athens or Rome of Old.

"Yet they would have us enslaved. Yet the Red-Coated Soldier with an alien tongue, though the language we speak be the same, would appear at our door to tell us, by Law of the faraway King, that whatever of ours he desires must be his for the taking.

"In England the property taxation by Representation is tax put on those small minority of landowners. We landowners here are almost all of us. We cannot be measured by English terms.

"In saying the Colonists are not to be emancipated from their dependence on England, would Parliament think us clinging children who would suffer a punishment and be glad for it? In calling us Nothing but Farmers, Cowards, and Ruffians, who pose no real threat, by chance would the English have awareness of a Gun in the hands of we Colonials?

"So let me say this. Let them not fear us, the better to have them Astonished when they learn, in the Province of Maine, *we do not miss a target when we Aim*. We drink no tea. Even now, as I write this, we have further news of the Closing of Boston, the Suspension of Massachusetts's Governing, the so-called Right of English officers never to be denied entry to the Home, Shop, Barn, or Storehouse of a Colonist. We know of the English hand at the throat, and say this: Should you think you strangle us when you squeeze, *we find better ways to breathe.*"

It was never going to be published in the paper. She had left it on the bedroom bureau for William to read, while she was out with the ox. She had planned that part carefully. She hadn't wanted him to read it in front of her, because she knew how he would look at her. She knew what memories would be stirred in him, which he'd want to always be buried.

She looked up. Smoke from the farmhouse hearth rose steadily, in thin, languid curls. The sun had cleared the top of the woods-covered hill behind the back fields, breaking through the fog in a lustrous, liquidy orange-pink. "We have got to give that hill a name."

Lavinia found herself talking out loud, and the sound of her own voice made her jump. She had to laugh at herself for that. The air smelled of water, salt, hay, burned-pine, dung, fish. Barn swallows were rustling. Somewhere in the nearby woods, a thrush was singing melodically, with a throat that was the same as a flute. There was no place on earth, she felt, more beautiful than her home.

A warm glow had fallen on the pines, the oaks. The sunlight in the trees along the top of the hill had a thin, white-yellow sheen. Maybe they should name the hill "Daybreak," she thought, or maybe, even better, one of the Wabanaki Indians might turn up, and could tell them the word, or words, for "the hill the sun comes up from."

At the door of the barn, she called out to the animals to let them know that she was there, that she was about to open the door. It was too bad that an animal didn't know ahead of time what was going to happen to it, she felt. Shoeing an ox was almost a luxury, like pewter dishes instead of wood.

But the old ox always loved the adventure of a trip into town, even if it meant the trauma at the blacksmith's of being secured and hoisted in the ox sling. Things would have been simpler if you could shoe an ox like a horse: but the poor big beast couldn't support itself on three legs. It would be led into a huge contraption that looked like an oversized gallows, with straps hung on pulleys to suspend it in the air. It would bellow its brains out, but who knew what it would think? There was always the possibility it might enjoy the sensation of giving up its own weight, of being lifted.

What an absurdity, with so many other things to be thinking about! An ox's pleasure!

Lavinia heard no sound. She had no indication that she was being watched, and crept up on, and then surrounded. Then she saw movement: crouching figures behind one of the haystacks, and more of them behind the old dory in the yard, the one Seth and Robert had brought up from the dock for repairs.

Then her eyes made out faces, smeared red, Indian-style; and leather breeches, and furs thrown over shoulders, and blankets, too, instead of coats. She saw feathers, and a quick glimpse of a part of a man's bare chest, with white, pale skin that looked like it had never before been bare in sunlight.

Those men were not Indians. She didn't need to recognize the state of their paleness to understand this. No hands took hold of her. It wasn't like what happened to William. She was not seized. They wouldn't carry her off.

There were guns in the barn and it occurred to her that she might be able to get herself inside, quickly. The one thought she had was that these men must not be allowed to enter the house. She thought, "I must stop them."

Even if she had wanted to cry out, she would not have been able to do it. She didn't hear the sounds of the shots. The power to hear had ceased. There was only one thing: an explosion of colors from the back of her head to the front. The colors were aurora-like, in a riot of different shades: yellow and red and orange, and then a blazing, astonishing white, as if the sun had left the sky at the top of the hill, and entered her.

When the second shot hit her, not in the head this time, but just below her left shoulder, she was already tilting sideways, like a tree that was chopped, and only needed a slight push to topple over.

Then they headed for the house.

CHAPTER II

THE WABANAKIS

J ACQUES WABANAKI DIDN'T give a damn what anyone thought of his name. He gave it to himself around the age of eleven, having decided to emotionally bind himself to the biggest tribe in Maine. Wabanaki Indians were also called Abenaki, with, for white people, four or five different spellings. Jacques liked "Wabanaki" better because it had no variants. Before he chose his name, he'd been called Little Moose, because of the way the top half of him did not match his short, bow-shaped legs. It was true that the droopy, woeful-looking shape of his face was somewhat mooselike.

At sixty, if you didn't count his height, he still gave the impression of a massive, broad, bulky man; his upper arms were incredibly thick. His face looked something like two different faces joined together lengthwise, and not quite fitting evenly. One eye drooped significantly lower than the other. It always seemed that the left side of his skin was darker than the other, as if he stood every day in profile under a blazing sun. His nose had been broken twice and never healed correctly, and it looked it. He had been raised—as an orphaned infant—by Jesuits in Norridgewock.

"We found you like Moses, but instead of in a basket, we found you naked in moss beneath a tree, howling in an ungodly way," the Jesuits had told him.

They'd had in mind a future for him as a missionary, but the only thing he'd ever been drawn to was iron, as though that were naturally the one thing to match his own strength: molten iron and fire. He had set himself up as the Tibbetston blacksmith over thirty years ago. He was the only Catholic for miles.

By the door of his shop hung a small engraving of the Virgin, which the local Calvinists, and even the Anglicans, found disturbing. He told people he'd made it himself, but he'd got it in barter years ago from an Italian adventurer who'd passed through, and needed shoes for his horse. It was no pious Mary with an infant in her arms and loving, holy, maternal eyes. As rough as it was, it was a clearly earthy, lusty, self-satisfied, peasant-faced Madonna, and the lowness of the bodice of her gown did not imply breasts meant only for the suckling of Jesus. A halo was around her head, though.

The settlers of Maine had never been anything like the old Puritans of lower Massachusetts—and God knew, there were plenty of them left, as dour as ever, with tightness in every one of their muscles, especially around the eyes, as if they suffered, all of them, all the time, from constipation. Maine people were a little looser.

In fact, unlike almost every other colony, the town charters here, at least in Tibbetston and Grilleyville, did not insist on a church, and did not make it a law that townspeople had to attend Christian services every Sunday, or be seized and put into the stocks. There wasn't a church here, and there weren't any stocks. God was more or less a private matter.

But still, it was always interesting how nervous it made Jacques's customers to gaze at his Mary. At the bottom of the engraving were the words, "True Queen of the One True Son of Maine," which he'd put there with a nail. He was proud of it.

How much of himself was French and how much was Indian he'd no way of knowing, so he called it half and half. After his wife, Naomi, and their three children, the people on earth who were dearest to him were the Mowlans.

Fourteen years ago when they took William Mowlan, Jacques led a search party to find him, and when he failed (as Lavinia's brother Patrick had failed), he went home to Naomi, took out the shears, and had her cut off his long, long hair, as black as a crow and already starting to gray. It was the first time in his life he'd had a real haircut.

He did not allow it to grow back fully until the day he went down to the shore to help William off the ketch that had returned him home, one-footed and as thin as a stick.

William had looked at Jacques's head with amazement, and knew at once what he'd done to his hair, and why. The emotion William had felt had made him look away. He said, "Thank you, Jacques." And then he said, "My friend, you look worse without your hair than I look without my foot."

So Jacques grew back his hair, and kept it that way. It went down to the middle of his back. The desire to do harm to Englishmen, any Englishmen, had never left him: an enormous desire, fiery and fierce, like all his appetites.

On the morning the Mowlans were murdered, he'd been busy with a new task: outfitting bayonets on thirty muskets, stolen from the fort at Augusta last week, and belonging to the Tibbetston militia, which he was part of.

He owned four rifles, three muskets, and four pistols. There was no one along the river who could match him when it came to using a bow. He made his own arrows. The English warships in the bay did not alarm him. He was a patient man, the way all blacksmiths were patient. It was the calm, confident patience that came from pure knowledge of what power really is. Molten, hot, fiery power was what he held in his hands every day.

The news that English officers might invoke the Quartering Law, and demand that farmers and townspeople turn over food and shelter to them, didn't worry him. If a Redcoat showed up in his yard or near his pond, or approached his shop, or either of his two houses, that Redcoat, he felt, was the same as someone running after a bear. He'd only be asking for a mauling. He didn't recognize English laws. He wasn't English.

Where, he wondered, was Lavinia?

It was already 9:00 in the morning. Jacques had put in new harnesses on the ox scaffold for the shoeing. "It is not like Lavinia to be late," he was thinking. The sound of an approaching wagon brought him to the side of the road.

A two-horse wagon carrying four people and double as many trunks and valises should not have been going so fast down narrow Surrey Road, even in autumn, when the dirt was hard packed. But those horses—in spite of the whip being lashed at their backs—had to ease up their gallop as they approached the town, where the road curved past shops and houses.

They might have slowed down anyway, as if they'd decided on their own what their destination should be. The blacksmith's. Like all other horses, they distinguished between two types of people: the ones who whipped them, and the ones who did not. They knew who their friends were.

Leyson. With him in the wagon were his wife's two sisters, Sarah and Jane, and his wife herself: weak little sour-faced, sharp-tongued, always-complaining Louise, who'd come up to Tibbetston to marry Leyson seven years ago, and would never let anyone forget she was a Dudley, of the Dudleys of Salem, one of the richest of the Massachusetts merchant clans, and Tory to the root.

The younger of the sisters, Jane, was a seventeen-year-old copy of Louise—fair and delicate, and just a little less brittle, so far, and completely out of her element in Maine.

But Sarah Dudley, at twenty-two, was altogether different. Where her sisters were like ornamental little figures of insubstantial glass, Sarah had plain good looks. She was as solid and broad in the shoulders as a Maine boy, and she looked you directly in the eyes when she spoke to you.

She was gold, solid gold, Jacques always said, which was the second best compliment he could pay a human being. His own wife and their sons and the Mowlans were of a much higher order: iron, and the marvelous ore it comes from.

Sarah didn't come up often from Salem. When she did, she usually spent much of her time riding alone, or visiting the tavern in Grilleyville, or here in town, although Leyson had forbidden her to do so. Jacques had heard that she was supposed to marry a well-off Tory businessman from Salem; it was hard to imagine she really would.

And here they were, the four of them, in sunlight and dust, in the cool, clear October air, thundering along the road into town as if demons were chasing the wagon.

The horses didn't come to a stop, but turned their heads toward the blacksmith's in a greeting that was almost a plea. At the reins, Leyson was hatless, disheveled. He was balding at the top of his head. Without his English wig he looked smaller and vulnerable, the way a sheep does, when it's just been let go from being shorn.

Jacques felt some sympathy for that. It reminded him of what it had felt like—physically, on the back of his neck, and in every fiber of his being as well—when his own hair had been missing.

Leyson looked frantic, scared. His wife and Jane were clinging to their seats. They looked even paler than he was, and more terrified.

As the wagon came toward Jacques, it seemed that Sarah Dudley was going to jump off. She'd partly stood up, with her head ducked, like someone about to take a dive. At that velocity she would have landed hard, in clumps of weeds and thistles and stone—or else she might have been hoping, or trusting, that Jacques would be able to catch her, which he would have been happy to do.

Jacques shouted as loud as he could. "Leyson! Whoa! Whoa!"

"Indians!" cried Leyson. He couldn't let go of the reins; he knew what his horses would do if eased up. Instead of pointing, he tipped his head quickly backward a little, indicating the slope of Surrey Road, and the farm, and the hill that had no name.

At the same time, Sarah's two sisters grabbed hold of her, pulling her down to the seat. It seemed amazing that those weak-looking arms had any strength.

They shot by. Leyson urged the horses on harder, then shouted over his shoulder, "I had nothing to do with it!"

Jacques caught a glimpse of Sarah Dudley, trapped and clung to, looking back at him, with the same look in her eyes as the horses. Her bonnet had slipped off. Her long, curly, loose hair, streaming like a banner, was exactly the same color as the turning maple leaves she was rushing by: orange-gold. If Jacques were twenty, or even thirty, he would have run after the wagon with his arms out, fully expecting to catch up with it. It occurred to him to get on his own horse and go after it, but the impulse left him as soon as it came. He felt an awful tightening in his chest, as if his heart had suddenly clenched up.

The wagon turned the bend and disappeared. Something was wrong. What Indians? If Leyson and the women were fleeing Indians, why the trunks?

They had packed. Maybe they had packed in a hurry, which certainly seemed the case, but they had *packed*. And Leyson was using the dependable, sturdy wagon instead of one of his carriages, which were built from an elegant, English-town model, and would have broken at least one wheel on that road, at that speed. And they wouldn't have fit all those belongings in a carriage.

Jacques reached inside his shirt and rubbed at his chest. There wasn't any pain, just a knotting. He stared hard up the road as the dust settled, as if Lavinia and the ox—and perhaps a few of the children—might materialize, coming toward him, waving, calling to him.

He remembered that Lavinia had promised him river fish later on in the day, which he was very much looking forward to. He didn't fish himself, not even in his pond, not that the raccoons, and sometimes a bear, ever left him anything to try catching. He just didn't like to fish.

Naomi had already started a pot of potatoes and onions for a chowder in the outdoor hearth near their summer cabin, behind the pond. It was still warm enough to be down there, even at night. Their main house, behind the shop, was sawed wood; the summer cabin was a simple, single room, built of logs.

The room only had a bed, a table, and two chairs. When their children were growing up, they were never allowed inside. It could only be reached by boat—by their canoe, although Naomi preferred to swim across the pond. It was always a vacation to be in the log cabin. It was the one place in Jacques's life where he could sit down—or lie down, as he loved the summer bed—without any sort of fire, not even a small hearth. He loved the internal coolness of the autumn nights. They liked to sleep there, under furs, until well into November.

He told himself that Lavinia would appear. Maybe Leyson's wagon had passed her, higher up on the road? Maybe Leyson had not done the neighborly thing and slowed down and offered her a ride, towing the ox behind?

No one was in the road. The sky was an empty, piercing blue. The river fog had lifted, and there wasn't even a cloud.

Maybe Leyson hadn't meant "Indians" literally. Maybe he'd said it because he thought it was an acceptable thing to shout out, from a perverse sense of a joke?

From where he was standing, Jacques could see the cove in the bay where, almost 150 years ago, when the smithy and the houses and the town were all wilderness, a four-masted English bark had anchored. A canoe approached the huge and marvelous ship, and in it were three Wabanaki sagamores and three of their sons, teenagers.

The Indians wanted to trade. They had learned enough English to call out their intention. They had furs, fresh game, and fish. Their experience with Europeans had not been hostile. They wanted anything metal they could get: knives, pots, buckles. And anything wool, especially blankets.

The account of what happened was written by one of the Englishmen on the ship. It existed, with accounts just like it, in a box in the storeroom of the little granite Catholic church down in Portsmouth. Some New Hampshire privateer must have stolen some officer's papers, which perhaps had been meant as letters back to England. The papers had ended up with priests. Jacques went down to Portsmouth six or seven times a year, and he always said he just wanted to visit with the blacksmith there—a friend of his—but really he went to Mass. He liked to hear Latin; it was something he required.

Jacques felt that the best thing about having learned to read, which the Jesuits had forced on him, was that things that took place in the past could come up to him clearly, as if they'd only happened five minutes ago. He could see with his own eyes the words on a page that spelled out the facts of *atrocity*.

That was the word the English writer had used himself about the Indians in their canoe, paddling toward the ship, a century and a half away. A priest had copied over the original words—the original papers had long since disintegrated—but Jacques, reading, had heard echoes of an Englishman's voice.

"Atrocity." The Englishman had used it to describe his outrage because the Indians had come out in their canoe on a *Sunday*.

The English had shot them all. It never occurred to the writer of the account that an English idea of "Sabbath," and "God forbids mercantile activity on the Sabbath," might be things that applied only to themselves. Only the devil would inspire "these Savages to Willfully Defy God's Law."

In shooting three men and three boys, they were striking at Satan himself, and they were pleased to say that after taking hold of the canoe and "putting the Savages into the Water to Hastene their Plummet to Hell," they had helped themselves to the pelts, the game, which, they felt, were rightfully theirs.

Jacques had memorized that account. There were others he'd memorized partially. He had often taken his children, three sons, to the church with him. Those accounts were their earliest lessons in reading.

"Lavinia might not be coming," Jacques said, out loud. "Something is wrong."

He made up his mind to go up the hill to the farm. He left the shop to his apprentice, a fourteen-year-old boy named James, who was sweating over fire tongs he was trying, badly, to get the hang of making. Not one of Jacques's own boys had wanted anything to do with smithing, or with clamming or fishing, either. The elder two had turned to wood, and had ended up in lower Massachusetts—far, far lower, in Nantucket, where they whaled. The youngest son hadn't left Maine, but he was more than a six-day ride away, near Moosehead Lake. The elder two had married, but he had not. He trapped and hunted. Everyone took him for a full Indian.

"Where is the Mowlan ox?" James the apprentice was looking forward to it. For the first time, he was going to be allowed to handle the business of strapping it; Jacques had promised.

"I have the notion to go and fetch it myself."

Jacques went past the main house, and Naomi wasn't in there; her loom and spinning wheel, which dominated the big front room, looked as though they hadn't been touched yet that morning.

He went down the path through the woods to the pond. The pond was completely surrounded by thick stands of trees—some were oaks, but most were high, massive pines, along with solemn old giants of hemlocks, with deep-green branches hanging low.

It was private, but still, there was probably no other woman in Maine, perhaps in all the colonies, who'd do what Naomi was doing. She stood thigh-high in the water, naked. She'd started doing this in broad daylight the very day their youngest child had left home. Her old brown wool shawl and a homespun dress, a sort of shift, were hanging on a branch of a pine.

She owned a dozen dresses just like it, some in wool, some in well-tanned hides; they were the only things she ever wore. The shifts had round, low necklines, loose sleeves, no buttons, and no waistline, but were gathered around her very ample middle with a belt made of hemp, when she felt like wearing a belt.

All the shifts were beige, gray, or brown, but Naomi didn't need dyes put into her clothes to be colorful. She was colorful enough as it was. She owned two other shawls, elegant and as thick as blankets, and a few petticoats and stockings, but would only put them on when they went to someone's barn for a dance, or there was a wedding; and then Lavinia would always step in, and lend her a normal skirt, which usually had come from Jossey. Jossey was always sending clothes from Boston up to Maine.

Naomi wore moccasins instead of shoes, but around home, when it wasn't winter, she was usually barefoot. Under the shifts she often wore breeches; this was a new habit. Last year when she had finished making him a new pair, she had got it into her head to try them on herself, and liked them very much. All she'd had to do was adapt the waist to fit her. But she also owned normal ladies' drawers.

She was fifty. She'd come from a family of clam diggers down near Bath, at Winnegance. Her body was shaped forever by all the squatting, bending, and digging she had done; her back had a permanent curve. Her hands were muck-accustomed, nimble, hard.

They had chosen this land for their house—first the main one, then the cabin—because of the pond. After she'd left home, she swore that she would never live anywhere except at the edge of fresh water, and she would never pay attention to tides, and she would never eat anything that came out of mud in a shell. All through her youth, she ate clams: raw, fried in corn batter, steamed in a pot, in chowders, fried in pork fat. She had felt that her stomach was more like a gull's than a human's. She never wanted to look at a clam again, and that included mussels and quahogs. If Jacques wanted to eat those things, he had to go to the tavern or up to the Mowlans' without her.

Jacques called out to her, "Lavinia should have come by now."

She was facing the other way, and turned at the sound of his voice. The water looked cold and glassy, and very black. But Naomi acted as if she'd just finished bathing in water poured there from heated kettles.

From the back, she looked almost like a slender woman. Her back was strong, and the hunching look of her shoulders made her muscles even better-defined. Her legs were as firm as if she were thirty.

The front of her body seemed to have been placed on the rest of her skeleton by mistake, and it never stopped making him happy that this was so. She was fleshy, wide, and abundant. Her belly was like the belly of a woman well into pregnancy; her huge breasts hung well down, past the bottom of her rib cage, like oblong melons. The chill had made her nipples erect and as reddened as strawberries.

Drops of water clung to her skin and shone brightly. She thought, at first, that he was telling her about the absence of Lavinia because he wanted her to know that, for the moment, he had no chore; he was free.

"Come in here with me," she answered. She was always trying to get him into the pond. He loved her. She was the most beautiful woman he'd ever known. She was the living embodiment of the engraving of Mary in his shop.

He reached for Naomi's shift, held it in his hands; he rolled it into a bundle and pressed it against his chest, as if that would make the fist in his chest turn back to his normal heart.

"I want to go up to the Mowlans'. If Lavinia can't bring down the ox, I shall bring it down myself. Then I'll want my fish."

"I heard a wagon. I thought I heard a voice that was Samuel Leyson's."

"It was."

"I thought he was shouting at you."

"He was."

"Has something happened?"

"I only want to go and get the ox. The boy is waiting."

"I wondered if the wagon was going very fast."

"It was."

She didn't ask him any more questions. By now she'd looked at his face more carefully. He didn't need to tell her that he was worried. They'd been married a long time.

In long, loose strides, she walked out of the pond. Her feet knew every stone at the bottom, every old bit of moss, every inch of mud. It was nothing like the low-tide mud of a clam flat. Some mosquitoes buzzed around her head, around her shoulders, but they were old, and half-dead in the air, like leftovers from summer.

In the air was the smell of onions in the pot on the embers, in the outdoor hearth across the pond. Some smoke rose up, too, just a little. Jacques couldn't see any frogs, but he knew they were there. It was supposed to be good luck if you looked at the shiny, unblinking eyes of a frog before setting off from home on any sort of journey at all, even a small one, as if the eyes would pass into yourself, and help you watch out for any danger. Jacques hadn't learned that from the Jesuits. He had learned that from his wife. She didn't know how to read or write. What she read was not written in words.

She said to her husband, "I shall go with you," and he didn't argue. When she came up beside him, he stood there without touching her, which was very unusual. Where anyone else would have been shivering with cold, Naomi was perfectly still.

Jacques handed Naomi her shift, her shawl, and she said, "Shall we walk, or take the horses?"

He estimated how much time it would take her to go into the main house for more clothes—some underwear or breeches; she couldn't ride a horse in just her shift, even though she'd often done so when she was younger. If she went into the house to put drawers on, it would take ages. She'd start looking around for little gifts and sweets to bring up to the children. She was especially partial to Mary Mowlan—"my little river seal, with the brain of a girl," she called her; she believed that Mary had gotten her love of being in water from herself, as if hereditary material had been transmitted from Naomi's body.

Well, if they walked up Surrey Road instead of riding, all she'd need were her moccasins, which were close at hand on the ground, where she'd kicked them off.

"We can walk," said Jacques. "I wouldn't mind the exercise." He rarely had the chance to get out and stretch his legs, but she knew he was lying.

She put on her moccasins. She put on her shawl and tied the ends in a knot between her breasts; it was a tighter knot than what she usually made, as if she wanted him to know that she understood exactly what was going on inside him with the feel of his heart.

It took them almost half an hour to walk up Surrey Road. They saw no one. Halfway up the road, he paused and acted as if he didn't need to stop and catch his breath and let his knees have a rest, but he was winded, achey. He told her who'd been with Leyson. He didn't tell her what Leyson had said, because he didn't want to think about it, but he described what Sarah looked like when she was making the effort to jump out of the racing wagon, and how he'd wanted to catch her.

They saw from the road that no smoke was coming from the farmhouse. There was no sign of children. Or hands, but that wasn't strange: the Mowlans' farmhands, with the harvest nearly over, only came up in afternoons. The boys' fishing boats were tied up below in the cove.

Without another word, Jacques and Naomi started walking much faster.

Naomi's eyes were better than his. She was the first to see that the door of the animals' barn was wide open. The two oxen were lying on the ground on their sides. If it weren't for the enormous dark birds circling high up, above the trees, it would have seemed that the oxen had taken it into their heads to lie down and sleep in the sunlight.

Then Jacques and Naomi saw the flies. The oxen had been shot. The horses were gone. The cows were gone. The chickens were gone, too, and so were the geese and the ducks, which the children had kept as pets. And the dogs weren't bounding down the road to meet them.

One of the dogs, Jacques remembered, had been wounded, but that wouldn't have prevented the others from doing their job as guards. Naomi reached for his hand, squeezing hard. The doors of all the sheds were open, too. The fish shed was empty. Apples from the apple shed lay everywhere on the ground, as if dropped.

"English," said Naomi.

Then the silence hurt their ears. The fist in Jacques's chest swelled up; he felt that something inside him would burst. This was what they saw: that all the Mowlans were lying on the ground, like a family that had decided to camp outside, or a family that had picnicked for breakfast and, having put away the trappings, had all sprawled out and gone back to sleep, not far from the front door of the farmhouse.

There wasn't a particular order to the lay of them, but Lavinia was a little farther off from the others. William, unlike the children, was face-down. His hands had been tied behind his back. Except for Lavinia, they were all in their nightclothes. The dogs were there, too, as still as rocks. Except for Lavinia and the dogs, everyone's throat had been cut. Lavinia had been shot, like the animals.

Here and there in the yard were pieces of furniture, as if meant to be robbed, but the robbers had changed their minds, as if the furniture proved too cumbersome to take. One of those pieces of furniture was the bureau from Lavinia and William's bedroom, with the drawers pulled out, having been emptied.

Against the front of the house, someone had stacked hay bales. Jacques figured that the original plan had been to burn the house down. He thought, with the part of his brain that rushed up to forge some comprehension, "That's why they placed the bodies outdoors. To have them found. Not destroyed by burning. To have them found, as a warning."

They had changed their minds about the fire, perhaps on moral grounds. Perhaps they had felt that, in burning down the house, they would have committed an atrocity.

Naomi went down on her knees to the ground, as silent as if she'd been turned to stone. They knew that their eyes would never allow them to stop seeing what they were looking at. Jacques felt the need to speak. Not to God, not like praying. He just wanted to raise his voice in the air.

"Lavinia Mowlan, born Lavinia Rouse, dead," said Jacques.

"William Mowlan," he said. "Dead."

"Margaret Mowlan," he said. "Dead."

"Mary Mowlan. Dead."

"Seth Mowlan. Dead."

"Robert Mowlan. Dead."

"Nathaniel Mowlan. Dead, and the animals, too, all dead, except for the ones they had stolen." His wife looked at him, willing him with her eyes to say more, but he couldn't think of anything else. He knelt down on the ground beside her.

Within the hour, his assistant from the shop came up looking for him: the poor boy stood gaping from the field, and couldn't bring himself to go near the yard. He ran back into town and brought others.

Word was sent to Boston, to Lavinia's sister and brother-in-law. Lavinia's brother, Patrick, was at sea; it would be a while before he learned what had happened.

Someone from the town thought to mention to Jacques that a messenger be sent to York, to Lavinia's friend, Winnie Goodridge, who ran the tavern there, but Jacques said, "I shall go to her myself."

Some of the people of Tibbetston had felt the burials should take place at once, but Jacques and Naomi decided on a postponement, so that the Avenses would have time to come up from Boston, which was important, as John Avens would need to be the one to conduct things.

The bodies were moved into the house. People brought food but no one felt like eating. Some people wished that Tibbetston had a church, so that bells could be rung.

On the night of that day, as cold as it was, Jacques and Naomi sat all night outdoors in the Mowlans' yard, resting their backs against the house, against the hay bales, in vigil, like two figures frozen in snow; the fog came in thickly. Sometime in the night, some twenty Wabanaki Indians—men, women, and older children—came down from their inland camps, and sat with them. They did not tie up the horses they had come on. The horses stood still, as if they knew, too, what had happened. No one talked. Everyone knew that, when something unspeakable takes place, the first answer to it is silence.

The day after the murders, Naomi stayed at the farm, with some of their friends, to wash and prepare the bodies, which were moved, covered in sheets, to the barn. The men built wooden planks for them. They put the house back together. They buried the animals. They shoveled dirt on the ground where the blood was. They lit the hearth fire; they lit dozens of candles. Word had been sent to Jacques and Naomi's sons, who would join them soon. Jacques got on his horse and went to York.

ᴀT THE TAVERN

M RS. WINIFRED GOODRIDGE—Winnie—was well-read in the subject of history. She was fond of telling new customers in her tavern, by way of deflecting their surprise and discomfort at meeting her, that if she'd been born in ancient Sparta instead of modern America, she would have been left in the woods to die of exposure, or be eaten by animals. If she'd been born a hundred years ago in America, to Puritans, she would have been drowned, as they'd have thought her a child of a demon. Even as a baby she'd been tiny, unusual, and under-formed.

She gave the impression of a shrunken-down version of the woman she perhaps might once have been, as if she'd compressed herself, like a piece of fruit in a drying shed. If you put her in a tub of water, she'd expand to normal size. She couldn't be called a dwarf because she wasn't quite that small. She was four feet two inches high, and her feet were so tiny, she wore a girl's shoes, although nothing else about her was childish, not at all. She was as healthy as a horse and still, at the age of fifty-six, she'd not lost any of her teeth.

Her tavern was always crowded, day and night. There was no longer a Mr. Goodridge.

Everyone knew she was a widow, and that her husband had owned a small foundry, but not many people knew more than that. She kept the details to herself, and she was not the kind of person who inspired personal confidences among her customers.

She'd come up to York from lower Massachusetts, near Plymouth, more than twenty years ago: the man who'd owned the tavern was a much-older cousin of hers, and so was his wife. They were childless, having lost three babies in infancy. Soon enough, they came to call her "Daughter."

She could not say that the way she'd felt about her tavern-cousins was love, or anything close to it. She was grateful to them, she was loyal to them, she was fond of them, she was good to them. That was the best she could do. The part of herself that was able to feel something like love was all closed up, the way the shell of a spoiled clam doesn't open, not even when you boil it or steam it.

She went into the tavern as a maid but did not stay a maid for long. What she lacked in physical size was more than compensated for. She had a big, strong, gruff voice—she smoked tobacco in a pipe like a man, and always talked loudly. After you'd found yourself in her presence for just five or ten minutes, you'd stop noticing how small she was, and you would never notice it again. She was badger-like in intensity and daring; she was smart, shrewd, hard-working, tough. When her cousin and his wife died, they left the tavern to her, and she'd been running it ever since, as a sort of small kingdom.

In a replication, inverted, of the relationship she'd had with her cousins, she took on as her assistants a married couple named Edmund and Silvia Church, who were devoted to her.

On the surface, she seemed every bit a worldly, scar-free, successful woman. Her husband's name had been Obadiah. Hobe, he was called. His physical size was normal; except to the people who knew him well, he appeared to be normal in every way. It was a good marriage in the brief time it had lasted.

Winnie Goodridge always called the strange, dark moods that took over her husband "his problem." Sometimes they would come as a result of something that went wrong in the foundry—some trouble with the big stone chimney, some molding that took on the wrong shape, some difficulty with the wood kiln, something off with the hammers. He never raged, never swore, never let on in a big, outward way that his mind would go as dark and as bleak and empty as the forge when the fire went out. But most of the time, melancholy would take him over for no reason at all.

The light in his eyes would go out, just go out. He might lie back in their bed after making love, and tell her how blessed their lives were, and call himself a happy man—and five minutes later, that unpredictable, hateful mechanism inside his soul would kick in. There he would be, naked and blank and lost to her, as if part of himself was always poised at the edge of a terrible pit of despair: he'd go plunging over the edge, without warning. It was no good to plunge in after him and try to bring him back.

She'd have to wait until it passed. He told her once—not in one of those fits, but calmly, objectively—that he'd married a wrong-size woman because he'd been sure no normal woman would have had him, and she had not felt hurt, but had agreed.

His foundry was the most successful one in southeastern Massachusetts. He was a hard man to work for: he was demanding and stern, but his turnover rate was low. He was fair, and he honored his contracts. Thirty-three men worked for him, including those inside the forge; the lumbermen whose full-time job it was to keep the kilns stocked with simmering wood, for charcoal; the colliers who gathered ore from the bogs, and the blacksmiths who worked with the molds.

Almost all of these men were indentured to him under a two-year deal: Scots, Germans, Irish. He had put up the money for their passage, and those who'd survived the hell of the month-long sea trip did not think that working for Hobe Goodridge was another form of hell.

Goodridge Foundry specialized in farm and home equipment: shovels, axes, pots, skillets, hearth irons. And there was always a market, in England as well as in the colonies, for new, pig-iron bars. England could not get enough of American bars.

Winnie handled the accounts. There was no way—short of smuggling, which took a great deal of thought and energy—to establish a steady trade with France or any other European market. By the middle of the 1700s, the might of England was greater than everyone else's combined, and no other country had anything near the force of their navy. What was made in the colonies, England felt, was meant only for itself.

It wasn't hard to understand that the foundries of England were slowly getting less and less productive, not because there wasn't ore, but because there weren't enough trees for the fires. It took nearly an acre a week to keep the kilns stocked. The supply of

North American lumber seemed ample, never ending, and free, like foam on waves of the ocean. There'd been foundries in the colonies from the time of the first settlements.

When Parliament shocked the colonies with the Iron Act, in 1750, there was a huge, initial surge of worry and rage, but every other founder in America figured out very quickly that it was a law that could be ignored or gotten around. Realistically, there weren't enough customs officers. The ones in Massachusetts had their hands full with Boston and Salem.

"All American foundries henceforth are permitted the manufacture of merchant bars only," was the gist of the new law. The idea behind it was that English ships would carry bars of pig iron to England, where English smiths and forgers would remain employed, crafting the bars into objects that would then be sailed to America and sold, at English profit, to the same people who could have purchased the local-made stuff at a tenth of the cost.

This was something like forbidding a piano player to play songs he'd spent his whole life learning, and telling him he must only bang hard on the keys, or play nothing but scales. Or as Winnie, who was practical, had put it, it was just like closing the door of the barn to prevent the escape of horses, after the horses had escaped.

In the fall of 1752, it happened that a team of customs men were in Plymouth and got word of Goodridge Foundry. Iron might have been the last thing on their minds, but they'd felt they ought to check up on Hobe anyway.

It would have been a simple thing for Hobe to hide the forge-workings and the molds and the finished products. All he had to do was point to the stacks of merchant bars and say, "Hello, English officers, all this iron is for you, just you alone, just as you see it," and as soon as they were gone, everything could have gone back to normal. Friends in Plymouth had sent word that the officers were on the way.

There'd been plenty of warning. Hobe Goodridge didn't have to conclude that he had come to the end of his foundry, that he would have to spend his life as if he were an unskilled worker, indentured himself, perhaps, with no contract to say when he would be free. He didn't have to panic that he was about to be investigated.

Maybe that was what it was, panic. Why should it happen now that an actual, external event had the power to trigger his problem, and drive him straight to the edge?

But it did, and Winnie never saw it coming. Two days before the customs men were due to arrive, Hobe took his old pistol and went up to the wide, frothy source of the stream that drove his big waterwheel. Winnie hadn't even known the pistol worked. He shot himself in the head. He left her no message.

She later found, on a rock of the huge main chimney, seven words, chiseled into the stone with the edge of a knife, or a nail. "ENGLISH, YOU WILL NOT HAVE MY LIFE." They could have been put there long ago, and not by Hobe; who knew? There was not a person in the foundry or town who would not have felt the same way.

They tried, just briefly, to keep the foundry going without him. His assistant manager was a thirty-year-old man: ambitious, soft-spoken Tobias Firth. Tobe, he was called. He had lived all his life in Plymouth. He'd been the one to find the body. Hobe and Tobe.

Out of a sense of duty he'd asked Winnie to marry him, or maybe it was only because he'd felt the foundry had a better chance of surviving that way. When she refused him, he went to where the iron was more plentiful: Pennsylvania. She heard from him now and then: in all these years, he never stopped writing to her. They were quick, almost anonymous notes, mostly about the foundry where he worked, which he now owned. He said often he would one day come to Maine, but he never did.

It was Tobe Firth Winnie thought of—strangely and vividly—when she learned what had happened to the Mowlans. It was as if a vision of Tobe Firth appeared to her, not as he was at thirty, but now, somehow: she pictured him gray-haired and fifty, with an iron man's powerful arms, coughing with an iron man's cough, with wrinkles around his kind, light blue eyes.

She didn't know why, but suddenly, she started thinking very strongly of iron—iron, iron, iron—and she could smell the old smells of the foundry all over again, and hear the roar of the furnace, the pounding of the hammers, the steady, creaking churn of the waterwheel; she could see in her mind's eye the molten glow of hot, liquid iron before it hardens. She felt that it was like being near an erupted volcano, without fear.

She wanted very badly to see her husband's old assistant manager, her old friend. It came over her as a craving.

"I must send for Tobe." She had the sense she would figure out why, sooner or later. She was not a woman who took her own instincts lightly. If there were ever a person who believed in holding trust in one's self, absolutely, it was Winnie: she had to be that way necessarily, because of her size.

She was sitting in the tavern at her usual table, in the relative calm of mid-afternoon. She had just had her dinner. She was doing the same thing she did every afternoon at this time: whittling with her good German knife. She wasn't an expert, but she was competent. The Mowlan children's playthings had always contained toys that Winnie had made them. They called her their aunt.

On that day, one of her maids had a daughter at home in bed with bronchial troubles; someone had built the girl a dollhouse, and Winnie was determined to furnish it. She'd already made a little table, a little bed, a little stool. She was working on a stick-doll to put into the bed when the Churches, the two of them, Edmund and Silvia, came over to her table, sat down, and looked at her with scared, somber eyes.

"Mr. Wabanaki from Tibbetston is on his way to see you," Edmund said. "We had word he was in distress some ten or twelve miles off. We sent a boy with the wagon to bring him the rest of the way."

"He rode hard. His horse gave out from under him," said Silvia.

Winnie put down her whittling knife. She'd already begun to steel herself for bad news. She'd thought, at first, that something might have gone wrong with the delivery of muskets she was expecting next week.

Winnie was an arms broker, extremely secretly, for the York militia, and she also dealt with other groups up the coast as far as Augusta, and south into New Hampshire. She trusted the privateers she was dealing with, but it was a risky business. But the Churches didn't know she was brokering.

It was not about guns. "Is Jacques injured?"

"He's hungry, we were told. The boy we sent has food for him, and water. We must tell you, there's been news." Silvia Church was pregnant, for the first time, and put her hands on her belly as she said this.

"Something has happened," said Winnie.

"Bad," said Edmund.

"It's the Mowlans," said his wife. "We don't know what exactly."

Not twenty feet from where Winnie was sitting was the long table that had been lavishly covered with platters of meats, and bottles of wine and Spanish brandy, and steaming kettles of chowder, and platters of cold, sweet, tiny Maine shrimps, and baskets of flowers, and cheeses and fruits and cakes and pies, for the wedding banquet of Lavinia and William Mowlan, how many years ago? Fifteen, it must have been. Fifteen.

In the corner behind Winnie was the table where Nathaniel Mowlan used to come and sit with the Churches, while his sisters and brothers played outside, and his parents sat visiting with Winnie. The Churches had let the boy go over the ledgers with them. Sometimes he wrote letters for them. His writing and spelling were better than theirs, and better than Winnie's, too.

The first time Seth Mowlan stood up on his own two legs and started walking was right here. Out in the washroom was the tub where a tiny Mary Mowlan had stuck in her head, fully, to see how long she could hold her breath underwater. (A long time.) Out in the yard was a five-foot-long piece of good, gnarled, heavy driftwood, which Winnie had been thinking of making into a walking stick for William. Once, a little drunkenly, he had taken up the dare of some of Winnie's customers to climb up on a table and stand on one leg without his crutch. People were placing bets to see how long he'd do it for, and he would have gone through with it if the table—a good one, oak—hadn't broken right under him, almost at once. Winnie had used the wood for many of her projects.

At this table, where Winnie was now, how many times had she sat talking with Lavinia? It wasn't possible to put a number on it. A lot of times. How many times had she gone with Lavinia in the carriage through York, so that Lavinia could look at her old home, her father's sawmill? A lot of times.

"Leave me be, to wait for Jacques," said Winnie to the Churches. "Please have one of the girls fix up the bed for him in my house, in the back room, and have her light the fire. Jacques shall need to rest. You said nothing of Naomi. Is Naomi with him?"

No, they said, he was alone. Winnie sat there. She willed her mind to be empty, and an image came up at the backs of her eyes, and with the image, a voice, a face. Maybe it was because of Jacques, maybe not, but the face and voice belonged to a Massachusetts Indian called Rabbit. Winnie remembered Rabbit.

Once, in the early days of their marriage, when Winnie was just beginning to get a glimpse of what her husband was like when his problem took him over, she had a conversation with Rabbit, who wasn't rabbitlike at all: he was slow and deliberate in his movements, and deeply, darkly brown.

Rabbit came in now and then to the foundry to trade skins for pots and knives. He acted as if he didn't care that almost every other white in the foundry compound went paler at the sight of him, and were quick to get out of his way, and never spoke a word to him, as if he were language-dumb, like an animal, when his English was excellent.

He was a short man, which was the reason why Winnie initially liked him. He liked to stop by the little office, where she worked at the foundry accounts. She would make him some raspberry tea, and if she'd been making a stew, she'd go up to the house and get him some. He had known her husband longer than she had. He knew about the moods, the problem. He had seen that look in Hobe's eyes, same as she did.

One day, not knowing if this was an all right thing to ask or not, but venturing into it anyway, she asked Rabbit what it was like to be an Indian.

He said, "It is like life."

No, she had argued, really, she wanted to know how it *felt*.

He said, "It feels like life."

Then she asked him what it was like to think about this land, and what had happened since white people came. He had smiled at her. He let her know that it was not a possibility for her to understand even a tiny bit of what it was like; but he let her know, gently, all the same, it was nice of her to try.

And he said to her—and she knew at the time, it was something she would never forget—"When you go to your church, what do they tell you is the single biggest difference between the mind of a beast and the mind of a human?"

She thought about that. She was never one for church. "We can talk, and we can have ideas," she offered. He shook his head.

"We can imagine revenge," he said. In his soft, gentle voice, the last word had a luxurious resonance. "We know enough to want it, like your angels."

That probably wasn't the last time she talked with Rabbit, but she remembered no other conversations. She felt that he had taught her a new word, as if she were a toddler. She was grateful to him. She felt that he had given her the word as a gift. On her own, it never would have occurred to her to put the word "revenge" in the category of things that constitute angels. But that, she felt, was where it rightly belonged.

"Winnie," said Jacques. He was standing right beside her. He held out his hands to her, and Winnie had to hold herself back from smiling. She knew Jacques well. She had never seen this expression on his face before—hard, grim, weary, with the tension that comes from held-back feelings—and it was not an expression one could meet with a smile. All the same, she couldn't help but wonder what Jacques would have felt about Rabbit's ideas.

Did Jesuits believe in angels? She almost wanted to ask him. She wanted to ask him anything, get him talking about anything at all, just to postpone whatever he was going to tell her.

He sat down beside her. His big hands enfolded both of hers. He was not a man for small talk. "The Mowlans. They are killed," he said. "The English would say it was Indians."

"Lavinia?"

"Yes."

"William?"

"Yes. All of them."

"It was white men?"

"It was English."

She looked at him. She said, "You did not come all the way to York just to tell me this with your own mouth, Jacques. You could have sent for me. There must be much to be done in Tibbetston."

"I had wanted to tell you myself."

"And?"

"And I want more guns," said Jacques.

Winnie nodded. She asked for no details. Not yet. She almost felt proud that she was a person who was closed up, all closed up. She could think right away of practicalities. She could think right away, as she'd thought the day her husband's body was found, of the one human feeling she still had left to her fully. She had no desire for intimacy, no desire for pleasure, no desire for joy. The desire for revenge had never really left her. "Thank you for reminding me," Winnie said silently, to the ghost of her memory of Rabbit.

"Jacques, your horse, what happened along the way?"

"I'll need the loan of one of yours," he answered.

"There'll be a funeral," Winnie said. "They will need to have food. I'll go back with you, with provisions."

"And guns."

"And guns."

Winnie paused. "You must rest now," she said. And that was when she had the notion that Tobe Firth, of all people, seemed to be standing in front of her.

"Good day to you, my old friend, tell me what you want of me," he seemed to be saying. He looked as if he'd just stepped out into daylight from the forge.

He didn't look at her the way he did when he had come to tell her that he'd found Hobe. He was looking at her gently, kindly, shrewdly, hopefully, the way he'd looked at her when he had told her he thought she should marry him.

Somehow Rabbit and "revenge," and Tobe Firth and "iron" were now joined together in Winnie's mind. Maybe this was because of Jacques, too. Maybe Jacques resembled both of them, put together. Winnie was seized with the desire to see Tobe Firth.

She called for Edmund and Silvia to bring Jacques back to her house. And she said to them, "I must leave this afternoon. Whatever we have in the storerooms, I shall want to take with me, and the linen tablecloths, and the set of pewter plates. But first, would someone bring me paper and my ink pen?"

She was going to write to Tobe Firth right away, and say to him, "Come to Maine. At once. You must."

CHAPTER IV

DECLARATION

"THEY WILL EXPECT YOU to offer some words, as you are the one in charge of these proceedings, Father Avens."

John Avens didn't correct Jacques for calling him "Father." Jacques Wabanaki, having been reared by Jesuits, would naturally, under stress and in shock, fall back on thinking that a man from Harvard College and a parish in Boston was the same as a Catholic. As fair-minded as John was, he held no respect in general for Jesuits. He wondered if Jacques ever thought about the priests who had cut out the tongues of Indians caught speaking their own language, instead of French. But this wasn't something he could have asked.

He said, "Jacques, I have nothing to say."

"But Father, everyone from every township on the coast, and well inland, is here for the burial. There is no one else. What must be done, must be done. We have no church, no one else to offer some ceremony."

The warships had left the bay and had headed down to the noisy, bustling, prosperous port of Falmouth. But the farmers who came for the funeral were armed, every one of them.

The burial was taking place at the end of the Mowlans' back field, with the coffins in a row. The heads faced, not the house, but the hill beyond, which still had no name, which was squat and round in the sunlight, and pine-heavy and very beautiful.

The pond on the hill could be seen just barely, all silver and bright, like a slice of liquid moon. Its strong, clear stream went rushing in its usual way to the Kennebec, as if nothing out of the ordinary had happened. The sun, people felt, should not have been shining.

John had no words of his own, no prayers. He would never again step foot into a church—not his own, not anyone else's. Beside him, like a ghost of herself, Lavinia's sister, Jossey, held her baby boy. His name had been Patrick, for her brother, but Jossey and John had decided to change it. There had not been much discussion about it. William Mowlan, whom they loved, had left behind no kin. The baby was now to be called Mowlan. Mowlan Patrick Avens.

John and Jossey's little daughter was with them, but not their other son, Little John. Eight-year-old Little John had been left behind in Massachusetts, with his uncle Patrick. Neither John nor Jossey could bear to think about what was happening with Patrick, except to tell themselves, "He'll be well, he'll be here with us soon, it's good that he's got his nephew with him."

The baby was wide awake, but made no sound, following the lead of his mother. Jossey was utterly silent. Shock had settled deeply into the very skin of her face, like a mask that might never come off. She was thirty-two years old. Gone was the vibrant, glowing, bursting-with-ruddy-good-health Jossey Rouse Avens. She looked like a woman of fifty or sixty who had never in her life had a moment of joy or contentment.

Jossey and John's little girl had been named Priscilla, for her long-dead York grandmother. Prissy, she'd always been called. Now her name was changed, too. Now she would be known as Lavinia. Lavinia Priscilla Avens. Vinny-Pris. She would not be able to understand why for a long time. She was six: a keen, lively, lovely, thoughtful child, with the deep inner solidity that comes from knowledge, at the core of onself, of being beloved.

The little girl had taken off her bonnet. She liked to feel the sun on her head. She clung to her mother's skirt and kept wondering why everyone was so sad, and why her five Mowlan cousins were not with her. She wanted Mary and the boys to bring her down to the river, where she'd take off her shoes and run about with them, and have the thrill, like any city child, of being terrified that crabs would jump out at her and bite off her toes.

She looked up at her father. "Papa," she whispered. "I want to go to the river."

"Hush."

"If you would please, Father," said Jacques.

"There is something troubling me, Jacques. My sister-in-law had been writing an article for a newspaper in Boston. I believe she would have had it completed. I should have liked to read it. I should have liked to deliver it, here today, but no one has said anything of having found it."

"My wife," answered Jacques, "had felt the same, and had searched for it. The robbery was extensive, Father."

"Then it does not exist."

"It does not."

"Then that's one more thing I shall have to reconcile myself with, somehow." In his hand, John held a long piece of thick paper, still curled from being rolled in a tube for delivery.

In other circumstances, the words in that elegant script would have given him joy. It had come from Philadelphia, from the Continental Congress. On October 10, the members of the Congress had drawn up what they called "Declaration of Rights."

"It would do well if you were to stand up in front of us and read what it says there, as you planned, in place of prayers," Jacques said.

"You do it, Jacques."

"I doubt these people would appreciate the view of their blacksmith, giving words as priest. Not to mention the fact that their blacksmith is a brownskin, and a Catholic."

"And you would have me speak well of a Declaration of Rights?"

"John, you must do as he says," said Jossey, quietly. She had not brought enough clothes of her own from Boston; they had left so quickly. The black skirt she wore belonged to Lavinia. So did the black shawl and black bonnet. The English had not robbed the house of clothing belonging to anyone but William.

John wore the same clothes he'd come up in from Boston. He wished he could get out of them. He felt his daughter was right: they should all go down to the river. They should all plunge into the cold strong Kennebec, where the tide might startle their souls into comfort.

What comfort? There was no comfort. The papers in his hand whiffled lightly. There was a breeze, salty and sharp and watery. They had been worried about taxes. About *taxes*.

But John resolved that he would not be a coward. He made his way to the seven oblong holes that Jacques and his friends had dug. The holes were all the same size. The seven coffins were all the same size, too. They had not made smaller ones for the children. In Massachusetts, perhaps, they would have done so, but this was Maine.

John would say nothing of God. He would say nothing of life everlasting. He hoped that, when he finished reading these words, every man standing before him in the field would have the hope put into their hearts that they could use their guns on as many Englishmen as possible.

"Declaration of Rights, adopted by the Continental Congress in Philadelphia," he said. His voice was loud, clear. He'd never been much for a pulpit, but this was different. He held firmly to the papers, and read.

"'The good people of the several Colonies of New Hampshire, Massachusetts Bay, Rhode Island, and Providence Plantations, Connecticut, New York, New Jersey, Pennsylvania, Delaware, Maryland, Virginia, North Carolina, and South Carolina, alarmed at the arbitrary proceedings of the British Parliament and Administration, having severally elected deputies to meet in a General Congress in the city of Philadelphia, proceeded to take into their most serious consideration on the best means of attaining the redress of grievances. . . .'"

He paused. Many of the people standing in front of him were confused, nervous. This was not the way one was supposed to conduct a funeral. He lowered the paper and said, "These are not normal times. I believe we all know that."

And he read the rest of it without pause. Resolved. That the colonies are entitled to life, liberty, and property. That they will never cede to any foreign power whatsoever. That Parliament cannot raise a revenue among the people of America, without consent of the people of America.

He read these words in a way he'd never done while standing

before a congregation, reading from the Bible. When he was finished, and the hush around him became deeper and deeper—in the moments before the burials took place—he felt a small relief and satisfaction. He knew, just like everyone else, it wasn't about taxes. It wasn't about revenues, not at all.

The last coffin to be put into the ground was Lavinia's. Jossey handed the baby to John and knelt down on the ground and said, in a clear voice, purely as a statement of fact, "Now I must learn to be alone." No one thought that such a statement was odd, coming from a woman with a husband she adored, and three sturdy, healthy children. Everyone knew how Lavinia and her sister had felt about each other.

"There shall be much ahead to redress what was done. We shall not forget what took place here," Jacques whispered to Jossey, as if that would console her.

Two days later, in the middle of a dark, cold, foggy and moonless night, an armed band of fourteen men—from Tibbetston, Grilleyville, and two coastal townships—rode on horseback up Surrey Road to Samuel Leyson's farm.

The Maine men had suppered together on lobster and potatoes at the Grilleyville tavern, and they had been drinking from tankards of hard Maine cider all evening. They were farmhands, a couple of farm owners, a couple of tanners, and a trapper; most of them were fishermen.

All of them (as Lavinia had described in her article) claimed direct descent from England and had, at one time—for most of their lives, in fact—thought of it in a fond, familiar way.

They'd called it "the home country," or just, "back home." No more. Some of the men had not known William or Lavinia personally, but they all knew Jacques Wabanaki. Jacques was not among them that night. He took a stand against undisciplined, rowdy, marauding mobs, especially when the purpose of the mob was purely bent on pillage. But he knew what was going to happen, and did nothing to try to stop it. Some of the guns in their hands had come from York.

The burning of Leyson's barn was carried out swiftly, efficiently. The animals were removed, and were taken into ownership by the first men of the group to get their hands on them. The blaze did not spread to the back woods, or to the main house, or the shacks beyond, which housed Leyson's slaves.

These shacks were empty of people. Leyson's slaves were slaves no longer. No one had witnessed them walking away from Surrey Road, and now they were making their way down the coast, hiding in good people's barns, looking for somewhere to go that would be safe.

In the main house of Leyson's so-called estate, most of the furniture was broken, as were most of the windows. The house was robbed of every object made of silver, and pewter, too. The buttery was emptied of all foodstuffs. So was the blockhouse-like shed where Leyson had his meats cured.

The only person who stayed on the land after Leyson had made his escape was his manager, a dour, nervous man from Maryland, who had anyway never felt comfortable here, and had been thinking he wouldn't be able to bear one more winter.

He handed over the keys to Leyson's strongbox without protest. He asked only to be allowed to pack up his things and be given one of Leyson's best horses; these requests were granted. There wasn't much money in the strongbox, just enough for everyone to get enough to go back to the tavern and eat another meal.

It only took a few hours for the barn to burn to the ground. There were two smaller barns, which were emptied of their stores of hay and corn and fruits, and left alone.

There was nothing indulgent or thoughtful in the act of refusing to set the main house on fire. The shattered glass in the windows, and the leaving of the door wide open, made sure that the weather would pour in unchecked, along with any bird or animal that might feel like nosing inside, or moving in. In a way, it was more of an insult to Leyson to leave his house standing there whole, abandoned and helpless.

Before the men left the scene, someone wrote a message to Leyson on a section of bedsheet torn off his own bed. The piece of cloth was attached to a long stick and stuck in the ground, flag-like. The message was written with the end of a burnt piece of wood. It said, "TORY."

No one was at the Mowlans' farm to hear the racket, the shouts, the smashing sound of glass. John and Jossey were staying at the Wabanakis' house. Jacques and Naomi, together with their youngest son, who'd come down from Moosehead, were in the summer cabin. But all of them, except Jossey, went up Surrey Road the next morning to see what had been done. John had felt the compulsion, out of decency, to shut the front door and put some boards on the windows, but the compulsion only lasted a moment.

Four days later, near the end of October, the fort in Grilleyville was approached—again, late at night—by a smaller group, who could not be considered a mob, although some of them had taken part in the action at Leyson's. This time Jacques went along. They had muskets, pistols, hatchets, and rope, but all they needed was the rope.

The four English sentries at the fort were young. Two looked barely old enough to grow face hair. They were bored, restless, chilled, damp, hungry, and miserable, and they had not had a full meal for a long time. Their teeth were going bad; their stomachs hurt. They hated Maine with all their hearts, and thought bitterly of their officers, who were, they imagined, lording it up in brothels and taverns down in Portsmouth, York, and Falmouth.

The four guards in their dirty, tattered British uniforms, did not offer any sort of resistance, and instead, begged to be allowed shelter in someone's farm, and food, as they were laying down their guns—not that they had much by way of weapons—and taking the parts of deserters. Jacques picked out two farmers and two lobstermen from the group, and assigned each of the English boys, separately, with rope-bound hands, to follow them home for the night.

It felt good to those four Maine men to take a prisoner, even a prisoner they felt sorry for, and had to nourish. The next day the guards were rounded up and put into an ox-cart for a slow, long ride down to Gloucester, where they were turned over to a new militia of fisherman who needed the release, from a Gloucester jail, of one of their leaders, who'd been grabbed and chained to a wall.

The court system and justice system in Gloucester, like everywhere else in the colonies, were now completely being run by English officers. The four guards were offered in a trade; no one knew what came of them. The Gloucester man was let go.

In the Grilleyville fort were two cannons, a small cache of gunpowder, no shot, six pistols, and six muskets of the type that would come to be known as "Brown Bess." That was all.

Word came from Boston that the new English governor had made a ruling on the murders. They were said to have been "carried out most despickably by Maine Native Savages that would break the Treaty of Peace." There was no day in court, no official inquiry.

There had been no witnesses. There was no official evidence to point to anything else, as if what went on in the wilderness of Maine was the business of the wilderness of Maine.

CHAPTER V

LEXINGTON

Around dawn, on october 19, 1774, the sloop *York Sawyer* neared Charlestown, Massachusetts, having come from stops at Falmouth and York.

The wind was brisk. It was lightly foggy. The cargo consisted solely of barrels of Maine-made rum, and the captain, Patrick Rouse, had no fear of the British blockade. He knew he wouldn't be barred from entry. The rum was for British soldiers garrisoned in the harbor islands, and in Boston, Charlestown, and Cambridge.

There were several thousand of them—bored, homesick, young, restless men, with nothing to do but stand sentry over a population of colonists who were very much at home, but were not bored at all, and were much more restless than they were. The soldiers had developed the taste for American rum. There was nothing like it in England.

Yes, there was always a possibility that drunken Redcoats, with almost no possessions of their own except their muskets, might lose their heads and go charging about the streets, and start shooting; but this would not be such a terrible thing. The so-called Boston Massacre of four years ago, a mob-action completely, had already faded into memory, as if it happened long ago in people's childhoods. Like everyone he knew, Patrick Rouse was waiting for something to happen that was real and immediate.

But the powerful Maine rum, with all that molasses, wasn't likely to incite anyone, not even the most trigger-greedy Redcoat.

Maybe it was because the molasses had come from the hot, jungle-like (Patrick imagined) West Indies.

He never drank rum himself, nor did anyone who crewed for him. They liked wine, and even more, they liked tart, hard, edgy Maine cider, which always made you feel a little keener in the senses, not dulled. He knew perfectly well that a little bit of Maine rum might inspire a Redcoat into looking for someone to bully, but almost no one drank just a little; it tasted too good. Sooner or later a tranquillizing effect would take place—not a heaviness, but a drowsiness, with immense satisfaction, like a baby at the breast, feeling smug and plump with milk.

It lived in a nightmare of a loop, this rum. Patrick's part in it was a small one.

He'd heard that a single sailor on a British merchant vessel could actually, by simply changing from one ship to another at the right ports, go through the whole cycle: sail to Africa to seize and take, in chains, as many people as could fit in your hold; then take those people to be molasses slaves on an island that looked, if you were not a slave in chains, like Paradise. Then sail to America, to Maine, to unload the molasses. Then pick up rum, sail to England, unload the rum—along with Maine wood, Maine fish, Maine potatoes, Maine apples (but not hard cider; the English hated it). Then you could get on another ship, sail to Africa, and do it all over again.

"God shall forgive me," was the way Patrick felt about his part in this. "God shall forgive me, and so would my sisters, if they knew."

Patrick would be paid for the rum in gold. There was nothing about him that would suggest to English customs officers he was not what he seemed: a Tory mercenary.

He had named his sloop *York Sawyer* in honor of his father, Robert Rouse. After his death, Patrick and his sisters sold the sawmill, thus severing all connections to their York home. The only tie to York any of them had kept was at the tavern: with Winnie Goodridge.

The money from the sale of the mill had been the means for Patrick of buying his first boat, a sturdy, fast schooner. Jossey and

Lavinia had forced him to take their shares. He had called that first boat the *Jossey-Vinna*. Jossey and Lavinia had always thought it was funny that, of the three of them, the one who was the most sentimental, and even, at heart, the softest, was their only brother.

The *Jossey-Vinna* had been wrecked in a gale off Falmouth: Patrick and his crew had been picked up by fishermen. As much as he missed the schooner, he had the small satisfaction of knowing it went down near home.

Now Charlestown was just ahead in the watery air, rising above its port very handsomely, with its trees and spires and hill-ness, and its solid-looking roofs. There was something about the broad slopes of the Charlestown hills that reminded Patrick of Tibbetston, of Surrey Road, and the hill that stood roundly and placidly behind the fields of his sister's farm, which had felt, to him, like his own home. He had an ugly little cottage of his own up near Augusta, where he rarely stayed, where he never wanted to be.

He'd planned to see the Mowlans next week. After he was paid for the rum, he'd go ashore, into central Boston, where John Avens would have been waiting for him for his trip to Maine. Patrick knew all about the Maine provisions to be smuggled past the boycott into Boston, and he meant to deliver John up there on the sloop. Lavinia and William and the children had been told that John would travel there by horse. Patrick's appearance had been meant for a great surprise.

"I know I'll never tire of coming up on this Boston town," one of the crew was saying. "A fine pretty town, a place I could live in, were it not for this demon in me that wants the sea."

"Myself, I shall be wanting a washtub and a barber," another said.

They sounded strange, distant. Something was wrong. Patrick tried hard to focus his eyes on the approaching line of the land, then the sky, with its pink-red sunrise glow. He hoped he'd never lose the joy of watching dawn from a deck of a boat. But he felt no joy. He had started to feel queasy.

At first it was only a shakiness, with a minor sensation of nausea, as if he'd been suddenly cursed, for the first time in his life, with seasickness. Then he tried to convince himself that it must have been something he ate. Like all sailors, especially captains of ships, he always made the effort to appear to be fearless, especially in the eyes of himself.

He had a well-developed ability to reduce all danger to a minimum. For supper last night he'd had beans and bread, and the rest of the smoked duck he'd got from Winnie Goodridge's tavern, back in York. For lunch, he'd had salted pork and potatoes. Long ago that morning, he'd had apples and corn cakes and sassafrass tea.

The three men on the sloop with him were Enoch Lister from Newburyport, who was as big as Hercules, with a thick black beard that he really took care of, and was vain about; and skinny little sandy-haired Asa Patch, from Boston, who was only seventeen; and George Huggins, from a township without a name, somewhere in Maine up the Penobscot River. Huggins wouldn't let anyone call him by his first name, not even his wife, because it was the name of the English king. He was exactly in the middle of the sizes of the other two, as if Patrick had planned it that way. Huggins and Enoch had been sailing with Patrick since the days of the *Jossey-Vinna*. Asa had joined them two years ago.

What he had eaten, they had eaten, too, exactly the same things, and probably more of it all. Nothing was wrong with anyone else.

Patrick began to retch, violently. Everything he'd had that day, he threw up, and when there wasn't any more, he kept retching, in spasms that were worse and worse. He couldn't hold himself up to lean into the salty, cool and watery air.

Someone brought him a bucket, then another one. Patrick was able to take off his pants and position himself at the second bucket just in time; he was overwhelmed with the worst diarrhea he'd ever had. Every mild rocking of the sloop became a torture. His forehead, and slowly, the rest of his face, his neck, his chest, felt as if he were sitting too close to a fire.

"He's fevering," someone said.

"Seems to me, it came on so quick, it will pass even quicker."

"We need another bucket."

Patrick couldn't tell who was speaking. His ears felt as if they were made of tin, distorting everything. Someone placed a bit of cool, water-soaked cloth against his face.

Patrick did not consider himself a religious man, but he found himself thinking of Jesus, on the last day of his life, walking up the hill with his cross. A woman from the crowd had moistened Jesus's face, Patrick remembered. He couldn't think of her name. He hadn't been diligent with the Bible, although his mother had tried with him hard. Why should he be thinking of Jesus, when he could barely distinguish words, when he couldn't control his own bowels, and could not stand up?

"What was the name of the lady giving water to Christ on the day two days before Easter," he tried to say, out loud. He felt sure he'd get an answer. Enoch liked to be tested on Bible information; he knew things that anyone else would find obscure.

But Patrick's voice had got all balled up, and was stuck in his throat like a lump. He felt desperate for something to drink.

The sun was all the way up. He felt hands on him. He wasn't retching any longer. There was nothing left; he was drained. He was being lifted, set down: he lay flat on his back on the deck.

Someone was washing him. *Washing* him, as if he were a baby and could not clean his own arse. The mainsail billowed over him with a terrible roar. The mast had grown higher in the last few minutes, and it was growing still. He thought he was watching it stretch itself up into clouds, and past them, and into the sun itself.

He thought they were approaching rapids, boulders, a waterfall as high as a mountain. He tried to cover his ears with his hands, and couldn't move.

Again, the cool wet cloth was on his face. He tried to suck it, and couldn't even manage that. He touched the tip of his tongue along his teeth, which felt very heavy and very dry, and along his dry lips. He thought he saw his mother bending toward him, his young, tall, strong mother. Her hair had been the color of cornsilk: he felt it brush against his cheeks, feathery-like. He was four years old when she had died. Jossey and Lavinia had mothered him as best as they could.

"Hush, you must be strong," he imagined his mother whispering. He imagined that she had dipped her finger in a bowl of maple syrup. As a tiny child he had thought of it as the perfect substance on all of earth. She rubbed his lips with it. "Veronica was the name of the woman who gave Jesus a cloth," he remembered.

"My uncle is at home today in Charlestown. I shall go there from the dock to ask his help." That came from young Asa. He was the only one besides Patrick who had family in Boston.

"Bring a wagon with your uncle, and we shall take him to John Avens's house."

"We shall unload the rum without you, Asa. Go quickly."

Patrick felt hands on him again. Clumsy, awkward hands. He was having his clothes put back on, by someone who, obviously, had not had experience in dressing someone else.

The deck felt lightweight, flimsy—had the wood turned into nothing stronger than leaves, bark? Patrick thought he smelled trees everywhere. He thought he was in the woods. Then he thought he was back in the sawmill.

A man's broad back—the man was hunched over, and seen from behind—appeared. He knew that man. Robert Rouse. Sawdust was all over him like dry, white-yellow snow.

"Patrick," he imagined his father saying. "Patrick, I am here."

"Father, am I going to die?"

"No."

"Vinna and Jossey and I sold the mill," said Patrick. "I bought a schooner with the money, but it was wrecked, and it was sunk."

"I know."

"I am sorry in my soul about that, Father."

"I know."

Then there weren't any more words. A blanket was placed on him. He tried to push it off. It was too hot for a blanket.

Was "Veronica" the correct answer? Could he still trust his brain to think a thought? The dark fuzziness that came into his head was extending itself very quickly, the way fog does. He knew he was slipping into unconsciousness.

No, it wasn't "Veronica."

He felt proud of himself that he'd got the right answer at last. "Lavinia," he thought. It was the same to him as if he'd felt his sister enter his mind. His beloved, excellent sister. What was the last thing he'd said to her? The last time he'd seen her was last summer: he'd gone up to the farm to help bring in the corn harvest. "Patrick," she had said to him, "Jossey and I are quite ready to have a sister-in-law from you, and should you not mind cooperating with that, we would be most grateful."

"I suppose you'd want nieces and nephews of mine as well."

Lavinia had squeezed his hand, had embraced him. "Half of a dozen of them, at the least, if only to have in this world some more of you. And as Jossey would say, they would be most attractive. You must not deprive the world of the chance look at their faces."

"And if I wed an unpretty wife?"

"You have enough good looks on your own to father the comeliest children who ever walked this earth."

"Ah, Lavinia, I would have thought you care nothing for looks."

"I am only repeating what came from Jossey."

And he had said, "It seems not to be my fate to be wed." She had smiled at that, and had not believed him. That was what he remembered: that smile of hers.

Patrick had been engaged to be married three times. Each time he'd thought, "this is it." Each time, a breach occurred somewhere along the process: it was always a breaking-off that seemed to Patrick like the attempted grafting of two trees, which didn't take, and left both trees scarred forever.

It was always, Patrick felt, his own fault, partly because of who he was, and partly because he lacked the insight to have seen the break coming ahead of time.

The first time, when he was seventeen, and in a hurry to establish himself, it was close to home in York, with the daughter of a lumber dealer his father often dealt with. The woman (Jossey didn't like her; Lavinia was neutral) could read and write and sew and spin and draw, and dance at town dances like a professional on a stage, and she was fair-haired and pretty, and conversed with wit and charm. Though he'd never done more with her than kiss her, and sometimes touch her breasts, under four or five layers of clothing, he was absolutely certain his life with her would be passionate, rich.

Then William Mowlan was taken prisoner, and Patrick had gone at once to Tibbetston. That was bad enough, but then he had made the "mistake" of taking off up the Kennebec to search for his brother-in-law, without asking permission of his bride-to-be, who, he knew, would have said "no."

In fact, he'd left York without telling her at all. She'd come up to Tibbetston on her own, where she stopped with Lavinia, and was horrified to find out that the closest friends of this soon-to-be sister-in-law of hers were the Wabanakis. In her own words, Jacques was a half-breed Indian Catholic blacksmith who had the arrogance to call himself for a whole tribe, when he didn't even know what tribe he was from. As for Naomi, well, look at Naomi: an unkempt, almost completely uncivilized wife, who was as unlike her pious namesake in the Bible as anyone could be.

Jossey had been right about that fiancée of Patrick's. That woman hated the sight of Jacques and Naomi's boys running everywhere unsupervised, and tussling with each other like animals, and stripping off their clothes to jump into the pond behind their house, as wild as minks. She broke off the engagement while Patrick was in Canada. He came back from not-finding William Mowlan, discovered he had been broken off from, and went back to try to find William again, and failed again.

The second time he was engaged he was twenty-five, and was wildly in love with a woman from Bath who was thirty, and a widow with two little sons; her husband had been a fisherman, lost at sea. Patrick had discovered, just a week before their wedding day, that what she had in mind for her second husband—it almost didn't matter who that second husband was, or what his interests were—was a lifetime spent close to home, with his two feet on dry land all the time, which was understandable. She had wanted Patrick to join his father in the saw mill, which he might have done, on a part-time basis—in the winter, say, when ice clogged the Kennebec and he was grounded anyway.

But the woman went beyond that and asked him to swear to God, on the memory of his dead mother, like a type of collateral, that he would never go to sea: not on a boat of his own, and not on anyone else's, not even to day-fish in the placid little bay. This should not have been the shock to him that it was. The body of the woman's first husband had never been found. Both Jossey and Lavinia had liked that woman, and didn't bear her a grudge.

The third time—and the hardest—there was a woman named Caroline Knox, from a township near Augusta. This was just three years ago. He'd met her at the fort there, Fort Western, while delivering rum and conferring with some guards who were secretly forming a new colonial militia, and were looking to deal with boatmen willing to take on the role of privateers, which he'd been, then, not quite ready to consider.

Caroline Knox was not as pretty as his other two almost-brides. She was somewhat horse-faced, and homely. She was a midwife, studied herbs and medicines, and was practical, independent, and brave. On the day she met Patrick, she'd been at the fort to command the guards to let her use one of the cool, dry ammunition rooms to hang plants for drying. She was always going into Augusta to deliver children, and needed a local storeroom.

Lavinia had been willing to start calling her "my sister-in-law" from the moment she met her, and the same had been true for Jossey. The way Patrick fell in love with her had felt real, deep, genuine, as if the other two women were only practice. He took her out on the *York Sawyer* and she loved it.

The first thing he told her about himself, in the confidential tone of a lover, was what it was like when the *Jossey-Vinna* went down, and how he'd always feel that part of him had gone with it. They made love in her homey, good-smelling cabin whenever they could. A few times, he went with her to the bedside of a woman in labor, and saw what it was like to behold a squealing, wet baby, when the cord had not yet been cut.

It looked as if his life as a married man was already beginning; he'd had no complaints about that. He'd felt a quietness and connectedness he'd never known, which lasted right up to the day when Caroline—in her bed, this was—leaned over him, propped her head on one elbow, smiled at him, and said, "After our marriage next month, you will of course be selling the sloop."

She said this as if it were something they'd discussed in great detail, and had agreed on, and she was only just reminding him.

He had looked at her with astonishment. Getting up from her bed, and dressing himself, he knew that after he'd walked out that door, he would never see her again. It had been hard to walk out that door.

Meanwhile in Maine and Boston, Lavinia and Jossey were having babies. Patrick had not yet seen Jossey's new one, whose name had been given as his: Patrick Avens.

Patrick knew the dates of all these children's birthdays; he gave the whole force of his affections to them. He was crazy about all of them, but there was one, more than any of the others, who'd found a way into the deepest area of Patrick's heart, like a crab that finds a perfect shell, and moves in, and plans to stay there forever. Jossey and John's little boy, eight years old. A prince of a child, in the best sense of that word. Little John Avens.

"I am not going to grow up to be a preacher like Papa. I am going to grow up and go to sea. I am going to grow up to be the second Uncle Patrick."

The boy had started talking this way when he stood no higher than Patrick's knee. He didn't resemble Patrick physically—he looked like John—but it was clear who was closest to him, of everyone.

It wasn't as if Patrick considered him a substitute child of his own. Patrick considered him, with a simple, abiding, powerful allegiance, as a mate of his soul.

"Uncle," he imagined the boy saying. "Uncle!"

And flat on his back, Patrick began to stir. It had been six days since he was taken sick on the sloop.

"Uncle. Uncle. Uncle."

Patrick thought he was hallucinating and hearing voices. "Uncle, Uncle."

He became aware of himself slowly entering a state of consciousness, not like waking from sleep, but more like being forced toward the surface of some dark, deep body of water, where he'd been—perhaps for far too long—submerged. His eyes flickered open, briefly, and made out light. Daylight. Land, not sea. Within walls. In a room, with shutters on a window that were partially closed. It was not a room he'd ever been in before.

A quilt was on him. He was lying on a narrow bed. Under the

quilt he was naked: he felt a surge of pleasure and relief to know the sheet he lay on was dry. His sense of smell was returning and he was thrilled to not be smelling his own urine, feces.

It was a small room, lightly furnished: there was a small table by the bed, and a chair with some clothes on it—his own waist-coat, jacket, breeches, shirt, clean. The sawed-wood walls were pine, fairly new. He made out the room to be a lean-to of a farmhouse.

He smelled something cooking—it seemed distant, but was probably in the next room. Meat in a pot: game, perhaps rabbit. This disgusted him. With a great deal of effort he was able to ma-neuver the quilt so that it covered the bottom of his face.

Almost at once it was yanked down to his chest. *"Uncle."* This was no figment of his imagination.

Patrick had no power of speech, not quite yet. His tongue felt triple its size, but he wasn't thirsty or hungry. Instead he had the curious awareness that, for however long he'd been in this bed, he hadn't gone without some sort of nourishment.

He felt no pain, no discomfort. He wasn't afraid. He only knew that he was weak, very weak, and he knew, too, that whatever he'd find himself waking to, it was going to be bad.

If it weren't for Little John, he would have given in, fish-like, to the powerful desire to sink back into the bed and shut his mind, and be submerged all over again. It was no use shutting his eyes. Little John was leaning over him, poking at his eyelids, prying them open. Patrick tried once to shake him off, but it was no good trying to resist him.

The boy placed himself on his knees, in a crouch, at the edge of the bed. He hovered over Patrick. Patiently, now that he knew Patrick was awake, he waited for those sleep-fuddled eyes to focus on him. Then he waited for a sign of the same old smile that said, "Sweet boy, no one on this earth is as dear to me as you, and noth-ing about that can ever be possibly changed."

Patrick smiled. The boy looked pale, as if he hadn't been out-doors for days. He stared at his uncle with urgency, gravity. His breath smelled milky, sweet.

With a deep breath, he burst out with it all at once. "Uncle. Make Papa and Mama change my name, too. Make them not change only my new brother and Priscilla. Make them act *fair* and change mine! I do *not* mind about Priscilla. I mind the *baby*. If the new baby shall *not* have Patrick for a name, then I shall have it. Uncle! I waited so long for you to wake! Make them change my name, too!"

And a big, unfamiliar voice boomed out from the doorway, "You little scoundrel! You had orders to let him be! You had orders to guard the door, not enter it!"

A giant, ruddy-faced bear of a man, about Patrick's own age, came lunging into the room. He grabbed for the boy—not roughly, but kindly—and hoisted him up in the air.

Little John, to Patrick's surprise, went meek. He made no protest; his expression was one of pure guilt. He was carried toward the door, as limp as empty clothes in the big man's arms.

Over his shoulder the man called softly, "Jackson Prout, I would be, Captain, at your service, once I dispose of this rascally imp. We were having him stand outside your door protective-like, so as to have something to put his mind to."

"Uncle, I have an ax, and I will be back *very soon*, as soon as they *let* me," the boy called out softly.

Almost immediately, the big man returned alone, this time with a small bowl of liquid, which he carefully set on the table. "The boy is well taken care of. What he told you as being his ax, we fashioned him a stick with a small bit of flint put on the end, not to be supposing we'd arm the little devil."

Patrick managed a smile, in spite of himself.

"Do you a world of good to be thinking on the fellow," said Jackson Prout. "They had felt you would hearten to have him near you. A good boy he is. Do you good to have a pleasant thought in your head, as what I would fear for you, is coming ahead, you would be in for a rough time of it, Sir. There are things you must be told in the fullness of time. As I was made to be the one to do the telling, I would say, in a position of trust, as being necessary, at the moment, we would be going ahead on, if you agree with me, what I would explain as being the slow side of moving."

Patrick had already made up his mind to trust him, because the boy did, even though it crossed his mind that this man might be insane. He didn't seem, somehow, to be truly a stranger.

"I know you," Patrick tried to say. He lifted his head and tried to prop himself up on his elbows, and fell back again.

"Captain, you'll want some aid before considering getting up. These last six days, being here with you, I was glad to be of use to you, by way of explaining how I would seem familiar. You were able to drink the minty tea we put up for you, and also as of yesterday you were allowing some broth to go in. The cook had killed a chicken."

Six days. Patrick heard those words clearly. But trying to make sense of what had happened to him—and what was happening to him now—was like trying to see ahead, in the middle of the night, in thick, gray-white fog. He remembered what it was like when he was ten or eleven, and first learning to handle a dory in York. He'd watched the fishermen constantly; one thing he had wanted to learn, more than anything else, was the secret of coping with fog.

He'd always known how quickly fog came, and how dangerous it really was—like a huge monster, with the power to blind you and, worse, with the power to make you fear it would swallow you whole. He'd felt there must have been a sacred, traditional knowledge, known to men of coastal Maine, as if fog were a thing one could be apprenticed to, then master.

In time, he learned the truth. The secret of handling Maine fog was to stay out of it, and, if you found yourself in it, lie low, and surrender to the faith that it will lift.

That was what he decided to do now. He remembered nothing of how he had come to be here. He remembered that he had been sick, very sick. He had been lifted. He had been moved. His head felt filled with after-effects of a nightmare, all vague.

The big man folded his arms across his chest; there was nowhere for him to sit in the room. Even if he'd moved Patrick's clothes off the small oak chair, or just sat down on top of them, which was probably more likely, the chair, as sturdy as it was, would not have been able to hold him.

He was dressed like a farmer, but to Patrick's fastidious shipman's eyes, the man was unkempt, messy. He wore an oversized, worn muslin shirt that looked as if it were made for a giant; it flowed over his belly like an apron.

For some reason, ridiculously, at the collar of the shirt, as if he couldn't make up his mind what occasion he'd ought to prepare for, he wore a formal, clean, new-looking English ruffle. And even more strangely, on top of his long, wild-looking, orange-red hair, he wore a wig. It was small for him, and slightly crooked; he wore it like a cap. The ponytail at the back stuck out from his head like a tail.

He noticed the way Patrick was looking at him, and motioned for Patrick to not try quite yet to speak. Quickly he took off the wig and unfastened the ruffle and removed it.

"I forgot myself. I see what I would seem, and I would not blame you for wondering on the condition of my mind. Today, I was playing the role of the English. In the firing practice, that would be. The boys what come in new, they like to have a human as would stand in front of them as their target, it not being the case they have gun balls, as you would ascertain, when they first learn the right end of a musket. Not that I would give the impression there was those as would not love the chance to have a shot at me, once they were here for a while, and had a taste of the training."

"Please. You must tell me."

"Slow as I said, Sir."

Patrick's voice was coming back. It was hoarse and shaky, but it was his. He hadn't meant to ask this question, but his brain seemed to be working quite without him. "Are you a Scot?"

"Well guessed. I am, until I die, and well beyond it."

"Your name is not Scot."

"Not as I was born, as you would guess."

"I do not understand what the boy was saying."

"He should not have come in, Sir."

"Where is my sister Jossey?"

"Waiting for you."

"And my brother-in-law?"

"Likewise."

"You know my family?"

"We are friends. Your brother-in-law, John Avens, is a man I consider ranking in honor among men of the highest honor, and your sister, Jossey, is well his match."

Then the other man went silent. Patrick changed tack. "There was a change in the new infant's name. Were it not so, he would not have said it. What would it be changed to?"

"It would be, as it was, same as you, Patrick. But now, with the Patrick put into the second place, with another in front of it, as decided by its mother and father."

"And the girl?"

"Priscilla would be likewise."

"And what would those other names be?"

"They would be, with Patrick, the name in the first was made Mowlan. With the little girl, it would changed to be Lavinia."

"As my sister Lavinia?"

"The very same, although I had not had the fortune of knowing her, nor her husband, Mowlan."

Patrick said, "Why would it be the names of the children were changed?"

"It would be, that was what was decided."

"Priscilla was the name of my mother."

"As I had heard."

"Where is my ship?"

"It would be as you would hope, waiting for you, with your men."

"What is this place?"

"A farm, the owner of it being myself. Four miles out from Lexington. I would say as there are not many what know of it, as there would be but the one road in, with a guard day and night."

"How did I come here?"

"From Boston, by wagon. It was decided, seeing as how it was necessary to have you in a place that, you could be in good line to be well, when the ones what love you, what would want to have the care of you, could not, as the necessity arose for them to travel."

"Please. You speak in riddles."

"Slow-like. You are far from well. A storm is up ahead for you."

Jackson Prout came over to Patrick and gently helped him sit up. Without being asked, he went under the bed for the chamber pot, and handed it to Patrick with a grin. Patrick didn't have the energy to summon up embarrassment for his helplessness: he was already resigned to his position as an invalid.

Jackson Prout kept talking—not cheerfully, but steadily, and almost lightly. He was trying to tell a joke.

"I heard tell that down in Virginia and Carolina they have got windows what open, with hinges or latch-work, not as here with our panes all leaded in shut. Gentlemen as I am told all very much enjoy opening their windows to be pissing into the flowerbeds of their wives. I have not had an answer to where on the window the latch would be, but I would very much hope, for the sake of the manhood of the southern colonies, it would not be in a lateral position, with a danger of coming loose. I would fear the sudden slamming down of a window-glass upon one, if you follow me, Sir. I would tend to believe it would not be an experience a man would recover from."

He took the pot when Patrick was finished with it. He left with it—no, he simply opened the door and handed it to someone standing there. Patrick hoped it wasn't Little John.

"The new ones in training, they sometimes are suited better to chores within the house," said Prout. "The boy is having his dinner."

"What o'clock is it?"

"Gone noon. You will want to lie down again, Sir."

"I can sit."

But Patrick fell back on the pillow. After a moment, he said, "Lexington has no harbor."

"The very truth."

"What harbor has my ship?"

"It would be in Massachusetts, same as yourself."

Then again, silence.

"If it was in harm," said Patrick, "I would be told that."

"You would."

"What is the day?"

"Thursday." Prout went over to the table for the bowl. "If you'd drink some soup, now."

For such a big man, he was careful and precise in his movements. He knelt on the floor at the side of the bed, where Little John had been. He slid one arm under Patrick and helped him sit up. The bowl in his big hand was steady; not a drop was spilled. The pain in Patrick's head—beginning as a slow, dull ache—had sharpened with every word he'd said, and now he felt as if he would not be able to bear it. He felt as if he'd been hit with an iron rod. But no bruise was there.

The broth went down easily. His nausea was gone. "We had a boy here when you had arrived, as was knowledgeable with plants, his mother being a midwife."

Patrick swallowed hard. In the broth were bits of leaves, and tiny sticks, and bits of something that tasted and felt like tree bark. He could not deny that the pain in his head was easing already.

"What name?"

"Otis. Gone now to your ship in point of fact. You will know him soon enough."

"What name of his mother?" It made sense to Patrick to suppose for a moment that in the time since he walked away from Caroline Knox, she could have married, given birth, and raised a son who was now fully grown. He wondered if he would ever be able to hear the word "midwife" and not see her face, as if in front of him, as if he could reach for her and touch her hair.

"He never said the name of his mother. I believe she lives nearby, in Concord. You'll do well to drink all of what's in the bowl, Sir."

Jackson Prout didn't hurry him. He held the bowl to Patrick's lips again and again. Now and then he paused and, lifting the bottom of his shirt, he found a patch that was relatively clean, and used it like a towel to pat Patrick's chin dry. This did not disgust Patrick, or even bother him. When the bowl was empty, he went back to the door, opened it.

"Uncle!" cried Little John. "Let me in!"

The door was shut. Prout came back with a heavy earthenware cup and a small plate. Mint tea, lukewarm. On the plate was bread.

"I believe I can feed that to myself," said Patrick.

"Be my guest, Sir."

But Patrick's hands were shaking too badly to manage. Prout sat at the edge of the bed. He broke up the bread and fed it to Patrick, dipping each piece in the tea.

"I would like to have the boy sent in."

"In time."

"I would like to be told how it happened that I came to be here."

"You had come into Charlestown, delivering your goods, which was done, and you took sick. They brought you—your good men, that would be—into Boston, to John Avens and your sister, who had in the doctor, and saw to it, afterward, as there was news of certain developments, you were brought here, with the boy."

"How was my sister Jossey?"

"Perhaps as you would expect, far from well about things, and most out of herself."

"And what was the opinion of this doctor?"

"That the sickness in you was brought on by no ailment of your physical self."

"You confound me. You would have me believe it was mystical, that I was puking and had been struck from my wits?"

"Not mystical. Explainable, like, you shall see."

"Perhaps I shall not. Where is John Avens?"

"He has left his parish, with your sister Jossey and the two little ones that now are Mowlan and Lavinia."

For the first time, Patrick realized that there was a small fireplace in the room, with logs glowing low. It was there all along, never being shut down, he knew, but he'd not smelled the good familiar scent of smoke and burning wood until now. He felt warmed. He felt that some part of his strength was beginning to come back, like the first signs on a shore that the tide is coming back in.

Patrick wondered, what sort of training went on here? Muskets, Prout had said. Training, muskets, target: there could only be one reason why a farmer would put on a ruffle and wig and stand up as a target for practice. He said, "I have no memory of how I came."

"It shall return."

"Have my men left my crew?"

Prout laughed out loud at the preposterousness of that. "It would be a hot day in December when that would happen."

"You say my goods were delivered."

"And paid for."

"And what would have come of the payment?"

"It would have come that . . ."

Prout paused, deliberating with himself, as if walking on shaky ground. "It would be that your men, the three of them, came to the decision to do a thing you would have done yourself, had you been in your senses, and walking about as your normal self, fully well."

Prout set the empty cup and plate on the table. Patrick lay back on the bed. "I want to rest." Sudden fatigue was pushing against his head, in place of the pain.

"You would want to stay awake. You would not want to waste the nourishment you have swallowed down on merely sleeping, when we would need to get you dressed."

"Please. I am very tired."

"And shaved."

Shaved? Patrick's fingers were as shaky as if they had no bones. "I would remove half the skin of my face."

"I shall take care of it."

"I think not," said Patrick.

"I think, Sir, you would do well to have yourself back to normal."

It was Prout who asked the next question. "What would you have done with the gold for the rum, had you been there yourself to collect it?"

That was easy. "Paid my men. Put up in Charlestown for a new mainsail. And some fittings were needing replacement."

"And the rest of it, if you would not mind the prodding."

Patrick was reluctant to say more. He'd planned, on his return trip to Maine, to stop at York to deliver part of the gold to Winnie Goodridge, for guns. What Winnie was doing at the tavern in York was not a business that would thrive on being well-known.

But here was Prout. He seemed to know everything. "Guns."

"Yes."

"You would have been wanting them. To have them."

"You know my friend Mrs. Goodridge?"

The big man shook his head. "I speak of your ship. What was decided to be done to it. At a cove of the Nahant Peninsula, that would be."

Even at his most fuddled, Patrick would know what everyone did—that is, every colonial connected with the coast. A cove at Nahant meant one thing only: the base of a secret militia of Massachusetts privateers who called themselves the Hammerheads, after the iron foundry that used to be in nearby Saugus. Hammersmith Foundry had been shut down for almost a hundred years, but Hammerhead Cove was thriving.

"Two four-pounders, and two six-. The fours with a five foot barrel and the sixes being slightly more," said Jackson Prout. "They were telling me, it is a fine, powerful boat. They were saying your deck is taking to the guns with a fine, keen pleasure. They were happy to be of service, in the cove."

Patrick didn't know any of the Hammerheads personally. "You would lose me," he said. "The name of my ship is *York Sawyer.*"

"Aye. Now being outfitted, Sir."

"You speak of *cannons?*"

"Aye."

"On my ship?"

"Bought and arranged for. Now, being put on."

"I would pretend I understand you, but I am, as I said, most tired."

"They had put their minds in place of your own. Once they had news of what was done in Maine, Captain, Sir."

Those words, "what was done in Maine," were delivered in a slower, lower voice. Jackson Prout stared hard at Patrick, gauging if he should go on, or wait. Patrick knew this, and looked at him as if he spoke a different language.

"The men had reasoned you would be interested in arming yourself, in such a way as to take up position with impunity, at sea and in the rivers as well."

"I have no interest in privateering," said Patrick. "I am interested in delivering goods, as would be ordered and paid for."

"Not anymore, as you will see."

"Why? Please, why?"

"It would not be that there is not a requirement for rum, as what your goods would constitute. You would be interested, as we are here, as I have been all the days of my life, since I was brought to Canada, as a boy, in perhaps doing harm to those what would be Englishmen, Sir. Specifically, English soldiers and their officers."

"You know that my brother-in-law Mowlan was taken captive?"

"Aye. Fourteen years ago."

"I shall see him and my sister next week in Maine, though they know not I am coming. It is meant as a surprise."

Jackson Prout said nothing, but his big, craggy, sunburned face took on a new expression: he looked harder, graver, even solemn.

"Uncle! Uncle! You shall need more firewood! I have wood! Let me in!"

"We have all we need and thank you, and mind how you stand guard," bellowed Jackson Prout.

There was a pause from the other side of the door: then the little boy knocked rapidly, insistently. "Tell Mr. Jackson, they are wanting him in the field to be shot at! He must go at once!"

Patrick said, "Would you now allow me the boy?"

"After you're dressed and prepared, as we would have need of the privacy."

Jackson Prout went out, silenced Little John, and came back with a bowl of water and a wooden plate that held a hair comb and a long-handled razor. The comb and the razor's handle were made of ivory. "Elephant tooth," it was called. One would not expect a farmer to lavish money on such objects.

"I would go to sleep now," said Patrick.

"That you would not."

The big man moved Patrick's clothes to the bed and got Patrick, wrapped in the quilt, to the chair. Patrick had never been shaved before by anyone except himself. But he submitted. He wanted to stop talking. He wanted to delay the knowing of what it was he needed to know.

Jackson Prout's touch was deft; he knew what he was doing. Patrick had a week's growth of beard; he had never liked being bearded at all, and began to feel glad for the chance to get rid of it. Anything was better than the asking of questions that brought answers he could not understand.

Jackson Prout took his time with the razor, and felt moved to talk about his life, unprompted. The razor and comb had belonged to his grandfather, in Scotland, not far from Edinburgh. His grandfather had been "what you would call, Captain, a member of the aristocracy."

His father, a second son, had been given the deed to a vast tract of land near Quebec; if the land were in Scotland it would have been the size of three villages. A great house was built, which was a version of an English castle.

"I was brought at the age of seven, hardly more than the rascally boy out there, and in time, there being war with the French, who I was expected to look upon as the enemy, what came to my mind was a loathing, very great, for good reason, of the English, and naturally it would follow I would find myself out of favor with those what were my family, and thus I came down from Canada. I had made a plan to go to Edinburgh, but what with stopping in Lexington, I came to see there were men what felt as I did, toward the king and the Parliament."

"How came you to change your name?"

"It was the name of the brother of my wife, what was killed in Virginia. Shot in the back, as he tried to make his escape, to be made an example of."

"Jackson Prout was a Negro?" said Patrick. "A slave?"

"Aye. Born in Virginia. Tobacco."

"And your wife?"

"My wife had made her escape the year previous. It was well I made the severing with my family. They would be people what would not take kindly to how I married."

"Is your wife here, with you?" If Patrick didn't have to be still—with the razor at his throat—he would have turned toward the door, imagining that a woman was there, as if on a stage, waiting for her cue.

"She is dead now four years, Captain. She took sick from the smallpox. I was spared. I was what nursed her."

"Have you children?"

"My wife could not bear, Sir. My wife had been scarred very badly."

"I am sorry for you," said Patrick.

"I had, Sir, in the years we had together, a better time of it, I would say, than what most men have in double the years."

Jackson Prout had finished his task, and patted Patrick's face, with the towel this time, not his shirt. Neither of them spoke for the moments it took Patrick to get into his clothes. Patrick was able to handle the comb, to comb his own hair. His hands were not trembling at all. Good.

Patrick was now standing upright in the center of the small room. "You look what I would say is presentable, Captain," said Jackson Prout.

He was supporting Patrick by holding on to both of his arms. When he let go, Patrick surprised himself by not falling over. He could hold his own weight, without wobbling. He felt proud of himself. His mind was in a state of alert.

The two men stood there and looked at each other. In a moment, he would not be the same Patrick Rouse he was now. It would not be his name that was changed, but himself.

"You have handled me well. Thank you," said Patrick.

Jackson Prout held out his hand. They shook hands formally. Their eyes met. "You might be wanting to sit, Captain."

"I want to stand."

"Aye."

"I believe I have followed your course very well. I believe I am ready to be told what you must tell me," said Patrick.

Jackson Prout did not look away from Patrick's face, not once. He spoke clearly, directly, slowly, without emotion. "It would do with your sister what lived in Tibbetston."

"Lavinia," Patrick said.

"Aye, her and hers. In Tibbetston, there was what the English said was Indians, what were not Indians at all," began Jackson Prout.

The logs in the fireplace were almost cinders. The room had become chilly. Autumn-yellow, late-afternoon sunlight came pouring in through the opened part of the shutters, without warming what it fell on. Patrick stood there and listened to everything he had to be told. It took a long time.

CHAPTER VI

SALEM

ONE THING PATRICK ROUSE had in common with Sarah
Dudley was this: each of them had decided on a solitary life,
having despaired, for different reasons, of finding someone who'd
put up with them, and simply take them for who they were. Each
of them believed deeply that marriage was something designed for
other people, not for themselves, as fishes were not designed to fly
through air. "Should it ever happen to me again that I'm attracted
in a certain way to someone, I'll flee that person immediately," was
pretty much how they both felt.

While Patrick and his nephew made their way up the coast
from Massachusetts to Maine, in a series of carriage rides, Sarah
Dudley was doing the same.

In Salem, Massachusetts, and in certain circles of Boston, Sarah
Dudley was ripe for marriage. Jacques Wabanaki was not the only
person who said of her "she is gold." She was considered a prize
catch, and it wasn't purely because her family had made a fortune
in shipping.

She wasn't as pretty, people said, as her younger, unmarried sister, and she wasn't as ambitious and clever as her sister who married Samuel Leyson and moved to his estate in Maine. She was
certainly very different.

She was popular. She could read, write, calculate sums, and answer general questions about countries and history. She could quote
at length from the Bible; she had memorized most of the psalms.
She could ride risky horses fearlessly. She could play the piano—

hymns only, as she'd never been allowed anything else—and she could sing like a bird. She could converse in sitting rooms; she was an excellent dancer.

But in all these things, she felt no pride or satisfaction. It had all been a matter of going through the motions and doing what was required of her, as a means to draw no negative attention to herself, on any level. She had made up her mind when she was still a little girl that she would *be good.*

"Please do not let anyone think I am a witch. Please help me keep being good." Her nightly prayers contained these lines every night of her childhood.

There were people in modern-day Salem who made it through a whole lifetime without ever once thinking about the fact that, in the streets where they lived, not that long ago, a girl who was said to be "bad" could be captured, even as she slept in her bed. She could be hauled into court for a trial, and be condemned to a hanging, or a drowning. The girl, the witch, had to choose which way she'd be killed.

Sarah Dudley thought about the witches and the witches' trials of Salem a great deal.

She would wonder, if given the choice, which way she would choose. Hanging would break your neck quickly, they said, but with hanging, first they'd put you into the stocks—always in the dead of winter, or at the height of summer. Was drowning easier? Maybe. Maybe you'd go down underwater with the hope that God would intercede, like a god from a fairy tale: you'd be changed into a fish or a turtle. You'd swim to the other shore and emerge a human again, completely free, completely yourself.

No one would ever tell Sarah how many people from Salem were tortured and destroyed for being witches. "Many," was the answer she had arrived at. No one wanted to talk about the old religion and the witches, or, if they did, it was always as a threat, as in, "Sarah, a girl that doesn't sit still at table is a girl with a soul that would develop to the soul of a witch, and Mama and Papa will not be able to save you, when they come for you."

Or, "Sarah, mind the care you take with that needle. Would you forget that they ascertained witches by how a woman held a needle when she sewed?"

There was only one thing she could honestly say she was proud of. She could embroider exquisitely, and had, at the age of sixteen, completed a large bit of tapestry that now hung in the Dudleys' foyer.

It was the only thing in her parents' house she loved. She loved it partly because she'd made it herself, but mostly because, when she looked at it, it took on an objectivity and remoteness, and was simply very beautiful, as if the maker didn't matter at all.

It was three feet wide and four feet long. It had taken four years to complete it. When she'd finished, her family begged for another, but she refused.

At sixteen, she had been ready to start calling herself a woman. She had felt very strongly that embroidery was not for a grownup, but for the hands of a girl who was sitting around in her parents' house, stuck like a bird in a cage, with a furious, almost uncontrolled impatience. Sewing wasn't just a way to be good. It was a way to handle the impatience.

Her tapestry was a winter scene done in white, gray, black, and brown threads. Much of it was snow. The absence of color was a shock; most embroidered works, at least the works of Salem girls, were meant to be pleasing to the eye, with colors like an imaginary, perfect garden of flowers. Other girls chose spring, summer. But Sarah didn't call it "Winter."

She called it "Waiting." One brown oak, stark and bony, stood at the top of a small, snow-banked hill. The sky above it was as gray as smoke. In a few branches of the tree were black silhouettes of birds, with heads tucked under their wings, as if a storm were on the way, and they knew it.

It was going to be hard to leave that tapestry behind. She had thought about telling her family, and most of the servants, too, that she was taking it down for a cleaning. But she didn't want to raise any alarms. She had already traded four of her silk brocade dresses, and her beaver muff, with a servant at a neighbor's house, a girl who could be trusted. In return she got a plain, working-class wool cloak, two much-patched wool skirts, and a homespun blouse.

She would use her gold locket for fare on the mail coach that would take her up to Portsmouth. She would not stay long in New Hampshire, just long enough to connect with the next coach. She would pay for the ride to Maine with two silver rings.

Along with the trade in clothes for her muff and expensive dresses, bought from London, she secured the services of the young fiancé of the neighbor's maid—Abel Brown was his name. Abel Brown drove a wagon for a dairy farm outside Salem, and came into town before dawn with deliveries of milk and cheese for the shops and taverns. It was in this wagon she'd be conveyed from home to the mail coach.

The Maine coach would get her to Falmouth. Falmouth was said to be civilized, but she didn't kid herself that, on her own, brave and careful or not, she'd be safe. It was a port town; it was big; it had nothing like her own neighborhood in Salem. She would not be safe for a minute. Her maid's mother, a widow, lived near the harbor, and had promised, for no payment, to meet her herself with a horse, wagon, and driver, and take her up the coast to Tibbetston, to Jacques and Naomi Wabanaki.

They knew she was coming. She had written to them, a brief, simple note, done hastily. "Please when I come to Tibbetston, will you kindly take me in? I know of the murders. I know what was done to my sister's husband's farm. I do not belong with my family. I must leave Salem at once. You are my only hope."

As for her own maid, another Sarah—Sarah Pease, who was thirty, and had been with her since she was born—great care had been taken to spare her the trouble of being subjected to the Dudley family's wrath, and the Leysons' as well, once they discovered she was gone. Sarah Pease wanted to remain in Salem, at least for now, not that she had a choice. The coaches would only take one traveler and, anyway, if anyone in Salem tried to go searching—with plenty of money for bribes—they would find it much harder to track one runaway than two. That part of the plan had taken the most thought, the most craftiness.

For the last three days, Sarah Dudley and Sarah Pease, who until now had never had a harsh word between them, had waged a loud, dramatic series of arguments: their shouting matches were carried out publicly in the halls, the sitting room, the sun room, and even in the Dudleys' enormous, luxurious dining hall, where the first rule of family meals was "maintain a hushed decorum."

Sarah Dudley would sit in her place at the table and pause in the lifting of a soup spoon to shout, really *shout*, at Sarah Pease, eating in the scullery with the other servants. "You must tender your quitting, Sarah Pease! I will not have you near me! You are a wretch, a layabout, and an altogether undesirable woman!"

Her family, appalled, concluded that it was time to separate her from her maid. In the point of view of Sarah Dudley's father, who owned hunting dogs, it was just like what happened with dogs: you could have two females together as long as one was a pup, but as soon as the pup was grown, those two females would go at each other to the death; it was just a law of nature.

No one disagreed with him. Samuel Leyson, who was staying at the house, offered to take Sarah Pease off the Dudleys' hands, but his wife wouldn't hear of it. On the day Sarah Dudley slipped out of her home to crawl into Abel Brown's milk wagon, Sarah Pease was taking up her new position as second assistant to the Dudleys' cook.

Sarah Pease had never cooked a thing in her life; she was a lady's maid. She wouldn't be in for a easy time of it, but it would appear that she'd be the last person on earth to know where Sarah Dudley had gone, or how she had managed it. Thus, no one in the Dudley family would think of Sarah Pease's mother in Falmouth as the person Sarah would be meeting.

"I shall come to you as soon as I can," was how Sarah Pease had left it. "I shall say my heart is broken from your sudden spurning of me, and I am fearfully distraught, and must now send to my mother, to come and fetch me to her home in Maine."

Sarah Dudley couldn't give her anything to use in trade, or to sell, for her trip: the Dudleys' servants were always being suspected of thieving. Sarah's father employed a servant whose sole job was to supervise the others. Their rooms were regularly searched, and sometimes, so were their persons. Sarah Dudley had two silver plates, inherited from her Dudley grandparents; she would bring them with her so Sarah Pease's mother could sell them. Sarah Dudley had no money of her own.

She wondered if they would destroy the tapestry when they re-alized what she had done. She wondered what they would say to the Summersons. Her engagement to Reuben Summerson had not been announced: her parents planned to do so at their dance on New Year's Eve. Now, she was free of the burden of having to break it off before it happened.

She knew that Reuben Summerson would not go looking for her; she wondered if he'd feel relieved she was gone.

The Summersons owned the biggest ship yard in Salem; at any given time they had five or six merchant ships under construction, and their hemp shop was one of the largest on the eastern coast. If it weren't for the building of the ships, they would have made a for-tune anyway in selling rope. Reuben Summerson, their second son, managed the hemp operation. She had known him all her life. He was older than she was, by twelve years.

He was a handsome, elegant-looking man, dark-haired and vi-brant: when he walked into a room, he brought with him a sort of visceral, powerful charisma.

His movements and manners were always just right for which-ever situation he found himself in. He had gone to college in Vir-ginia. His time away from New England—especially the winters—had given him an ease and deliberateness, and put a slow, drawly cadence in his voice. He had never handled hemp himself; his hands were long and smooth.

His first wife had died in childbirth, with their first child. He had moved out of the house where he'd lived with her, and he was having another built, just outside Salem, with fourteen rooms, on two hundred acres of Summerson land. He had admired the mansions of tobacco plantation owners in Virginia and the Car-olinas, and wanted one for himself. Of the three Dudley sisters, Sarah, it seemed, would be the one with the biggest house.

With a sort of sleepwalking-type unawareness, she had agreed to marry him. His first wife had not been dead for long when this happened, and it had seemed to Sarah that the actuality of it would never come. Agreeing had seemed a way to be left alone.

Perhaps she might have gone ahead with it. She knew, from the few times she'd been alone with Reuben Summerson, he was not a man who cared about emotional intimacies, or confidences; he was aloof, polite, gentle. He seemed to genuinely find her wonderful in every way—perhaps he looked at her the same way she looked at her tapestry. She had gotten the idea that being married to such a man might have its benefits.

One afternoon in early October—a Sunday, and the shipyard was closed—he came calling on her, to go out walking with him.

She took his arm. They nodded to people they passed; they took tea at the house of one of his aunts. He had seemed agitated, excited: he liked the way people admired them. He seemed to stand taller, with his shoulders drawn back even more than usual, as if, in her presence, his chest had expanded. He took some brandy at his aunt's.

After tea, they strolled down past the shipyard. Did she want to see the inside of one of the hemp sheds? She did, very much.

She remembered that it was dim and shadowy. She remembered great loops and coils of rope hanging everywhere, and giant, loom-like apparatuses, standing in shadows and dust. The air was thickly dusty. It had never occurred to her that she ought to be wary of him. It had never occurred to her that he might have been some-one who, in a flash, changed completely.

She had never, until this moment, been handled roughly by another human being, in any way at all. "My darling," he said.

The brandy made his voice sound even more lush, honeyed. He got hold of her arms and led her—she dragged her feet; she tried to stop him—to a lean-to at the back of the big building, where he had a private office. There was a desk, a chair, a cot.

She was put on the cot. His weight on top of her made her think she was going to be crushed. She fought him even harder when she realized he was thrusting his hands up her skirt, for her drawers. "I'll not put seed inside you until we are wed," he told her.

No one had ever told her that what went on between a man and a woman would hurt. No one had told her it could be like this. She had the awareness she might never be able to walk again, as if he would cripple her.

Her belly felt oozed with semen when he pulled out of her. It was sticky, like syrup. It was different from the blood between her legs. When she saw that she was bloody, she thought she was suddenly menstruating; it was just about that time of the month. When he got off her, he came back with a bowl of water and a towel.

"You are still a virgin, Sarah," he said, in a quiet voice. He seemed to be waiting for her to say something to him by way of thanks. He seemed to be waiting for her to speak to him of love. That was how he acted.

She was able to get out of the shed while he fussed with grooming himself. She knew she could run faster than he could, even though she'd never in her life had a reason to *run*.

It was dusk when she made it back home, alone. Her family was gathered in the west-side drawing room. Someone was playing piano. Someone must have told a witty story; there was laughter. She rushed to her bedroom, stripped off her clothes, and gave them to Sarah Pease to have them burned.

The next time he called at the Dudley house, she refused to see him. And the next, and the next. Her family didn't seem to think it was strange that she ignored him. She was probably just simply getting nervous about her engagement, it was felt.

She didn't hate him. She spent no effort of feeling on him at all. It was the same as if the man who came walking up the cobblestones toward the Dudleys' front door, with his hat in his hands, was completely, absolutely unknown to her.

She looked down at him from her window—and let him see that she saw him—and she was as blank as if he were a stranger.

"I shall never marry. I shall never have a man near me," she vowed. She left a letter full of untruths to her family. She said she was leaving for England, to visit with distant relatives of theirs. And then she went to Maine.

CHAPTER VII

PORTSMOUTH

"UNCLE, MR. PROUT said your ship has cannons."

"So I'm told."

"When will we get to your ship?"

"As I told you before, you won't be taken on it until you're tall enough that the top of your head is level with my shoulder."

"I'm that tall now."

"You're standing on a rock."

"I want to go back inside the tavern. I want to talk to the lady who smiled at me when we passed through."

"I saw no lady."

"You *did.* She is a traveler as we are, but they found she can read and write, so she's stopping here to write letters. For the people who did not do their lessons, Uncle, and cannot write themselves."

"How would it be you noticed that?"

"So did you!"

It was true. Last night and again this morning, in a dim corner of the tavern—and it was crowded, mostly with militia men who'd been on training exercises—a woman in her early twenties, in a dark, servant-type cloak, which she didn't take off, was granting the wishes of customers who wanted letters written.

Patrick didn't know where the letters were intended to go. He'd heard a man saying to her, "Write to my father, Eli Bowen, to say I have work with a cooper, for there is plenty of money to be made in barrels, and I shall one day take over the shop."

The tavern owner had given her ink, paper. It was good for business. Walking past her, Patrick had the feeling he knew her. He couldn't quite place her, and it seemed too much trouble to try. He shook it off, but his thoughts kept going back to her, in a vague, troubled, inarticulate way.

"Uncle, we must go back inside now."

"We'll be stuck inside the carriage all day, and the roads will be rough. This is time to get air and exercise. You are a child. Mama would tell you, take air and exercise."

Little John was bored with traveling the long route up the coast from Lexington to Maine. He was ragged and dirty. They had stopped last night at a tavern in Portsmouth, New Hampshire. They weren't supposed to stay the night, just for dinner, but the carriage driver had claimed that one of the horses was badly shod, and must be taken to a smithy. The driver was a lanky, energetic boy of nineteen or twenty, one of Jackson Prout's trainees.

There was nothing wrong with the horse. The boy had found the militia men, all much older, to be friendly, and had been quick to announce himself as a Minute Man. "In training," he didn't add.

The boy was enjoying his small taste of celebrity. Everyone knew that the Lexington militia thought of itself as the best, as a standard-setter. It probably didn't happen in Newburyport that the captain of the trainees put on a ruffle and wig to be shot at.

Again this morning, conversations ran as freely as the cider and ale. They compared their feelings about different types of flints, and how big of a tinderbox to carry, and if a buckskin bag was most durable, and how many powder horns should be part of their packs. Three, it was felt: a tiny one for measuring the gunpowder, a small one for powder for the flash pan, and a full-size one for the powder itself.

They wondered at the wisdom of the Brainy Whigs in Boston who kept insisting that, if it came to the point where shots were fired, the first shot would have to be British: no American would be the aggressor. They wondered if it was merely to conserve ammunition.

They talked about the meaning of *defenders*. They compared the differences between rifles and muskets, and agreed that, overwhelmingly, a rifle, which was harder to get, was superior for the relative ease of loading it, and the clean quick whiz of the shot, and, most importantly, it was a thing they knew how to use, which the British did not.

The British scorned American rifles, it was felt, as they scorned whatever wasn't made in England. But once they got a feel for the barrel of a rifle staring at their heads, and held by a colonist who was hiding behind a tree—the tone became braggardly very quickly—they would need to learn appreciation for a rifle.

It went on and on. Patrick could not take part in these discussions. There were as many militia men gathered in the tavern as there were Apostles.

But there was no Jesus. Patrick would have liked it if there was someone who perhaps could play the role—some local militia leader, some larger-than-life man, who perhaps wasn't merely human, who would quietly sit in the center of things and then get up and, on the way to leading a battle charge, raise his arms and work a miracle, such as raising some people from the dead.

There was no hero. There would be no miracles.

Meanwhile, the woman with the ink sat confidently, serenely, transcribing people's messages. She seemed to have a firm hand. "Deliver it to the vicar as he is the only one what can read," someone had said to her last night.

She was alone—an astonishing thing, a woman traveling alone—but there was an older man who kept hovering close by, and Patrick knew by his clothes and manner he was a mail driver. He didn't seem in a hurry; the tavern owner kept plying him with food and drink.

In the last couple of days he'd tried to explain to the boy why his parents were in Maine now, instead of Boston, and were saying they would stay there for good. It did not seem to bother him that he had left his home. He was interested much more in adventure, and he was with his uncle.

"You will not see your cousins and your Mowlan uncle and aunt," he had tried. "Because they are not going to be there, not ever again. They are gone to heaven."

That's what you were supposed to say to a child, Patrick felt. Fresh air, exercise, heaven.

"A bad thing happened," Patrick had explained. "A singularly, unthinkably bad thing."

"But how can a thing be unthinkable, if you're thinking it?"

"You sound like your father."

"I shall not be a preacher. I shall have a ship."

"It's unthinkable because, until it happened, it would not have been a possibility to have imagined anything like it. Some people have committed a terrible crime."

"Papa says they used to make people put their heads outside in a wood block if they did something bad, and other people spat at them all day. Papa says there was more crime done against people that made crimes, than the crime they did."

"These people aren't like that."

"Are they English?"

"Did Papa tell you bad people are English?"

"No, Uncle. You did."

"I did?"

"When we were leaving Mr. Prout's farm."

"I do not recall. But you must have it in your head that you will not see the Mowlans. All of them are gone now, John, but you must remember them always."

"When shall we get to Aunt Lavinia's farm?"

"We shall not go to the farm. I told you, Mama and Papa and Priscilla and the babe are in a good house, the blacksmith's house, waiting for you."

"She is not Priscilla. They had the changes. She is Lavinia, and my brother is Mowlan, from now on, for forever. When we were back in Boston and they had come to tell us everyone in Maine was dead, Papa and Mama made the changes and said they shall last for forever."

"Very well then."

"I made up my mind. I want to be called Patrick instead of John."

"But you're John already. Do you remember the blacksmith's house?"

He nodded. "When we were there last, Mr. Wabanaki let me make a nail. He said when I come again, I shall stand on a stool and hammer a fire iron."

"Then you shall."

"I shall bring my cousins with me."

"No. They're gone."

"So am I, and so are you." He thought Patrick had meant that they had taken a journey.

"Robert is gone, Seth is gone, Nathaniel is gone, Mary is gone, Margaret is gone, your aunt Lavinia is gone, your uncle William is gone. You must not expect to see them. They are gone."

Patrick kept wanting to say their names, over and over. When he tried to picture their faces, especially his sister's, nothing was there. He was terrified of the strange new blankness that kept rushing into his mind.

He wondered if he would ever have a clear thought again. He realized that if he didn't have his nephew to take care of, he'd be in much worse shape than the very bad shape he was in.

Patrick and the driver and the boy had slept last night—the three of them in one bed—on a soggy, hay-and-horsehair mattress, in a room that smelled badly of mold. But at least they'd eaten well—quahogs and roasted venison for supper, and good bread and fried pork and boiled apples for breakfast. For the first time since he'd been sick, Patrick had the satisfaction of a full belly, which was doing all right by way of staying full.

"I want to go back inside and sit with the lady."

Little John must have wanted his mother, but wouldn't admit it. Patrick knew the feeling. He said gently, "Would you ask her to write someone a letter for you?"

"I can write myself."

"Who would be the person you would write to?"

"My cousins, Rob and Seth and Natty, and I may call him Natty, not Nathaniel, he said, though no one else may. And Mary too, but not Margaret. She is only three. I would write one letter to all of them and say they must be ready to bring me to the river, as soon as I have arrived, to look at ships. If I must go to Mr. Wabanaki's house, I shall first look at ships."

"John, do you know what it means when someone is dead?"

"Jesus was dead."

"Not like Jesus. Like Grandfather."

"Grandfather died."

"Then you know if someone is dead, you cannot see them?"

"Mama says she can see Grandpapa."

"Mama must have meant that sometimes when she is asleep, and dreaming, she dreams of him. So do I."

"It was not that she was talking about her dreams."

Suddenly, the boy jumped down from the big rock he'd been teetering on; his face changed from somberness to a wide, happy, excited grin. "Here she *is*, Uncle."

Sarah's cloak was hooded, and she reached up to grasp hold of it as she approached them. Her thin face was tired, haggard, but she did not seem to Patrick to be in distress. She seemed sure of herself. Her hair had not been washed, by the look of it, for several days, but it was honey-brown and still lustrous, and hung loose around her head, like a young girl's. It struck Patrick how pinched and severe so many women always looked with their hair pulled tightly back. Sarah let go of the hood, and did not conceal herself.

Patrick felt weak, and as empty through his body as if he'd eaten nothing for days. He wanted to touch her hair, and had to put his hands in his pockets; the desire was too much to bear. He knew he had met her before. He knew, too, that when he'd met her, when she'd been visiting the Leysons, it had not been unpleasant.

The boy had never met Sarah before, but rushed to her side and, as if he'd known her all his life, stood before her very closely, tipping back his head, looking up at her, like a dog that would give you no choice but to pat it. Patrick hated himself for the anger that lit up in him when Sarah placed her hand on Little John's shoulder, then the side of his face.

"I am John Avens! But you must call me Patrick!"

"I am Sarah."

"We have no need of a scrivener," Patrick said coldly.

She looked at him over the top of Little John's head. Her eyes met his directly. He could not look away, as much as he wanted to.

"We know each other, Patrick," she said quietly. "I have no words to say to you to offer comfort for what happened to your family. Please. I cannot get out of my mind what was done."

There was no doubt she was sincere. It was not hard for Patrick to figure it out that she was honest, she was genuine, she was kind. But that irritated him all the more.

He remembered seeing her on horseback, too, riding fast on

Surrey Hill Road, thinking no one was watching her. She wore jodhpurs, not a skirt. She did not ride sidesaddle like a lady. She rode like a man.

The horse he had seen her on belonged to Samuel Leyson. She was a Leyson—if not by birth, then by circumstances. Her sister was Leyson's wife. She was a Dudley, of the Salem Dudleys.

Like Leyson, they were Tory to the root.

"I have heard that your brother's farm in Maine was pillaged," said Patrick.

"He is not my brother. He is the man whom one of my sisters had married."

"I was glad of the news of the wrecking of his farm, all the same. I am not ashamed to say so."

The desire to give himself over to the need to have something in his hands—her hair—that was soft and warm and unmasculine, gave way instead to a powerful wish to do her harm. He took his hands out of his pockets and found that, incredibly, they were shaking.

Once when he was eight years old, the news came to York that a family in a nearby village had been set upon by Micmacs. There'd been a father, a mother, several children. The amazing part of the news had not been the fate of that family, but the fact that this was the first time anyone had heard of that tribe causing trouble, never mind becoming warlike. The Micmacs had been peaceable.

The children had not been killed. One of them, a sickly boy, was left behind to tell the tale of what was done to his family, but the others were taken (and were never heard of again). Perhaps the Micmacs desired white children to be used in trades, as barter for the release of other Indians who'd been taken as hostages. Perhaps a Micmac had been kidnapped. The British were always kidnapping Indians and bringing them to London, to be shown like a prize exhibit at a fair.

As the story went, the Micmacs had forced those children to watch their parents be killed, which was unthinkable. And then they'd forced those children to watch their parents being scalped.

This was what Patrick had on his mind. The scalping. He pictured himself at the same age as Little John.

He saw himself lying on his back on the floor of the saw mill, near a window, in a cascade of yellow, sawdusty sunlight. A book was in his hands but he wasn't reading it. His father was at work. The sounds of the mill were deafening, but Patrick was deaf to it anyway. He'd never known anything else. He'd only just heard the story of the Micmacs and he could not get it out of his mind.

Safe inside the sawmill, eight-year-old Patrick touched his fingers to his forehead at the line where his hair began, and imagined scalping. He thought about a knife blade, or a hatchet blade. He thought about a blade in his own hand, and he found himself taking the part of the Indian.

He had pictured a boy he knew, who lived at a farm outside York—a bully, a brute, who had taunted younger children, and whipped horses—and he pictured himself grabbing the boy in a headlock, and thinking, objectively, as he raised the blade to his scalp, "This will be no different from slicing a rabbit, or a squirrel."

This fantasy had come to him so strongly, it had registered in his brain, he realized, as an actual event. He could not believe he had in him such violence, but once the discovery was there, there was no undoing it.

He saw himself a scalper. A terrible, icy terror had made him start shaking so badly, his father, along with some of his men, rushed over to him and pulled him up to his feet, thinking he was having some sort of a fit. He had sobbed uncontrollably, and sputtered, "Papa, Papa, I know what it means to *scalp*."

"But you are only a small boy."

"But I *know* about it."

"Indians shall never harm you," his father had said to him.

Patrick had been patted on the head. No one, except himself, would ever think of him as someone who sometimes ought to be feared.

And here he was, with a woman who was a Dudley, of the Salem Tory Dudleys, who had slept in the home of Samuel Leyson, her relative.

"God help me," Patrick said to himself. "When I looked twice at this woman's hair, I found myself desiring a blade in my hands. May God forgive me."

Little John had turned to look at him over his shoulder. His expression was puzzled, worried. Why should his uncle, who never spoke harshly, speak harshly to this beautiful, wonderful woman, who was letting him lean his head against her, just under her breast, with a smell of wool and sweat, and a feel of warmth and softness?

"I have left my home," the woman said. "I would be obliged, if you should meet up with any members of my family, you would not say you had seen me."

"Your family are not people I would choose to speak with, of any matter at all."

"And I must tell you, the life I had lived before, is no longer the life I am leading."

"That would be true for many of us."

"It is possible there are people from Salem who might be looking for me."

"You are a runaway then."

"I am. I had left word I went to England, and it will be some months before they know that to be untrue, yet I am worried."

"You are a runaway, like a slave."

"That I am."

"I would wonder what bounty is on your head."

"So would I."

Patrick bowed his head. He got hold of himself. The hardness and coldness went out of his voice. "Please forgive me," he said. "Please. I have not been well."

Little John cheered up. "Uncle! Her name is Sarah!"

"I know."

"Sarah!" he cried. "Our driver is a Minute Man! We know the soldiers in Lexington! We're going to Maine!"

She smiled at him. "So am I."

"You must come with us! Uncle! Say she will come in our carriage!"

"There is no room."

"There is! There is!"

Patrick went over to them. He took hold of the boy's hand.

He said to her, "You travel alone?"

"I'm riding with the mail," said Sarah. "I'm going to meet a friend, who is waiting for me in Falmouth."

"We shall take you there," said Patrick. "As we are passing by anyway."

He allowed his eyes to look at her face, and her hair. He wanted to ask her if she was afraid of him. But then he felt he didn't have to. He felt that she was standing there, meeting his gaze squarely, and asking him the same thing.

CHAPTER VIII

AT SEA

P ATRICK TRIED TO BE glad that his crew was still his crew, even with the addition of the new boy from Jackson Prout's farm in Lexington. His name was Otis. He was the son of the midwife from Massachusetts. Patrick hadn't asked for this new one. He didn't want him. But nothing could be done about it. If war was coming, one's own will was as frothy and insubstantial as foam on top of a wave.

There was going to be a war. Was that correct? And then what? Exchange one king and one set of lords for another?

He wondered if he was expected to be jubilant, slapping his crew on the backs, all stirred to a giddy new emotional height, taking pride in their marvelous accomplishment. He felt no pride. He was disordered, shaky, unsure, nervous. The fever was gone completely—that is, his temperature was normal. But he felt that it lingered, like a fully remembered nightmare. The fever seemed to be deeply inside him, heatlessly.

It was the middle of December. They were headed to Portsmouth—back to Portsmouth, for him. There would be no Sarah Dudley this time. This time, he wasn't on land.

They'd had word that Paul Revere rode up to Portsmouth earlier that week to warn the militia of a coming British action at the fortified Castle of William and Mary.

The first act of the gun-decked *York Sawyer* was to waylay a British frigate coming down the coast. It seemed as if the *Sawyer* had volition of its own, and would follow its own command—the command of the guns—like a living, breathing, enormous and fearful creature, with no choice from God but to obey its own instincts.

The *Sawyer* crept up on the frigate silently, in the dead of a moonless, cloudy, starless, frigid winter night.

The English crew consisted of eleven men, all of whom appeared to have never spent time at sea before in a northeast American winter, as mild as this one was. There was one officer, with nine Hessian mercenaries who'd been pressed into service as seamen, and did not seem to like it much. And one older, leather-faced man at the helm, who reeked of rum, and gave the impression that he was a marvelous, gifted pilot, perhaps the best in the world, especially when he was drunk, and all he wanted was to be left alone to do his job; they could steal whatever they liked.

The officer was about Patrick's age, and similar to him physically. Patrick made a half-hearted attempt to summon up hatred for him, but all he saw was a weary, baffled man in wet, dirty clothes, rocking in the dark in the middle of the sea, as far from his home, he might have felt, as if he were dead.

Perhaps the English crew had been numbed by the cold into a dull sort of stupidity, or perhaps they had no reason to care what happened, as long as they were not harmed. Even in the darkness they saw that, broadside of them, very closely, the barrels of wide-mouthed cannons were pointed at their heads. They could tell from the positions of Patrick's men that the cannons were loaded.

Patrick envied them for one thing: they didn't have a reason to want to fight.

There wasn't a fight. Patrick told his crew that they were sticking to the creed of the Lexington militia. Do not be the first to open fire. Fire only in response. In every instance, the aggressor must be the English. It was a question of being *defenders*.

Defend what, exactly?

"Lavinia," he thought. "Shot," he thought.

He thought, "Did she hear it? What was the last thing she looked at? If she'd heard the shot, did that mean she didn't die instantly?" Just because there could be no answer to these questions was no reason, he felt, not to keep asking them.

His crewmen wanted to try out the guns. They could have

blasted the frigate and watched it sink, like a ship made of stone, but they obeyed. It seemed noble of Patrick to hold to standards, to maintain discipline, to believe in principles, even when no one but God would have known which side shot first.

There was something about Patrick that was chivalrous, they felt. Or religious. Since his sickness, he seemed, more than ever before, in every inch of himself, a man who was absolutely confident of himself.

There wasn't any shooting. If a single ball was shot, Patrick felt, he would, at the sound of the explosion, go out of his mind. He felt that the act of keeping those guns still was the one thing that stood this moment between himself and madness.

This was as clear to him as the bitter cold and the roiling, rolling black waves. He knew what form it would take if it happened. It would be something like that terrible helplessness back at Lexington, lying flat on his back, in a bed he didn't know, in a room he'd never been in before: but this time he would not be asleep, or barely conscious. He had figured it out that to go mad was as simple as this: it was to always have nightmares, when you're awake.

Maybe that was a type of war. To fight to hold on to one's mind. For a reason, not like a mercenary. He tried to think of a reason, and then the one he came up with was completely unacceptable. Of all things, he found himself wishing to go one day to Salem.

He imagined the Dudley family's house. She had described it. He hadn't wanted to listen. But he hadn't asked her to stop talking. He imagined himself—smelling of sea salt and damp, sweaty clothes—walking into the house as if he'd anchored the sloop on the Dudleys' front lawn.

"I wish for you to know what it was I had left," she had said to him. There was a painting, was it a painting, had she painted? There was something hanging on the wall, big: a tree on a hill, snow, gray sky, birds. It had taken her four years to make it.

She had described it to him as if she were telling him about a map that laid out the whole workings of her soul. He never should have let her ride in the carriage with him and the boy.

"War," said Patrick.

He stayed with the ship and let his crew take care of the pirating. The new boy wished they had proper swords, like in a story, instead of pistols and hatchets and knives. Asa, who should have known better, solemnly promised him, "We'll get them from the Castle for the next time."

When the frigate was boarded, it turned out, all that was worthy of being taken, besides muskets, powder, a couple of knives, and all the shot on board, was a piece of mail. The frigate was on its way to delivering—first to Boston, then to London—a dispatch from the governor of New Hampshire.

The English ship didn't even put up a show of trying to go after the *York Sawyer*. The helmsman and the officer—and this wasn't just Patrick's imagination, although no one else on the crew claimed to have seen this—actually held up their hands in the air and saluted them. Not a word had been spoken.

Now that it was over, Patrick's crew had gone wild with victory. Their whoops of joy sounded joyless. They sounded like screeching, frenzied gulls.

His return to the sloop had been a thing of great ceremony, of great pleasure. "Captain," they still called him, as if nothing were different.

There they'd been: big, Hercules-like Enoch Lister; and the skinny teenager, Asa Patch, who had an uncle in Charlestown; and Huggins from up the Penobscot; and this boy sent from Lexington by Jackson Prout.

Otis Rawley. His mother was a midwife; he was vouched for; he had knowledge and experience with medicines, herbs. He was barely seventeen and called himself a gunner, but you could tell he'd never been around cannons, at least, not at sea. The only boat he'd ever been in was a fishing canoe on a placid little Lexington pond. The others had accepted him well enough.

"Good to see you, Captain."

"Sir, you look well."

"I am glad to be one of your men, Sir. I have got myself familiar with the sloop. I shall not disappoint you."

"The time in Nahant was well spent, Sir."

Their words sounded tentative to Patrick's ears, like questions. He wondered if they thought he was sick in a permanent way. He told himself he didn't care what they thought.

They'd chosen to stay with him, to wait for him, in spite of his fear, or perhaps his hope, that they all would have given up on him. They might have separated to join different privateers; they might have combined their forces with the Hammerheads in Nahant.

If they'd left him, he felt, he would have gone back to Falmouth, to the spot where he'd left Sarah and his nephew. He had trusted her absolutely with Little John, and he knew he was right to.

He called himself a coward. He had not been able to continue the journey up to Tibbetston. He made it seem that getting to the sloop was the one thing that mattered. He hadn't had to explain himself; she knew about ships. She had not tried to stop him. She hadn't even argued with him.

He knew exactly how careful he needed to be. He wasn't going mad. He could figure out what he needed. He couldn't go up there and find himself on that farm, looking at the graves, as if, as long as he could go without seeing them, they didn't exist.

But more than that, he did not want to allow himself to be anywhere near Jossey. He knew what she would be like. He knew exactly what she would say. She would talk about the saw mill, how it had smelled, how the noise turned your ears to stone, how they'd loved it, how they'd lost it.

Lost, lost, lost. She'd say the word like an incantation. She would count on the fingers of one hand the number of people who had been members of their family. Father, Mother, Lavinia, herself, Patrick.

Slowly, fingers would be lowered. She would do this with great concentration. Down would go Mother, down would go Father, down would go Lavinia. Mother was the thumb, Father the middle, Lavinia the finger that takes a wedding ring. Two fingers would remain raised. He was the index, Jossey was the pinkie.

When you hold your hand in this manner, you are making the sign for the devil. He'd learned that somewhere, long ago.

He looked at his own hand and saw what he'd done with his fingers, and was embarrassed and ashamed of himself. He was supposed to be *commanding*.

He just wanted to be back in Falmouth to undo the moment when Sarah Dudley was saying to him, "Good-bye for now, and be well, and I shall see you again soon enough."

He should have stayed with her. No, wait, that was wrong. He should never have invited her to ride in the carriage up to Maine. He should never have memorized every detail of her face, her hair, her expressions. He should have said to her, "When you first came and spoke to me, I had images of scalping you."

He should never have said, "If you are going to be there anyway, take care of my sister Jossey." He should never have said, "Describe to me this tree you made on a hill." He should never have said, "One day I shall go and visit your house." He should never have said, "Now I shall carry the look of you with me."

The woman who'd been there to meet Sarah was the mother of her maid: a lean, austere woman, holding out her arms. That was a first for him. A woman who had a maid. Who had a mother. Who was waiting with her arms out.

The two women, falling on each other, embracing, had a beauty and solemnity that reminded him of figures in a Bible story, but he couldn't think of which one. Until he'd got sick, he had never been reminded of the Bible at all, not since he was a child. It wasn't madness, he decided. But his brain seemed to have been altered, like his ship. In his own bones he was a stranger to himself.

It was easier to think in terms of "when I was taken so ill," instead of, "since my sister and her husband and children were killed."

He resolved to guard himself more closely. He felt he would not breathe correctly until he was somewhere close to Sarah Dudley again. Maybe it was part of the fever. He could not remember what it was like to have a will of his own, instead of being cursed like this.

Her face was appearing to him everywhere: in the clouds, on the side of a boulder, above the shoulders of people he passed. Her image was burned in the backs of his eyes. He saw her bird-like, in bare branches of almost-winter trees. He pictured her in the cloak she'd been wearing, and then he pictured the cloak falling off her. He craved her the same way that, exhausted and weak, he'd crave sleep without dreams, in a silent room, in a dry, solid bed.

He hated what was happening to him. He understood for the first time—having never thought of it before—that this was what it must be like for someone who wakes up in the morning craving rum and, having had it for breakfast, must have more.

"Do not go mad. Do what I must to not go mad." That was all

he could do. He wished he knew how to pray. Pray! It occurred to him that the desire for comfort was dangerous.

It seemed to him that except for the Tories he was the only person born in America who did not want a war.

The fact of it was, the *York Sawyer* with its new guns on deck—six, piratized, *British* guns—was not the same ship. Everything about it was changed, unnaturally, and almost unrecognizably. Patrick knew he would never be able to get used to it. Standing on shore, looking at it for the first time, was like coming upon a giant-sized, sleek, swift seal that someone had captured, and had weirdly fitted out with horns or antlers.

How strange it felt to remember himself at fifteen, sixteen, when his fantasies had been packed with dreams of guns. And again, fourteen years ago, when William had been taken into Canada. He had yearned for the very cannon he now owned.

This was owning? They'd put on the guns without his knowledge. He vowed to keep them silent.

Now it was festive on deck. No one would complain of the cold. No one except Patrick felt the usual heavy oppression of a night sky like this at sea—with no land in sight—when the darkness was a dirty shade of gray, and mountains of gray-black clouds hid the stars. Their victory—as hollow as it felt to Patrick, and in spite of how easy it had been—had warmed and delighted them.

They had put the stolen dispatch in his hands. They wanted him to read it to them. "The lantern light is too feeble for me," he told them, but in truth, his hands were too shaky. He passed it to Enoch, who passed it to the new boy. Maybe there was comfort to be had in the knowledge that he was no longer the only one on the *York Sawyer* who could read.

"It is well for us to have you with us, Mr., Mr.," Patrick said, and paused. It was the first time he'd spoken to the boy. He couldn't think of his name.

That wasn't madness. That was just a question of having a lot on his mind. And some natural resentment. The boy probably had a store of who knew what herbs in a pouch somewhere. He'd been sent, Patrick figured, to look after him, like a nursemaid.

The boy beamed with gratitude at being addressed at all. Patrick tried to make light of it. "Mr. Son Of A Massachusetts Mid-wife," he finished, and everyone laughed.

"Call me Otis, Sir. When I had trained with Mr. Prout, I hoped for such a place as this, seeing battles, with you."

"Would you presume to call our small bit of pirating a battle?"

The boy was shiny with intelligence and excitement. "I would not, as no shot was fired."

"Let us hope it remains so." They thought he was gallant for his even-headedness, his calmness. They thought that in his heart he was begging for an actual fight, as much as they were.

No one on the crew was alarmed that their captain's hands had trembled so violently, he could not hold a piece of paper. They wanted the news. It was the first time there'd be any sign of action. No one could say that what happened in Portsmouth was not a battle. They were awed by it. "Our boys took a fort," they kept saying.

"The letter here which I have, stolen by us," said the new boy, "is meant from the governor of New Hampshire, to the king of England."

"No," corrected Enoch. "That would not be so. It would be meant to get to Governor Gage, that devil in a red coat, as what commands Massachusetts."

"But then it would go on to the king?"

"Aye."

"Then I shall stay with what I said. To the king."

A hush fell over the sloop. Patrick watched the clouds. He thought of his sister Lavinia. He thought of all of the months when William was a prisoner, tied and bound, piloting on waves just like these. All those months as prisoner, keeping himself alive, *for a reason,* and look what it had come to.

There was no William. William, his brother. William's throat had been cut, they had said. He realized it had happened in the house. He had been wearing his nightshirt.

Patrick had his own type of counting. First, the English cut off William from his life on his farm with his wife. Then they cut off the chance of his unborn child to be born. Then they cut off his health. Then they sawed at his leg, so that his foot was cut off. Then, last, they put a knife to his throat. Did they wake him in his bed?

"I am going to believe William and my sister did not see their children destroyed," Patrick decided.

The boy read out loud in a clear, strong voice. The writer of the dispatch had not taken pains to be passionless.

"In the afternoon, Paul Revere arrived in this town, express from the committee in Boston. Before any suspicions could be had of their intentions, about four hundred men were collected together, and immediately proceeded to his Majesty's Castle, William and Mary, at the entrance to this harbour. An insurrection took place. They attacked, overpowered, wounded, and confined the Captain, and thence took away all the King's powder."

"Which we shall remove to Boston, as we would share in the victory and be spurred by it!" cried Enoch.

The boy grinned. He was loving this. He affected an English accent, and the effort made him looked pinched, comical.

"More numbers were assembled, and brought off many cannon, etcetera, and sixty muskets," he read. "The town is full of armed men. I most sincerely lament the present distractions."

"Ha!" cried the crew. "Ha ha ha ha!"

"Lament," heard Patrick. He repeated it. The crew thought he was joining in the mocking.

"Lament." The wind threw the word back into his face.

The sloop was turned toward the north. There was no sign of dangerous weather. There was plenty of food on board, and drinking water, and extra coats and breeches, and heavy wool blankets. Somehow with the guns, the *York Sawyer* was able to go faster, as impossible as that seemed.

CHAPTER IX

WINNIE'S PLAN

"M RS. GOODRIDGE, you desire to take my in-laws' farm and build a *what?*"

"A foundry, Mr. Avens."

Winnie thought she had made herself clear. They were sitting side by side on the settle by the hearth in the Wabanakis' big front room. John and Jossey Avens were calling the Wabanakis' house their home. They would never live in Boston again.

The hearth fire was stocked and glowing. Outside, where twilight had come very early, the darkness was as black as if the windows were coated with tar. Winnie Goodridge had been in Tibbetston for three days, and would return to York in the morning. But first, she'd had something to say.

Winnie's plan was still very sketchy but she pretended she had it all worked out. "I am a businesswoman. I would purchase the Mowlan farm, or lease it."

"But what do you know of iron?"

"A great deal."

"No ore is found in these parts for iron-making, Mrs. Goodridge."

"We shall find some, I believe, to the north, in the woods near Moosehead, or else, failing that, we shall send for it from Massachusetts, near Saugus, along with the rock which is best for mixture, from the Peninsula of Nahant."

"An embargo has been established," said John.

"We shall find a way around it."

"There is no furnace."

"We will make one."

"The farm is well high above the river. There is no water for the wheel."

"There is a powerful stream on the hill beyond, which you must have seen many times, Mr. Avens."

"You are speaking of preposterous things. You are shaken as we all are. You speak of this because you wish to have a scheme, to answer, I think, what was done to my wife's family. There is no answer to what was done, Mrs. Goodridge."

"Do you speak as a preacher, or a man?"

"I am no longer anything else but a man, as sits with you."

"You will not return to Boston?"

"We will not. My wife would not want to leave Maine, not again, not ever."

"But you would not choose to live at the Mowlans' farm?"

"That would be out of the question."

"You will live on here?"

"That would remain to be known. Our friends cannot stay in the summer cabin for much longer."

"Jacques and Naomi would move up to the farm, Mr. Avens. They would live in the house. Besides a good manager, what would be needed most would be a smith, and there is none better than Jacques."

"You spoke with them?"

"I did."

"And would this manager be yourself?"

"I must return to York. There is a man on the way here, a good man, whose whole life has been spent in iron. He is coming from Pennsylvania."

Iron was in Pennsylvania; even a child knew that. For the first time, John Avens regarded Winnie Goodridge with something more than an indulgent, slightly patronizing attitude. A foundry on Surrey Hill? It was as out of the question, as completely mad, as Jossey staring into her own cupped hands, imagining that Lavinia, as near as the air, was trying to reach her.

There was nothing hysterical about small, odd Winnie. She had placed a woodblock on the chair before sitting down. Her feet were far from touching the floor; her legs dangled like a child's. Her eyes were level with Avens's. He saw her to be a formidable presence; he'd never met anyone like her.

"I have no say in what becomes of the farm. It is left to my wife and her brother."

"I know," said Winnie.

"Then you speak to me as a courtesy only?"

"Not only. We would have need of you in the forge."

John could not remember the last time he threw his head back and laughed out loud; but the expression on her face was so serious, he couldn't help it. He wondered if she knew that the most intensive physical labor he had ever done was as a boy on his father's farm near Dedham, and even then, except for haying-time and the harvest, he'd not done much.

There had been no course for working with iron at Harvard. The most lifting he'd done in the last ten years was when he had helped put up the new pulpit in his church—and he'd managed that so badly, the workers made him sit down on a bench and just pray for them.

"And what, Mrs. Goodridge," he said, smiling, "would be made in this forge?"

"The militia has need of gun balls."

Ah, now he could go safely back to being aloof: he could sit back and wonder at the workings of a mind like Winnie's—grief and shock and rage, or not. "But a musket, Mrs. Goodridge, takes lead and grape shot."

"I would not speak of muskets, although, Mr. Avens, the making of them would not be out of consideration, as Jacques would know the mold."

"You propose to make *guns?*"

"Not at the start. At the start, balls, which are not complicated. For six- and four-pounders."

That took a moment to sink in. "For cannon, Mrs. Goodridge?"

She nodded. "And where would come the money for this?"

Winnie climbed down from her chair. The talk was over. Her face was inscrutable. "I have money, Mr. Avens," she said softly. "And good night."

CHAPTER X

FAITH

JOHN AVENS HAD BEEN putting off answering the many letters that had followed him to Maine. Most were condolences, or news from his parish, or bills. He would postpone them a little longer. He did not have the patience or the ability to sit still and concentrate on anything that did not have to do with war.

He had admitted to himself that there was going to be a war, and the knowledge made him feel sick to his stomach, and thrilled, both at once. He wondered if this was how it had felt in Troy, when the Greeks showed up with their devious, clever, war-machine horse. He tried to picture himself as a Trojan soldier, and failed. The Greeks had won at Troy.

There was only one letter, he felt, that deserved an immediate response. His friend and old classmate, Jonas Emerson—a minister, too, with a parish in Cambridge—had written to say that his thoughts were with him and, if the conditions in Boston grew any more inflammatory than they were, could his family, but not himself, come to Maine?

"My dear John, last night I supped with a party that included Samuel Adams," Jonas had written. "A garrulous, stout, undisciplined, utterly unnerving man, who quite possibly is deranged, but most definitely is a genius. If he has his way, the troops in our midst would be destroyed all at once, as if the colonists would thunder about like Titans, or summon Zeus to shoot them down with lightning bolts, as if it were all that simple. Yet I know of your decision to have left your home, your church. Know that in your grief, in your despair, and that of your Wife, I am forever your Friend, and share your mind."

John had put down the letter and wept. All he could say by way of answer was, "At the first sign of exchange of shots, or the first sign of provocation, send your Family to me at once, and I will take care of them."

He poured himself some brandy someone had given him after the funeral. He drank it down in one gulp.

It was nearly midnight. He was sitting by the Wabanakis' hearth. Jossey had fallen asleep. He knew that for himself, sleep was a long way off, if it came to him at all.

He had tucked his little daughter next to Jossey in bed, but now she came to him, climbing up into his lap. She was wide awake. She wanted to talk. When he looked in her eyes he saw miniatures of his own; he knew his own soul was partially mirrored there, and his anger, his bafflement, his despair. And his new, stubborn will to want to fight, even if he wasn't sure how.

He put his arms around her and feared they were not strong enough to contain for her some measure of safety, peace. Images of her two girl cousins flickered in his mind, like memories of a dream. He held his daughter tighter.

She'd been crying for days, and must have run out of tears. She wasn't feverish, she wasn't sick. Her forehead was clammy, sweaty, not like a child's, but like an adult's. She'd been laboring hard at thinking her private thoughts, same as the grownups around her. That was one thing that happened when evil took place; you could count on it. Evil. Children stopped being children.

"Papa, why did you and Mama change my name?"

"Because that is what we decided."

"Must I answer if someone still calls me Pris?"

"Yes. You can be Vinny-Pris now. You can answer to both."

"I want to go home to Boston."

"Hush. You have not slept well for days. You must sleep now, like Mama. The Wabanakis have given us their house, and this is going to be our home."

"Is Mama ill?"

"She is sad."

"Are you?"

"Yes."

"Will it ever go away?"

"I don't know," said John.

"Is Mr. Wabanaki an Indian?"

"He is."

"Is he going to kill us?"

"No. He is our friend."

"Did Indians kill my cousins?"

"No."

"Did English?"

"Yes."

"Did Indians kill my brother?"

"He is with the Wabanakis. You know that. You know that I brought him to the farm to stay there with them for a while, so Mama can rest."

"Is Mama going to die?"

"No."

"How do you know that?"

"Because I am your father, and I say so."

He didn't know if she believed him, or not. She put her head against his chest, and fell silent. Her breathing was light, soft.

It was snowing. The village outside was as silent as a tomb, and so, it seemed, was all of Maine, and all the world. The wind had stopped; the rush of the river was muted.

You could stand outdoors in Maine in a snowstorm and feel as if you no longer were on earth. There was sky, whiteness, more sky, and more whiteness. You couldn't even see trees. He had learned very quickly that here, in winter, you do not go out after sunset unless you absolutely had to, and you never went out alone.

The fire was glowing in the hearth. Snow was melting on the other sides of the window panes.

Boston was a world away, a lifetime away. He missed the solace of laid-out streets, and buildings clustered tightly, and the routines of daily, intricate commerce, even in a city under occupation. He missed what it was like, in rain or snow, to walk along a street and be able to duck into a shop, or the storefront of someone's office. He missed the warehouses, the docks, the elegance of the stately houses. He missed the way the stars, above roofs and spires, seemed so distant, and so carefully, rationally planned: in Maine, if it wasn't stormy or foggy, the night sky was like a riot of dazzling, impossibly bright, round white fires, overlapping each other and seeming close enough to touch. He wasn't used to the hugeness of this sky. It still frightened him.

He missed the noise of human life packed closely together. He missed Cambridge, too, for its orderly quiet and peace. When he was at Harvard he never imagined he'd live anywhere else. He missed his friends and some of his parishioners. He even missed the sight of soldiers amassed in lines on Boston Common for drills—and for routine acts of local intimidation. Their red coats were vivid and remarkable, as if a flock of young cardinals had taken over the trees, where before there'd been drab sparrows, starlings, doves.

Cows used to graze on that Common. Children played games; people shouted to each other, rushing this way and that, importantly, even urbanely. The cows were gone. Everyone was gone but the soldiers. Nothing was what it had been.

But at least with British troops so closely by, there had always been a feel in the air that at any moment something was going to happen. Something big.

What was it he had said to Lavinia, in his last letter to her? "In Boston we are like powder in a musket, waiting for the spark to be lit." Something like that. He had never in his life fired a gun, had never owned one. Now he had a rifle and a pistol.

There weren't any soldiers in Tibbetston or Grilleyville, or anywhere along this part of the coast. He wished there were. It was said that more warships had entered the harbor at Falmouth. Soldiers were everywhere in the streets, the taverns.

If it weren't for his wife and his children, and the work he now had to do, up at the farm, if this business with building a foundry took hold (which he had doubts about), he would have harnessed one of Jacques's horses, and gone down to Falmouth, galloping like crazy to the only city in Maine, like a lone, heartsick, avenging hero. What he'd do if he'd got there was anyone's guess, including his own.

The rifle and pistol weren't loaded. He didn't know how; he didn't even know how they worked.

When he knew his little girl was asleep, he didn't get up to move her back to bed. She could sleep there all night, in his arms. He wouldn't stir; his arms would be just like a safe, good, concealed shelter, in the hollow of a tree, that a rabbit has just fled into. That was something he could do. Sit still, give shelter, and pretend that he still held faith in all the old things he'd held faith in, somehow.

CHAPTER XI

CEREMONY

JOHN AVENS WAS HAVING his first Maine winter, so he did not appreciate the fact that, unlike every other before it, this winter was establishing itself as mild, almost tranquil. It had barely gone anywhere near freezing. The bay was a limpid, bright blue, as still as a bay in a painting.

On the Kennebec, it wasn't cold enough for ice layers, but here and there, like strange, harsh-white boats, large chunks of snow-crusted ice floated by on the rushing currents. The wind was its same old blustering, salty self, but there wasn't any icy, whiplike lash to it. People could walk outdoors and not have their eyelashes coat with frost; they could breathe without having their lungs hurt.

It had snowed, lightly, in big, soft flakes, on and off for the last few days. What snow had stuck to the ground gave everything a sheen, a gentleness, a clarity. Surrey Hill never looked as lovely as it did in snow and winter sunshine, and this year was no exception.

On the first Sunday of the first snowfall, Jacques and Naomi Wabanaki carried out the same ritual they'd held when their three sons were very small. They went ahead with it this year, even though their hearts were as heavy as lead, and they were barely settled into their new home, at the Mowlans' farm.

They had moved up the rest of their belongings, and their bed from the summer cabin.

Their three sons were nearby: the elder two, Perley and Simon, had left their homes and come up from Nantucket, and were staying at the inn in Grilleyville. It was off-season for their whalers, but they would have come anyway. "There is going to be war," they kept saying. "Perhaps not next year, perhaps not the year after, but there is going to be a war."

They had never shown the slightest degree of interest in metals and forges, but they had learned of plans for the foundry. Their feeling was, if there was really going to be one set up, they wanted in, and so did their brother.

Philippe, down from Moosehead, who refused, in his mother's words, to be domesticated, had set himself up in the barn. He'd brought them hides, smoked game, and four ducks he had shot on the way. It was all they could do to get him to come into the house for meals.

The three of them were strong, big men, and except for Philippe—"Fleep," he was called—they were worldly and rugged, and somewhat battered, like any natural thing that's constantly exposed to the elements. Fleep was outdoors more than the others put together, in spite of all those days his brothers were at sea, and he still looked as smooth as a boy, and as wide-eyed. His brothers were sunburned, tan. Fleep was brown. He was the tallest and the most agile—and the most leaderly, too—as if to compensate for his place as the youngest. Where Perley and Simon had booming, big voices, accustomed to shouting above wind and waves, Fleep spoke quietly, and only when he had to.

It was getting harder every year, around the time of the first-snowfall ritual, to recall what they were like as little children. But that's what Jacques and Naomi were doing. It helped that an infant was with them, pink and squawking and vigorous, punching at the air with tiny fists, and sucking happily on an icicle-like stick of maple syrup.

Jossey's baby. Mowlan. He'd curled up in Naomi's lap. John had come up last night to turn him over to their care; he would soon be brought to a wet nurse. John had not spelled out for the Wabanakis what had happened. He only said that their little daughter was having nightmares and doing poorly, and was begging to be brought back to Boston. As for Jossey, he'd said, "As you would understand, she is distraught, and is deeply in mourning." He didn't say, "The milk in her breasts has vanished."

It was almost noon. Jacques and Naomi had fasted since yester-day afternoon, and now they'd sit down to a small, spare meal of broth from the ducks, and corn cakes. They shuttered the windows and lit three candles, brought up from their house, one for each of their sons.

Their sons had been born close together, within the space of less than five years. They were just like a litter. One year, in early winter, when the first snow of the season had come—and it had come very early, in a raging, swirly fury—Fleep, who had barely started walking, had somehow managed to get himself outside.

He'd been in the smithy. But it wasn't Jacques's fault he'd gotten away; the whole family was there. No one remembered the door having actually been opened. One minute the tiny boy was there, standing upright on his wobbly, skinny new legs, and the next, he wasn't.

His brothers went out of their minds. They all went rushing outside, scattering in four directions, screaming for him: the calling of his name kept sounding like the bleating of crazed, scared sheep. Jacques made a solemn vow to his Jesuit God that if no harm came to his child, he'd spend the rest of his life giving humble, grateful thanks; he would never forget what it was like to fear that his baby was gone forever. And Naomi was doing the same, but her God was like a giant, of sky and water and tides and mud and wind, a God of a girlhood spent on clam flats: mighty and awful, but also quite possibly benign.

Simon and Perley were the ones who knew exactly where to look. The pond. A coating of ice had already crystallized the sur-face, but it was as thin as paper.

Fleep wasn't trying to walk on the ice. Fleep was trying to fly. His brothers found him at the very edge of the pond, standing on the trunk of a spruce that was felled the year before in a wind-storm. Jacques had leveled it; the broken-off wood had splintered badly, and he had worried that the two older boys would climb up it and be impaled.

That trunk was five feet high. How Fleep climbed up it, with the wind so strong, no one could figure out. But there he had been,

with his arms outstretched, in his flimsy homespun shirt and knick-
ers, barefoot. He hadn't needed warm clothes in the shop; no one
did. They had the forge.

His eyes were amazingly shiny; his expression was one of pure
joy. He had thought that the wind would carry him to the other
side of the pond. He hadn't said so; he still hadn't started talking
in sentences. He just kept pointing, first to his own scrawny chest,
then to the place where he wanted to be. In the air. "Bird," he told
them. "Bird, bird, bird."

Well, he never tried that again, that they knew of. For a couple
of months he was kept with a rope around his waist, which someone always had the other end of. But that was how the ritual
started.

On the night of the day he'd gotten away, when the three boys
were in their beds and fast asleep, Jacques and Naomi, still stunned
and shaken, sat down and felt that it was time to count their blessings. Three candles were lit.

The first time, with the boys as unformed—as bursting with
possibilities—as troughs of liquid ore, their parents got it into
their heads to decide what each would be like as men, as if they actually had a say in it.

When they lit the first candle they said, "Perley will take over
the forge one day, and he will clear the woods back of the summer
cabin and build a house with two stories, and be prosperous."

When they lit the second, they said, "Simon will go to college,
and be bookish, and be a man of the law." When they lit the third,
they said, "Fleep will love staying indoors, and he will become a
physician and run his own apothecary."

And Jacques asked Naomi if she wanted any of them to have a
talent or yearning to dig for clams, and Naomi said, *no*.

They felt like supernatural beings in a fairy tale, bestowing
these fates on their children, but more, they lowered their heads
and felt the powerful sense of what it meant to be a mother and a
father. "Please let nothing happen to them to harm them," they
said, praying to their two different Gods.

Now, in the flickering candlelight, and the dimness and shadows of the Mowlans' house, their new home, it was as if, all over

again, their child had just been found, just hours ago. The Avenses' baby had fallen asleep.

Jacques said, "All the same, none of them did anything we wanted. We have two of them hunting whales, as far away from us as the other side of the moon, and a third that thinks it stupid to sit at table and use a knife and a spoon."

He said this every year. Naomi usually agreed with him, but this time, looking around at the walls and the hearth, and the shuttered windows, with the terrible silence in her ears of the closed-off rest of the house, she pictured Lavinia's face, and then William's, and then each of the children's, and she answered, "Jacques, there will soon be war, and I am glad of it."

CHAPTER XII

NIGHT OF THE TEA

"Lavinia," whispered jossey. "Can you hear me?"
Jossey had been talking to her sister all week. She knew that John had promised Lavinia that, on his next visit to the farm—the visit that was supposed to be happening now—he'd spell out for her in detail what it was like that night at the harbor last winter, with the tea.

On the day of the funeral when everyone else had left, Jossey and John had lingered by Lavinia's grave. "Tell her what you were going to tell her, John."

John, of course, refused to do so. In a minister-like tone of voice he had chided his wife, as if he needed to make a comment on reality. "The dead have no ears to listen," he'd pointed out.

"Perhaps, talking to my sister would be the same as praying."

"I do not pray any longer, Jossey."

Jossey felt she would have to make the best of it herself. She was careful not to speak to Lavinia out loud. It would have been too upsetting to John and the children.

She lay under quilts in the Wabanakis' bed, missing her baby, missing Patrick, missing her sister most of all. "Lavinia!" she whispered. "I *know* you can hear me. I am ready to tell you what happened on the Night of the Tea."

Her version, she realized, would be considerably different from John's. But she started out objectively, as he would have done, sermon-like, with facts.

Remember the false sense of relief in Boston when that tax act was lifted? Imports of glass and paper weren't taxed any longer, but tea was? And then, in the spring of last year, the East India Company was awarded a monopoly, so that Americans importing tea from other companies had their trade cut out from under them? Shopkeepers were to stock only East India tea, and John had said, "Something is going to come of this. Something big."

But he hadn't known what. No one had known what exactly to expect. And when three English ships with the tax-burdened, newly monopolized tea came to dock in Boston Harbor, they had, by law, twenty days to take care of the unloading.

Unloading did not happen. It was put out in a general way that anyone who attempted to touch the tea would have tar poured on their bodies, which would then be covered with chicken feathers. Everyone in Boston had seen this happen once or twice to Tories; even the shopkeepers who wanted the tea most wouldn't dare go near it.

The deadline for unloading the cargo was December 17.

The night of December 16 was frigidly cold. At the Old South Meeting House, they held the final meeting on what to do. It was rowdy and noisy: then the signal to proceed to the harbor was given. Once they went forward into action, they were all very quiet, and remained so, and hardly spoke.

The hill above the ships was lit with so many torches, the air seemed brighter than daylight. They used tackles and blocks to haul up the chests from the holds. The English did not fire on the Massachusetts men. The Massachusetts men were careful not to harm anything but the tea, and they were successful with their care. One of the English captains kept repeating, "Thank you for that, my good sirs, thank you for that, my good sirs."

The Englishmen did not worry that they would be dumped overboard with the tea. It was civil.

It was terrible to see that there were colonists who pretended to take part, but only filled their pockets with tea. On shore were shopkeepers who offered payment on the spot for the pilfering. Some of those who attempted making off with the tea were set upon; one poor man who perhaps saw a means to a quick profit was removed of his coat and hat and splashed with a bucket of icy harbor water.

Many of the men painted their faces to seem as Mohawks. They looked nothing like Indians. No one had known for certain that the seizure of the tea chests would not result in shots being fired. There were some who were prepared for a battle. There were some who were even hungry for it, even greedy.

Jossey had thought that her husband had gone to the hill that night to only watch. He cared greatly to have moderation in his parish. He minded the importance, as he'd said, of remaining aloof to political matters. But he could not merely watch.

Little John woke when John came home, but thankfully not his sister. It was very late. Perhaps the boy knew that a thing had taken place of great meaning. "Papa, where were you and what were you doing?" he cried out. It alarmed him to see his father's face, dusty with the ashes he had used to blacken it. It alarmed Jossey, too, but not for the same reason.

She had been sewing by the fire. She had been mending a sheet.

"I was mending the sheet, Lavinia," she said, "and thinking about the day when Patrick came to tell me the schooner had sunk. How long ago that seems!

"It must have been the combination of the sheet in my hands, like a new white sail, perhaps, and the knowledge of what was going on at the harbor. How could I think of ships and not think of Patrick? You would do the same yourself. As close as we always were, you had always been closer to Patrick. Do you recall Father saying, 'Lavinia and Patrick, they may be different in age, but they are hatched from one shell'? Father used to say you and Patrick shared a soul between you.

"So I sewed on the sheet in my hands that night, and found myself weeping for Patrick, who had to tell us the ship he had named for us had gone down. I believe I had not wept at the time when it happened. Do you remember imploring him to get another, and name the new one for Father, as you and I now had our names forever on ship-planks at the bottom of the sea?

"When Patrick lost the schooner, I believed that it was the most dreadful thing I would ever know. I had thought, 'Patrick's loss is worse than death.' He had worried so much that we would mind it that all the money from the sawmill was gone.

"That was what was in my mind when my husband came home. I had been weeping for the schooner, and felt as low in my senses as I ever had been. John had put Little John back to bed, and came and stood beside me.

"He thought I was weeping because I'd feared some harm to himself. It was not a customary thing for him to be out in the streets at night on any business but with his parishioners.

"He had not cleaned his face. He took the sheet from my hands.

"An excitement was in his eyes. Anyone who knew him would know from his expression that he had not just come home from church. I had never seen him quite this way before. 'I cannot bear to see you cry,' he said. I did not tell him I was mourning the schooner.

"I had thought, he is going to talk to me about liberty, he is going to talk to me about ideals, he is going to talk to me about politics, he is going to talk to me of the possibility there will one day be a war and, if there is, it would all have begun in Boston. I had heard all this before. I thought, if he talks to me of those things, I shall cover my ears with my hands and go to bed.

"He did not talk to me of those things.

"He shook out the sheet and laid it down on the floor, as one would put a rug on the ground for a picnic. He said, 'Jossey, I would like it very much if you were to take off your clothes.' 'But it is cold,' I told him, and he answered, 'Not for very much longer.' He was not required to ask me more than once to lie with him on the sheet.

"Lavinia, on the floor. We were different that night. I cannot describe to you how, as there are things that must not be known of a man and woman except to the man and woman.

"That is all I can say. If carriage wheels just before dawn had not startled me awake, my children would have found us as we were. I do not recall the hours of a single night passing as quickly as those did.

"Later in the day, I said to John, 'I believe I might have conceived last night.' He was hesitant to think it might be so. You know what he is like. He will always refuse to get up his hopes for a single thing, no matter what it is, until facts present themselves that are irrefutable.

"But I was right. I had told you in a letter when I was bearing this second son, 'Lavinia, this child has been brought about in a most extraordinary way.' Perhaps you had thought I might have been reflecting on a religious subject, keeping in mind that after our daughter was born, it was felt I would bear no more children.

"But I had meant, Lavinia, on the *floor*. All *night*.

"It amazes me how the people of my husband's parish would say of him that he is not a passionate man. We have named the child newly, changing the Patrick we gave him at birth to a name for the middle. Mowlan Patrick. I know that we had decided to save the names of Mother and Patrick for children of mine instead of yours. But we have made the changes. Our little Priscilla is Lavinia now. Lavinia Priscilla. She will soon have mastered her alphabet. She resembles you! Lavinia! I *know* you hear me!"

CHAPTER XIII

GUN BALL HILL

JOSSEY REFUSED TO GO into the tavern or the inn in Grilley-ville, on principle. She felt that women who entered public places were automatically profane and unrespectable. She could not have cared less that this was Maine, not Boston, and she was Maine-born herself, and was no longer, officially, a duty-bound minister's wife, with the duty of setting a good example.

It was the last night of the year. If Jacques and Naomi wanted to put on a supper—with, what, ten people altogether, or eleven, twelve?—it would have to be held right here in town, at the Wa-banakis' house. Jossey was careful to keep calling the farmhouse "the place were Jacques and Naomi were living," and she was doubly careful to call the Wabanakis' house the place where she was tem-porarily staying, and not (yet) her home. Everything seemed to her to be temporary, suspended.

She could not understand how Naomi, a white, Maine-born woman like herself, was able to spend even one hour in that farm-house, knowing what had happened there. Naomi didn't complain of sleeping badly or feeling the slightest little jittering of her nerves. Jacques was a different case, and so was that woods-wild son of theirs, sleeping in the barn. Indians, Jossey felt, were not the same as white people. If emotions had their own sets of skin, the skin of Indians was thicker.

But Jacques was the one who'd been quick to say he understood her when she laid down some rules. She had made up her mind that if she went up the hill to the farm, it would only be to tend to the gravesites. If someone offered her food or drink while she was up there, she would have to refuse it.

All she could think of was Persephone, in the story of being kidnapped by the god of the Underworld.

Just because Persephone ate a tiny piece of fruit in Hell—it was only a seed, really—look what had happened. It was bad enough that the demon abducted her, but then Hell had claims on her life for forever. Nothing could be done about it, even though she was the daughter of the Goddess of Spring.

"Jossey," said John. "What are you thinking?"

Three, four, five times a day, John came over to her, cupping the sides of her face with his smooth, bookish-man's hands, or pressing a hand on her forehead as if she were a child, and he was feeling for a fever.

In Tibbetston, everyone thought of the end of December as a symbolic, hopeful thing, as if "1774" was a horrible creature that had menaced them, had caused them unspeakable harm. But now it was wounded. Now it was slinking away, conquered. It was never, ever returning, and neither would anything like it.

What was Jossey thinking? It was not a possibility to answer that question with, "The story from the Greeks, of when the order of things was destroyed, and the world had no Spring." It would not be all right to stand there and meet her husband's anxious, scared eyes with the truth.

A husband, she felt, had a right to be privy to the mind of his wife. Or at least, he had a right to be convinced that the mind of his wife was like a room in a house he could enter whenever he wanted, with a door he held the key to, even if, he might feel, she did not have a key herself.

"I am thinking of what spices from Naomi's cupboard I shall put into the stewed apples for the supper," said Jossey.

"And that would be all?"

"That, and how John and Vinny-Priss shall love the company at supper, and staying up late. And how nice it shall be to put on my good shawl and wool skirt from Boston."

A parishioner of theirs had packed up their clothes and many of their belongings, and had sent them by hired wagon to Tibbetston. It seemed to have made sense to everyone—even people who didn't know about the plans for the foundry—that Jossey and John would decide to stay in Maine. It wasn't as if there was a shortage of preachers in Boston who'd be willing to take over John's duties. It wasn't as if their Boston roots were tough, deep ones, not even for John, who still had a long way to go before he felt at ease in Maine.

Maybe, Jossey had thought, when all this business of war was over, she and John and the children, all together again, could move down to York.

These were idle thoughts, thoughts of a future, thoughts of hope, and they did not last long in Jossey's mind, but still, the children could do worse than be raised in the place where she'd been a child. She could make friends with the people who'd bought her father's saw mill.

Everyone was saying that once the war started, it would not last long, as if, at the first few signs of resistance, the British would go skulking off, back across the Atlantic, as finished and defeated as the year.

1774. It had been the best year of her life: she had loved her Boston house, no one had been ill, her two older children had flourished, her baby had been thriving in her arms; and she had loved her husband with a new, deep, peaceful and passionate certainty, and she knew he'd done the same in return. Then, like a terrible, permanent change in the weather, the best year became the worst.

It was suddenly so easy to tell lies. Seasonings for the cooking of apples, and the pleasure of their daughter and older son, and dressing up for the evening in her fine Boston clothes.

Did she sound convincing? She must have. John beamed at her with relief and kissed her lightly, like a cousin or a neighbor, on the cheek. She realized that all she wanted from her husband was that he left her alone. She had never felt this way before.

She did not feel robbed or bereft of her baby. She missed him, but now it was with a sort of detachment, a sort of measured indifference.

The oh-so-*capable* Jacques and Naomi had managed to get him fed just fine, and then they'd found him a wet nurse, down in Winnegance. Jacques had invented a suckling-thing from some sort of animal bladder, which they'd filled with boiled cow's milk, diluted with sugared water.

It was entirely possible that tiny Mowlan Patrick Avens, who had never cried or fussed half so much as his brother and sister, never once felt the lack of his mother. Naomi had told Jossey that the baby considered the bladder as a familiar, beloved sort of toy, and was allowed to have it next to him in his cradle.

The wet nurse had come up to fetch the baby herself: she was a daughter of one of Naomi's nieces from the clam flats, who'd given birth to a son a little over a year ago.

Apparently, this niece had plenty of milk to spare. John had given her some money, and so had the Wabanakis. "It shall only be for a couple of weeks," they all said.

There were moments when Jossey, sitting down to a meal with her husband and Little John and Vinny-Pris, or sitting with them in front of the hearth before bedtime, had the feeling that the other child had never been born at all. Naomi had said that the niece was bringing Mowlan Patrick out clamming in the mud with her, tying him in a pouch on her back, like an Indian, even in the cold harsh winds, which was probably good for one's character, but she might have been jesting.

In John's parish there'd been a well-liked family called Loudon: a father, mother, three daughters, two sons. The father was a manager of a harborfront warehouse; the mother had a small workshop, attached to her house, where she made candles that were always in demand, and were scented with bayberries, expensive vanilla, and pine. When that family came into the church, the air changed, as they carried these fragrances on their persons, in a pleasing, welcome way.

They had often visited the Avenses socially. When it came time for the eldest daughter to marry—a sturdy, healthy, no-nonsense girl named Eliza—it was arranged that she should travel to Delaware to make the acquaintance of a distant cousin who lived on a farm there. Somewhere around the time the two had been born, the family had decreed they should wed.

An aunt of the girl's—a sister of the candlemaker—went along, too. There'd been three carriages and a wagon making the trip, along with several young Massachusetts men on horseback, who were on their way further into the South.

But they never got far. Somewhere along the way—in New York, maybe it was—they were set upon by a crazed band of attackers, half of them British soldiers and half of them Indians. There had not been much by way of specific information, as most of the members of the journeying party had been killed. They were shot, stabbed, who knew what else. Everything worth stealing of their possessions had been stolen.

The girl, Eliza Loudon, along with a tough old man from Concord who owned and operated one of the horse teams, were the only survivors; they'd been left for dead at the side of a swamp, where they were found by a mail rider two days later.

The old man was too weak to come back, and never did. Eliza's father, with a couple of men from the church, went down there to bring her home. "Her eyes had looked at things of unspeakable evil," it was said of her. Before her journey, her dark brown hair was thick and long; when candlelight shone on her, it was as lustrous as if lit from within. But the girl who came back had hair the color of ashes.

The softness was gone with the color. It was coarse, harsh hair, as dry as a broom. How could that happen? The vitality had gone out of her as swiftly and easily as summer rainwater soaking into the ground.

What a shock it had been to look at her! There was her same face, her same young skin, her same self, with an old woman's head of dry, hard hair: how could that *be?*

The family had left Boston soon afterward, for a farm somewhere in New Hampshire. Jossey had wondered from time to time how they were doing, but now she wished she knew where they were exactly. She wanted to write them a letter. "Dear Loudons," she would have written. "We are connected."

She wanted to tell them that she understood what it was like for Eliza because, even though her own eyes had seen no horror, it had happened that, a little while after the day of the funeral, the milk in her breasts had dried up to nothing, although her baby had pulled and pulled at her, like a small angry pink baby pig.

And now Jacques and Naomi and their sons, and her own husband, too, wanted a celebration?

And there were two strangers to cope with as well: the man from Pennsylvania who'd arrived in Tibbetston the day before, to talk about this nonsense-business of starting a foundry, and that new girl Sarah, that awful, oh-so-earnest, oh-so-deferential, oh-so-smug Sarah Dudley, who came from Tories in Salem. It had been Sarah Dudley who brought Little John to Maine, instead of Patrick.

Sarah Dudley was staying at the farmhouse. They had opened up the lean-to for her. She'd joined up with Jacques and Naomi—who knew her, who adored her—as if she were a long-lost child of theirs. She was sleeping where the Mowlans' two oldest boys used to sleep. Jossey hated her.

When Jossey had asked her, "Where is my brother, Patrick?" what had Sarah Dudley done?

She had smiled. And not like a stranger, either. She had met him at a tavern. She had attached herself to Jossey's son—in fact, Little John looked at Sarah Dudley as if he'd pledged his life to her service. He was going around saying things like, "I shall pray to God for Sarah to not get older, so I may catch up, and then, when we are equal, we shall marry."

"Your brother who sends you his love has gone with the sloop," she had answered, and her face had lit up with a *smile*. She didn't care that Jossey was standing there with the feeling that a hole was in the air where her brother Patrick should have been.

They wanted a celebration!

The new man's name was Firth, Tobe Firth. "Iron Man," they all called him. Jossey acknowledged that he was an old friend of Winnie's, and was thus connected to York, but that wasn't enough for Jossey to feel obligated to try to warm to him.

There wouldn't be any foundry. Jossey felt sure of it. They were all getting carried away with idle dreams. What good could come of their talk? Did they really think it possible to put up a furnace, a kiln? To haul in ore from God knew where? The men were acting more like children than the children.

Jossey boiled the apples whole—plain and whole. She did not quite trust herself for very long with the paring knife. She didn't know what to make of the spices on Naomi's shelves, and she didn't want to ask her, because she didn't want to speak to her.

"A picnic in the snow! The last night of the year! We shall make sun balls! A picnic in the snow!"

The two Avens children were shiny with pleasure and glee. Jossey forced herself to smile at them, pet them, indulge them, as she bundled them into their coats. Little John seemed to have grown two inches or so in the time he'd been away from her.

Outside the Wabanakis' house, in the back by the pond, in the cold, foggy, early dusk, the wild son and his brothers built an enormous cooking fire. They talked among themselves in loud, hearty voices. The new man was here, and Jacques and Naomi, and Tory-born Sarah. Their voices boomed out with loud, energetic talk, like voices of people who are happy.

They talked about iron, gun balls, war.

"We shall have a waterwheel set up at the base of the hill by spring!"

"We shall have a manner of baptism!"

"We shall have a furnace as hot as the fires of hell!"

"We shall be making balls by Easter!"

John went outdoors, came inside, and looked at her face like a man who is checking the weather and fearing the worst. He never left her alone for very long.

"Jossey, have you done with the apples?"

"I have, quite nearly."

"Sarah Dudley has said we ought to name the hill for our new enterprise. That hill had been unnamed, so Jacques told me. Sarah has been inspired to name it."

"The new enterprise would seem to me to have as much substance, John, as a bubble."

"Perhaps a bit more than a bubble. Perhaps you shall be surprised at what the future shall provide. At the stroke of midnight by the Wabanakis' clock, Jossey, we shall turn to the hill and call it by its new name."

"Perhaps Lavinia knew its name, John. Perhaps there is no need."

"Lavinia is gone. What are you thinking?"

"I miss Patrick."

"If that would not be the only subject on your mind, you would tell me?"

"Tell me the new name."

"Gun Ball Hill."

"Very well. You might stop asking me these questions about my thoughts, John."

"Yet I would be answered, Jossey."

"I miss the babe," she lied. "I fear he shall grow used to being away from us, and he shall forget us."

"He is too young to grow used to anything at all, except being nourished, and kept warm and safe, and knowing he is loved. We shall all be back to ourselves before long."

He touched one hand, lightly, to her chest, the way he'd bless one of his parishioners, as if the touch would coerce her milk, as if he had that sort of power. Then he touched the side of her face, and she knew what the next thing that came from him would be. Just because he would climb on no pulpit to preach didn't mean he would ever really stop preaching. He always had the right words ready. He would have to speak of hope. He couldn't help it.

"We must have hope, Jossey."

"Yes."

"Especially on this last night of the year."

"I well know, John."

"The last is always darkest."

"The fire they've made is bright, John."

"Yes, it is. And we are with friends. Do put on your cloak and come outside, as the others are gathering."

"Yes, John."

"Mama Mama Mama! The last night of the year! We shall not go to bed! A picnic in the snow!"

They loved Maine! No one cooked outdoors in winter in Boston! What a perfectly splendid thing life was! No more sorrow! Everything was so grand!

A pot the size of a washtub was set up for a stew—nothing fancy, just a simple chowder of cod, potatoes, and corn, and boiled, tiny pink Maine shrimp (which Jossey had helped peel). There was no fresh game. Jacques and his sons had gone out in the woods that morning, with John and the children trailing behind, and that girl, too, that Sarah, and they'd found nothing to shoot, not even squirrels. They hadn't even seen any birds. And there'd been no tracks in the snow at all, not even of mice.

Wasn't that strange, when the winter was proving itself to be a mild one? Jossey had wondered about that. Was the land really cursed? Would the curse stay forever? It was looking as if they'd have the same sorts of problems with finding fresh food as the early colonists, so long ago.

There'd been a game in the woods with the children, thought up, no doubt, by Sarah Dudley. Vinny-Pris called the game "Starving the Early White English Settlers to Death." Or maybe it was the influence of Wabanaki Indian blood—weren't those children spending too much time running wild these days? They were forgetting their Boston manners. As for Little John, who knew what he'd picked up when Patrick had him? Patrick had taken the boy into taverns!

But Jossey couldn't think of a way to summon up the energy to try to rein in her children. Out in the woods they remembered the stories their Mowlan cousins had told them of the first coastal colonials, who had thought that the American woods and soil and waters, with barely any effort, would heave up bounties of food for them, endlessly; or it would rain on their heads like manna.

No one knew how many early colonists had died of hunger in a Maine winter. A great many. You could not walk far along the coast without knowing that your feet were walking on someone's bones—even down in York, that was true.

Jossey had grown up with it. "Lavinia," she said to her sister. "Do you remember the twenty-six?"

Down in York, not far from the saw mill, there was a crude, small old burial ground, with just slabs of rock for headstones, no names. These were the graves of twenty-six English sons of lords who had never done a lick of work in their lives, and had come to America in the middle of the last century with the idea of getting rich very quickly. They kept standing around waiting for someone to feed them, which they were used to, but which, in Maine, had not happened.

They hadn't known how to fish, and had not been curious about trying it, and it wasn't as if the Indians would have helped them, even if, at first, they'd been so inclined. The sons of lords had guns and plenty of ammunition, and would shoot at anyone who came out of the trees who wasn't white. In their last days, it was said, they went out of their minds, drank saltwater, and chewed and swallowed pine bark.

Once, thinking about their situation—and the story of the twenty-six sons of lords was known to every York child—Jossey had spent a lot of time imagining "hunger so bad it kills." She had sucked on a bit of pine bark herself, and swallowed a handful of ocean water, and had gagged and spat it out, and had wondered, "How could they be so unintelligent as to come to a strange new land with guns instead of food, with ammunition instead of seeds for planting?" She had felt no pity for the stupid early settlers, and neither, she remembered, had Patrick, although his perspective was different.

Patrick was always taking the point of view of Indians. Indians must have watched the stupid Englishmen. Patrick had wondered, "Did Indians, watching from the trees, *smile* when the Englishmen died? I hope so!"

As for Lavinia, she'd had a perspective of her own. Every now and then in summer, when they were children, she went to the little cemetery to place wildflowers by each of the twenty-six stones, with the feeling that, just because those sons of lords were murderous, ignorant, pompous, tiny-minded, and greedy, they had not deserved to die from having nothing to eat. Sometimes Jossey gathered flowers with her, and helped her scrape off bird droppings from the stones, but their motivations were not the same.

Jossey had felt that the only time her eyes could bear the sight of those graves was when they were clean, decorated.

"Lavinia, you have always been a better person than me, and so has been Patrick," said Jossey.

She wasn't feeling self-incriminatory, and she wasn't feeling sorry for herself. She was simply, she felt, stating facts.

"Mama! We played we were here in old times, starving to death!"

"Mama! Guns! We found no food, but hunting is wonderful!"

They had *played*. They had pretended it was a hundred years ago and they'd had nothing to eat for days, that there was nothing in store, that the supply ship they'd been waiting for had been sunk in a gale, and then the one that was sent to replace it had crashed into rocks and was smashed; seals and gulls had eaten their provisions.

They'd imagined themselves doomed. And they had sprawled on their backs in the snow and played at *dying,* all of them, the children, the horrid, Tory-born Sarah—who acted just like a boy—and that rough, loud, barrel-chested, rigid-armed Iron Man, Tobe, who wasn't acting like a stranger, but like a relation, with his silly dreams of a furnace at the base of the hill; and the wild Wabanaki who didn't have a proper name, and never washed his hair; and his two older whaleboat brothers from Nantucket, who never washed anything of themselves at all.

And John could only keep peering into her eyes as if she were ill.

What had Jossey been doing in the house in the village? Oh, resting. Did she speak to anyone while they were gone? No, of course she hadn't. Who was there to speak to?

"Lavinia," Jossey said quietly, "I am the only person in Maine who has respect, and the only one who grieves, and I am very, very lonely. If my husband asks me what I am thinking one more time, I shall scream."

Nothing answered her except the ticking of the clock, ticking down the minutes of the last day of the year. How could anyone imagine that the new one to come would be better?

But here they all were. They could not stop talking in a holiday way about their adventures; you'd think they had all known each other all their lives. They had formed themselves into a band, a unit, a family, quite without her—as if she wanted to be included! They said it was amazing that inside the house she had not heard their cries. Jacques and Naomi had heard them, had put on their coats and gone to meet them on the way back.

Oh, they'd had a fine time of it. They had gone out like hunters. They'd imagined shipwrecks. They had huddled together in the snow; they were hungry, hungrier, and they had starved. They had rested on the ground as if dead. They had died, and then they'd sprung back up to their feet as if Jesus had appeared from behind a tree, and worked a miracle on them.

And they came back to Jossey all ruddy, laughing, stomping their feet and counting their blessings and feeling lucky. "It was only a game! We are better off than people who are dead!" cried out Little John, and his sister cried out like his echo, "A game! A game! A game!"

It was perfectly all right, they said, that there was nothing out there to shoot. There was plenty of stored-up food. They would put on a fine supper anyway, a marvelous, convivial supper.

They came back from the woods *laughing*. They acted as if everything was operating in a normal set of conditions.

It was just like the story of Persephone. But no one else was worried. No one said it was awful or alarming that they'd been out there for hours, and nothing in the trees and brush and rocks and hollows, absolutely nothing, was alive and moving around.

They would have their celebration.

"Jossey," said John. He'd come up behind her as she was bending over the bowl of apples on the Wabanakis' big wood family table. He'd startled her but she did not turn around.

She thought, "These apples are going to taste dreadful. No one will congratulate me on my one contribution to the meal."

Well, fine. She didn't care, she decided. If Naomi wanted spices in the pot, let her come in and add them herself.

"I'll come outside to the fire in a moment, John."

"Turn around, Jossey. Please do."

She actually would scream if he spoke even one syllable of what-are-you-thinking to her. He could not know her mind. If there was a door to it, it was closed. He had no key. And if he did, he could put it into the lock all he liked: it wouldn't work.

He'd let his children make a mockery of solemn, terrible things! He did so himself! The husband who was her husband in Boston was not this man!

"Are you weeping, Jossey? Is that why you will not look around?"

"I am as dry in my eyes as in my breast," she answered.

His hand came onto her shoulder, not pressing, not heavy, but light, gentle. She tilted her head slightly, leaned back against him, just a little, as if her own weight on her own two legs was too much to be able to handle, in spite of her efforts to put up a good front. His other hand was on her. He smelled like outdoors. His clothes, his hair, all of him. He didn't smell like Boston. He smelled like Maine. "Here is something wonderful for you," he said softly.

Before she knew what was happening, he covered her eyes with his hands like a blindfold and managed to wheel her about, so that she was facing the doorway.

He moved his hands. The door was open. The blaze of the huge cooking fire lit up the darkness in the yard with a burst that made her blink hard, and it took a moment to understand that the figure in the doorway was not one of the Wabanakis, not anyone she would have expected.

For a moment, she thought it was one of Naomi's male relatives, come to return the baby, or to bring him for a visit. In fact she did not believe her eyes. She realized that she must have hardened herself against any further devastation: she must have, without knowing it, convinced herself that she would never see her brother again. Convinced herself to never get her hopes up.

Here he was. The thought came at once into her head that it was entirely possible he'd not come to see her, not only her, not at all. She didn't care!

She would tell him what Sarah Dudley had looked like at the mention of his name, she really would. She didn't have to like Sarah Dudley, but she would be generous! Here he was! She would be anything, anything, anything, just for the sight of him, and for the feel of his arms around her. He came toward her and she knew that the tears that suddenly started pouring out of his eyes had waited for this moment, like water behind a dam, which had just given way. "Patrick," she said softly. "Patrick, Patrick, Patrick, Patrick."

CHAPTER XIV

PATRICK AND SARAH

S ARAH DUDLEY loved the Wabanakis who were her family now, and Jossey and John and the children. If milk could flow in her breasts—if only she could tweak them and make it happen!—she would wet-nurse the infant herself, to save Jossey the sorrow of being apart from him.

They had planned to go down to Winnegance once a week to look at the baby, hold him, remind him of where he belonged, but that had not happened: there was too much else to do; the wagons and horses could not be spared.

Sarah thought of her new life as a sparsely furnished room—which was not hard to imagine in Maine—containing nothing but essentials. Simple furniture, everything homemade, everything solid and resilient, just like her almost-completely-made new self. Nothing luxurious, nothing Dudley, nothing Salem, nothing imported at huge cost from Europe.

Like Shakespeare's Juliet, she wanted to change her name, but for a different reason.

It embarrassed her to remember the old Sarah Dudley who'd made a thread-work of the word "Romeo" when first learning embroidery. Every other girl in Salem was making pretty work of psalms, prayers, and platitudes for daily living, like, "Patience Is My Virtue," and she was spelling out "Romeo" eight inches high and ten inches wide, in every bright color of thread she'd gotten her hands on. She'd known what would happen if anyone saw it except her maid, so she took it apart as soon as she'd finished it, and called it practice.

In her new life, there was not supposed to have been a Patrick Rouse.

They were walking side by side, in their heavy coats, out beyond the farmhouse, in clear, glittery, winter-morning sunlight. Now and then one of them would accidentally—it seemed—bump into the other, or their arms would brush, and they'd quickly, deliberately pull away, and say, "Pardon," and behave as if the contact caused them physical pain, like a kick.

There was something Patrick needed to know, something that was twisting around inside him. He could not believe how hard he was finding it to speak to her. He wished all over again he'd never met her. He wished there was no such person as Sarah Dudley.

"There shall be war," he said. "It is no longer a cause for speculation."

"I know that, Patrick."

"The siege of the fort in Portsmouth cannot be undone. We shall see a hundred other actions just like it, soon."

"You need not have so much glee to speak of it."

"You would call what I have in me *glee?*"

"You speak like a boy, excited over a game."

"No. In war," he said, "one's life is not one's own."

"You'd waste the last minutes before you leave, in talking to me of philosophy?"

"You asked me what was most on my mind."

"Then tell me. I expected an honest answer."

After a moment, he said, "Iron. I would show you where they plan to have the furnace."

He pointed. They'd been walking across the field toward the hill. The ground was lightly crusted with a hard, crunchy snow. It wasn't icy.

Snow in Maine was different from snow in Salem. It was shinier and whiter, here, somehow, and made a lot more noise when you stepped on it. It had never occurred to Sarah before, in all those years of getting ready to have the rest of her life—her real life—that she would never want to see her home again, and would never even miss it.

Iron, he was talking about. He was pointing his finger at emptiness. The furnace. He wanted her to imagine what he imagined. He'd been talking to Tobe Firth about iron, and tried to make it seem that iron was the only thing on his mind.

"It shall be astonishing," he said.

Now that it was time for him to leave, he was prepared to believe in the existence of the furnace, as crazy an idea as it was. He could almost picture the vertical layers of the towering shaft—stonework, brick, clay, sandstone, with one layer molded into the next—and the horizontal layers as well, the chimney, the tunnel head, the limestone, the ore, the charcoal, the crucible, the air duct, the inferno, all of which he wanted to describe to her with somberness and care.

His head was filled with foundry and iron information and he wanted to pass it along to her, and have her think it was a gift. But in his absence, she would be watching it built for real—built and then working, without him.

The temperature wasn't anywhere near freezing, but it was cold. His breath made mouth-sized white clouds in the air. Sarah wanted to grab each one; she had the crazy idea to pluck those breaths and pop them into her own mouth like something to eat, like berries.

Jossey had told her that, fourteen or fifteen years ago, when the English came to the farm to steal William, Lavinia had been out in the road picking blueberries. Jossey talked about Lavinia a great deal.

"The Enemy must be avenged for my sister," Jossey told Sarah.

The Enemy. Those were words everyone was saying all the time. Was Sarah wrong to be thinking of Shakespeare, was that Tory of her?

She tried to imagine what it was like for Lavinia to have seen her husband taken—taken from home, right in front of her eyes. Patrick was not being stolen to pilot an enemy ship. He was leaving of his own free will.

He said, "I had not been told where they plan to build the kilns. I believe I shall wonder of that. Perhaps it would not be a nuisance for you to write to me when they have decided."

"I would not know where to send a letter. One cannot address a letter to the care of the sea."

"You are right. But I would be able to receive post sent to Nahant, or Portsmouth, or to the care of my crewman's uncle in Charlestown."

"Then perhaps I shall."

"Thank you." He felt he was wadded in some kind of extreme politeness. He had never been this polite in his life, not even at table the few times he'd been to well-off houses, and had to handle himself as if harnessed.

He pointed to where he suspected the kilns would go, a sheltered area at the far end of the field, where the road was a buffer from the sea and the bay.

He said, "They must use dried wood as charcoal, so that, in the burning, the oxygen would be removed from the ore, you see, and that is the secret of iron. Removal of the air from the ore."

She didn't feel that it was necessary to tell him she did not understand how air could be contained inside something that was, basically, a chunk of solid rock.

She had decided to try to make an effort to take an interest in what he was going on and on about, but her ears especially picked out the part about the "removal of the air." Those words were just rubbing it in. She had already realized that, that was what she felt would happen in Tibbetston—in all the world, maybe.

The air itself would feel gone when he went back to his ship, which he was very nearly ready to do.

"After you leave, I think I'll not be able to breathe the right way," was what she didn't say out loud to him.

"Jacques already started designing the bellows," he said. "But I would believe they have not yet conceived the waterwheel. As for the crucible, they have had some disagreement."

They had reached the bottom of the hill, and would have to turn and go back. She stopped abruptly and so did he. Instead of turning, she looked at him, and said, "I would not be guilty of seeming to know what a crucible is, Patrick. I should like to be told."

"It's the chamber near the bottom of the furnace, for the ore to pass through, I would say, when the ore's been molten, and changed to iron."

"Empty of air," she said.

He wondered if she were mocking him. Her voice was edgy, tight. She wasn't trying to picture what he was picturing. He wanted her to believe in the furnace, to see it as if it were already there. What was he supposed to do without a furnace to be believing in? He wanted her to say she believed it would be standing there when he came back. He wanted to talk about when he came back.

"I believe they'd use limestone as a flux," he said.

And he waited for her to ask what that was, and she didn't. He felt that his two hands would be soon transformed into terrible, un-usable, inanimate things, like wood stumps or rock, if he didn't get to touch her, even if it was only to touch her shoulders, or put a finger to her lips, or her chin.

He said, "But I would not tell you more, as I have told you the full extent of what I had learned of it, except that, there must be a mixture of things. The stuff of the mixture is the flux, which they were saying shall be limestone, put into the ore."

"The ore," she said. "And why has no one said a place where this ore would be brought from? Did I not hear Mr. Firth tell you the cost of bringing ore from Massachusetts would be too high?"

"Fleep Wabanaki says there is ore near Moosehead."

"I've not been in Maine very many days altogether, but I would know there is a great distance to Moosehead, Patrick."

"There'd be wagons, oxen."

"Still, it's long way away," she said.

"There must be optimism," he said.

"There must be truth," she said.

She was missing the bigger picture, he felt. She wasn't doing her part.

He looked at her grimly. It occurred to him that a woman who'd leave her family, without sending news of where she was—not even to say she was alive—was perhaps not a woman who could be trusted, even though her family was deserving of being shut from her life. He willed himself to get rid of the desire to touch her. He decided to start to look forward to what it would be like to be free of her. It didn't work.

The awful thing was that for the first time in his life a woman was standing beside him and—face it!—he had the idea he might love her, and she was not, incredibly, forbidding him to go to sea, as if "forbid" were actually something he would allow a woman to do with him.

"I would be a fool to trust her" became the final thing on the list he'd been mentally compiling. He'd been adding to it for days. It wasn't so much that he'd studied every one of her faults—at least, the ones he'd discovered so far. It was more that the list of things against her was based on hard facts and circumstances.

"I would rather, Patrick, that we not speak of iron any longer," she said.

He felt as if his skin were transparent in front of her. He felt that she had developed a sort of smugness with him, a superiority, something like that of a mother with her child, not that he knew from his own experience what that was like. It reminded him instead of Jossey, the old Jossey, with her children, always knowing best.

He had never felt so *inferior.* She seemed to be looking at him as if she'd gotten the idea that she could read the workings of his brain, as if reading a book, or simply watching a wagon wheel turn, while he, confused and stupid, kept getting everything wrong.

What he wanted to know was, when he came back to Maine, whenever that was, would Sarah Dudley still be there and, if so, was she still going to be there for *him?*

He wondered, was that all right? Had he the right to that? After what happened, had he the right to happiness?

"We must turn back," Sarah said.

But she didn't turn around. She turned her face toward him with such a look of sadness—no, not just sadness; it was deeper than that, it was a look of despair, raw and bare, and he knew he would give anything he had to never see it there again.

"Let someone else captain the *Sawyer,*" he expected her to say. "Do not go to sea, not now, not ever, not with guns on your deck, and not without."

Now, he wished she would do him that favor, if only to have a reason to stay here longer with her, explaining why he couldn't do what she asked, which would take him hours, maybe days. He could do the explaining in her arms!

They'd throw Fleep out of the barn for a while! He'd rack his brain to find the right words, really search for them—"I cannot breathe as I must, not ever, really, without being on my ship, Sarah," or, feeling manly and confident, "I have my duty to think of," which would probably be words he would choke on.

He didn't have a duty. The outside world was a place he could very, very easily give up going to. He could get himself a dory or another schooner and fish; the Kennebec was as powerful—perhaps more so, at times—as the outside ocean, even if you never lost sight of land when you were on it, except in fog.

Jacques's two whaling sons were taking care of all the fishing, but once they started working in the foundry, that would be that, and also, they wouldn't be here forever; they'd go back to Nantucket, perhaps soon. Or they would join the army and go to war.

Then what? Who would provide for the farm, the village, the foundry? What about barter for the traders? And even when the construction was finished, there'd be lumbermen all the time for felling trees and filling kilns, besides all the other workers. It would take a lot of fish! It wasn't as if Jesus would come walking toward them with one Maine cod, which he'd multiply for a hundred hungry people!

So who would do the fishing?

Not Jacques, not John Avens, not even Fleep, whose idea of a boat was a birch canoe, self-made, and anyway, even though he'd not lived away from the river and the sea for very long, he'd always felt more at home on lakes and ponds. He didn't require tides, currents, the sight in your eyes of no land, just water and air and sky. Was that what Patrick ought to point out to her, that he required tides and currents, as another person required, say, a home?

"What I require," thought Patrick.

The Kennebec had probably twice its natural share of salt. No one who fished the Kennebec lacked for brine. If he had a new schooner, what would he call it?

That was easy. Then he listened to what she wasn't saying to him. She wasn't saying, "Stay here with me, Patrick, and let your pirate sloop sail without you, as you have men to handle it just fine. And they had put on those guns without asking you."

"Patrick," she said.

She was looking at him directly, but her eyes took on an objectivity, a neutrality, the way people always look when they deliver bad news, and want to hurry and get it over with. This was not a good time to describe to her that he wanted Fleep to let them have the barn for a couple of hours, alone.

The despair in her expression was still there. "I do not regret the hours we have had in the company of each other these days. You must know, I could not marry you, should you have considered such a thing, and which, had you not, but might later, I am glad to have forestalled, Patrick. Should I have spoken for no cause, let it be between us I had not spoken of it, at all." It was delivered like a speech.

He didn't know what to answer and just blurted out the first thing that came to him. "I had thought, before you spoke, I would have a new schooner, the name of which, I had thought, would be your own."

"I hold no pleasure in my name."

"But I do." He didn't know if she was pleased with that or not.

She said, "I was betrothed in Salem. I shall not be again."

"I was betrothed *three times*," he shot back. "I said, myself, those same words, *three times.*"

He wondered if he sounded like he was bragging. He said quietly, "Say my name."

"Patrick. Patrick Rouse of York. And of the sloop called *York Sawyer.*"

"Say yours."

"Sarah Dudley," she said. "Sarah Dudley of . . . of . . . of . . . here." It was her turn to look stupid, fuddled. She looked around at the ground, at the place where the furnace would go, at the hill that rose up in front of them, and the river and the cold blue winter sky. At everything that wasn't him.

He was just about to say, "Say both names together," when a cry rang out from near the farmhouse. They jumped apart from each other, guiltily, although they'd not been standing closely.

"Uncle! Uncle! Uncle!"

Little John was outdoors without a coat, in just his breeches and shirt and the buckskin vest Fleep had made him, which he never took off, not even for bed. He was waving wildly, and hopping up and down as if the ground he stood on were on fire.

"Uncle! The wagon is here for you! They are waiting! I am packed! I am going with you! I am going to sea! I am going to sea!"

"I think," said Sarah, "he will not grow up to be a preacher like John."

"Or a foundryman."

"Or a farmer."

"Or a blacksmith."

There was a pause. She said, "Go. I shall write to you when they have chosen the place for the charcoal."

"Thank you. I think perhaps it would be wise to have someone hold on to the boy as I am leaving."

"I'll make sure his father has him well in hand."

"I'd rather you would hold him yourself."

"Then I shall."

"There will be a time I shall find myself in Falmouth. Perhaps you would be going to Falmouth to see your maid and her mother?"

"I think I may not, as Sarah plans to come here soon."

"Then we shall not meet in Falmouth."

"I think not."

"Very well."

When they started walking back to the house, he held out his arm to her, and she took it, and he decided to take his chances on what he really wanted to say to her.

"I would have the hope when I return here, which I shall, as soon as possible, you would be here."

"I have nowhere else to go, Patrick."

"Neither have I, but I am going there."

CHAPTER XV

THE TORY

I‍T WAS A Saturday night in the middle of January 1775. Things were getting a little out of hand at Winnie Goodridge's tavern. It was hard to tell exactly at which point the rousing flow of hard Maine cider and rum changed course, but somewhere around 9:00 in the evening, all by itself, it seemed, that point was unalterably reached.

There were no warships in the York harbor. No one had seen an officer, sailor, or even one soldier, for weeks. The enemy presence in Maine had gathered and fixated itself in and around the hub of bigger Falmouth, to the north. But all the same, the feeling was a feeling of danger, and of potential attack.

At first, there was a muffling of conversations, which was no small feat, as the place was packed with men and women from town, as well as from outlying farms and settlements. Most of the York militia was here. A few were with their wives or girlfriends. All the chairs and benches were filled, and there was barely room among the standees to turn around, or even raise an elbow. Some of the farmers brought their own cider in flasks, but Winnie didn't care; she was profiting nicely.

Even if she'd seen what was coming—if she hadn't been so busy—it probably would have happened that she wouldn't be able to stop it (if she'd wanted to). She had not seen it coming.

There was no leader among the customers, and there was no single source of instigation. This would not be the first time at Winnie's when a crowd of people, lathered up, started thinking out loud about the subject of fighting the English, and when and why and how.

But always before there'd been someone—a doused-up tanner, or a farmer or fisherman, or a sawmill man—who'd step to the center of attention and take on the role of rabble-rouser, saying something like, "Liberty for us, and death to all English!"

The spark would be lit. Someone would take it up and say something worse, or something more eloquent, and someone would echo it and think of something else.

"God willing, may the king and his lords choke tonight on their suppers, as they had tried to choke us!"

"God willing, may the English governor in Salem fly to hell!"

"God willing, likewise with every Tory!"

"God willing, may every Tory kiss the farting, red arse of Satan!"

There'd be shouting and stomping, and the tables and chairs would shake. Winnie might bang on a table if it got too loud, but usually, as fervent as it could get, the only effect overall would be emotional: an outpouring of pent-up feelings, then a sense of relief, temporarily, as if that's what a tavern was for.

This was something else; this was spontaneous. Ten, twenty, thirty people seemed to have all started thinking the same way at the same time. The laughter all stopped; the shouting and the rowdy, raunchy jokes stopped, too.

The difference in the atmosphere was like the difference between fooling around in a wrestling match, and going at it for real, except that, in the tavern, everyone was on the same side.

A grim, belligerent seriousness took over, and suddenly, Winnie's customers were standing up straighter, in a state of alertness. They were pushing back their shoulders and steeling their jaws. No one said, "Let's talk about war." No one said anything at all, except, in whispers at first, then a bit louder, there was mention of the name of a man, with the word "Tory" in front of it.

Tory Edwin Norwood. And the men of the York militia were looking around quietly and nudging each other, as if saying, "Well, seeing as how the new year is here, and things are bound to be changing, why don't we go ahead and have some action *right now*."

It wasn't as if they could rush to a fort like in Portsmouth; their small fort by the sea was in their hands already, and anyway, it had never been fully English in a military way; it was a sea-merchant-run operation for the protection of goods, not people. They could have stormed the jail and released hapless colonists, chained to walls because they refused to pay English taxes, but the jail wasn't run by the English, and it happened to be empty. And there weren't any ships to stand up against, not even one stray British gun-decked dory.

Edwin Norwood was the closest thing to an Englishman in the town of York. He was thirty-six years old. He was unmarried, and though he had an occupation, no one had ever seen him involved with it, other than walking around by the harbor, police-like. But everyone knew he was a lawyer with a Boston firm that specialized in shipping, specifically in the import-export business.

Edwin Norwood had probably been sent to York against his will, perhaps as a punishment for some lawyerly transgression. He was a thin, lanky man, sharp-nosed, thin-skinned, bony, and pointy all over, as if God had designed his body with extra angles. He was already graying and slightly balding.

No matter how soft-spoken he was, or how mild, or how polite, or how decent—and no one had cause to complain of him; he'd never raised his voice or cheated anyone—he could not escape his appearance. He couldn't supersede the basic impression everyone had of him: lordly, aloof, untrustworthy, and too sharp, too stern, and too pointed. Too *not like us*. He had an air about him of always seeming to be marking his time, just like someone who is serving a prison sentence.

This was his third year in Maine. He quietly complained of the cold and the wind every winter, and would never make the effort to get used to it, and he never stopped shivering and groaning, no matter how many layers of wool and pelts he put on. He had no friends in town or in the villages or countryside—no friends, period. The two old women who lived with him had no one but him; hardly anyone in York except for shopkeepers ever spoke to them.

He'd been sent to York from Boston to keep an eye on what was coming and going on the merchant ships. If a load of insured Maine lumber was being put on a ship for England, it was Edwin

Norwood's job to make sure that the ship set sail, intact, not that he had anything to say about what went on once the ship reached open sea. If a ship was suspected of heading for Boston to defy the embargo, he sent word to have it watched. He was only concerned with comings and goings. It could not have been a particularly interesting way to spend his days. He never went onto the ships, or spoke with sailors; he just watched.

He traveled to Boston every couple of months, but usually he was in town, walking this way and that along the harbor, the shore. His eyes were as sharp as the rest of him, and it often made people feel nervous to be looked at by him, even in passing, just to say, "Good day." He made you feel guilty and worried, as if he'd found out about any secret pleasure or vice you'd ever had, or anything you'd ever done that was wrong, and he was waiting for the right moment to use the information against you. That was how people in York felt about him in general, besides the fact he was Tory.

He lived with his widowed mother and a very elderly aunt in a little gray stone house, with a wide, gently-sloping, English-style roof. No one at Winnie's tavern had ever been to England, and could say they knew what an English roof was like, but they were sure that's what it was. The house was a fifth of a mile down the road from Winnie's. Edwin Norwood had not built the house; in fact, it was being leased for him by his Boston employers, from a fur trader named Dodge, who now lived in Portsmouth. The fur trader had built the house with stone because the one he'd been born in, in the next village, had been burned to the ground in a Wabanaki raid.

It was the only stone house for miles. Everyone else had wood. Stone, it was felt, was *English,* and so what if it was American rock, from a good Maine quarry.

And the shutters on the windows? English shutters. And the vegetable garden in the back? An English garden. And the post? Didn't Edwin Norwood and his mother and aunt think the mail wagons were only for themselves, and didn't very large quantities of letters and parcels go out of that house every week, bound for England, the original home of the mother and aunt?

No wonder they rarely talked to anyone and, when they had to deal with merchants, they pretended they suffered from throat diseases, and were always hoarse.

When the militia had first started organizing, and then again last month, when they were starting to say that, when war began, which they were certain it would, they'd leave Maine to join the Continental Army, what had Mr. Edwin Norwood contributed? Not one coin, not one drop of lead to be melted for shot, not one gun, not one tin box for ammunition, not one strip of leather for a pouch, and not even a promise of clothing or blankets, when even the poorest farmhand and the unluckiest fisherman had measured out some part of their households as donations.

No, it couldn't be said that anyone had knocked on Mr. Norwood's door to ask for help, or stopped him and mentioned "necessary goods for the new militia" on one of his harbor *spy* walks— for wasn't that what he really was up to, when you thought about it?

It wasn't that he got up at Town Meeting to speak out against the organizing. He always went to Meeting, and never once had said a thing. There were plenty of smart, loudmouthed Tories in Maine. Most of them were connected in one way or another to ships and trade. Edwin Norwood pretended he barely knew those men. He sat alone at Meeting, and made it clear he was only there because he was a temporary citizen who understood the concept of duty. He stayed apart and aloof, with his sharp pointed beak of a nose, and his watchful, shiny eyes, like a man-sized bird. A lean, confident, highly competent bird of prey, that would be.

His silence, people felt, told everything. He didn't need to walk around with calling cards in his pocket that said, "Edwin Norwood, Man of Law, and Your Enemy."

Alone among the other Tories, he tried to hide it, which was doubly insidious, people felt, and made him look like a coward. There was no room in Maine for loyalist cowards. He'd have to go. That was it. Tonight. He'd have to go.

There was no one who took the role of commander. The militia prided itself on its inner structure, which was based on a soul-deep, blood-strong conviction of "democracy," which was another way of saying, "All of us are leaders, and all of us are equal."

Maybe in Boston, it was felt, they were planning a new government that might more or less resemble the old one, with a king of America to replace the one in England; but in Maine, and especially along the coast, it wouldn't fly.

This was basic and incontrovertible. You could not live long among the giant Maine trees, the giant Maine boulders, the giant Maine wide-open sky, and the giant Maine surf and the sea, without getting the notion, quite naturally, that the leader of yourself is yourself, in all things.

So no one person stood up and said, "Come along, we shall make an attack on the English stone house down the road." It seemed that they'd all figured it out on their own.

To Winnie, it seemed that, at some point in their meetings and training exercises, the men of the York militia had managed something extraordinary—and now that she'd thought of it, she remembered she'd seen this when she was up in Tibbetston, too. The militias had developed an intricate, below-the-surface system of communication, as if they were linked to each other's minds, like a stand of trees that shared the same roots.

When nine men of the York militia—with another half dozen men, and as many women, too, just behind them—put their coats on and left Winnie's tavern, it appeared that they were going out in the road for a festive New Year's post-midnight stroll. A few of the men had knives, and a few had pistols, and a few had both, but most of them were unarmed.

Why did Winnie put her cloak on and follow? She would ask herself this question many times. Because she wanted to see what would happen. Because, in spite of the we-have-no-commander militia mentality, she felt responsible for the conduct of her customers, like a grownup in a crowd of children, even though her customers had quitted her premises, and nothing she could say would matter to them at all.

And war was coming, was perhaps here already, and she was part of it. She'd consigned herself to the idea of fighting the moment she'd made up her mind to take over the farm in Tibbetston, for the foundry. One of these days, the gun balls in the pouches of Maine militiamen would come from her Tibbetston furnace: every time they'd load a musket, they'd do so because of her. But she didn't want to merely wait around in York for the foundry plans to bear fruit. She wanted something to happen now, and she wanted to be there when it did.

But mostly, Winnie Goodridge went out in the cold winter night, in the wake of what had turned into a mob—a grim, silent mob—because she remembered how much she truly understood the value of a certain set of necessary instincts and desires.

Her old friend the Massachusetts Indian who called himself Rabbit, the very opposite of what he was like, had really gotten it right when he'd told her all those years ago that the one thing that separates a beast, fish, or bird from a human was not what they told you in church. It wasn't the ability to think, plan, imagine, and have a soul.

The difference, in fact, was the ability of a person, in the right set of circumstances, to feel a rational desire for revenge, and then, with the righteous mightiness of a Christian angel, act on that feeling, pure and simple.

A bear might lunge at you to remove you of your throat if you went too close to its children, but once you'd escaped it, and went home to your bed, it would not show up later on, knocking at your door with an army of its friends, having tracked you. The brothers and sisters of a cod you'd caught on a line would not lie in wait to destroy you the next time you fished. A thrush in a tree could flap and rail all it liked when a crow came raiding its nest, but it would never join up with other songbirds, and plot ways to strike back at any winged, dangerous, predatory thing that came their way.

That was the beauty of being human, she felt. You get to strike back.

Winnie had learned this lesson even better than she'd realized. She had started to shiver badly, but it wasn't only because of the cold. An image formed in her mind, as if someone were slowly drawing a picture for her. She made out the shape of the hill behind the Tibbetston farm—the hill whose stream would soon run the waterwheel for the foundry. Then she made out a small detail she thought she'd forgotten, from the day of the funerals. She remembered it now.

She pictured herself back at the farm, trying to hide herself behind her role as a sort of traveling tavern keeper, who'd only come professionally, to supervise the hospitality, and not because she had loved Lavinia and William and the children. She'd been helping the village women lay out the tables set up in the lower field for the funeral lunch. Her eyes had sought something to stare at that was not some part of the grave sites.

She'd felt ill, and wondered if she'd have to bolt away on her own and be violently sick. A knife was in her hand. The roasted ducks had needed carving, and the job had fallen to her. It had happened that someone bumped into her, someone with a bowl that was filled to the top with dark, mashed cranberries, which were cooked in a pot with molasses, and were still a little hot.

Some of the berry sauce had splashed on Winnie, and some had landed on the knife, mostly on the handle. But enough of it went onto the blade to have caught her attention.

That was the image. That was what she remembered. That red along the line of the blade.

She'd been thinking about her husband anyway. Every funeral, no matter whose, was one more time to think about him more vividly than usual, and she had looked at the colored blade and thought, "If it weren't for the English, I would still have Hobe, and if it weren't for the English, we would all still have the Mowlans."

She'd felt remarkably clear-headed, calm. The sick feeling in her stomach went away as soon as she said to herself, "What a marvelous thing it would be, if the stain on this blade were not from berries, but from the body of an English solider." Any English soldier, she'd felt, would have served the purpose just fine. She understood the basic law that went along with revenge. There was nothing particular about it.

"Edwin Norwood!" someone shouted. "Edwin Norwood! You come out here!"

A powerful current shot through Winnie's blood. Something in her went cold, hard. It occurred to her that this feeling was something she should probably make an effort to get rid of.

She did not make the effort. She wished for it to be stronger, harder. "Scare them and hurt them, hurt them all," were the words that popped into her head, as if she were sending a message to the militia, as if she were part of their under-the-surface communication system.

At the front of the mob-crowd of her customers, three or four lanterns had been lit, as if magically, as if people had pulled them out from the folds of their coats and cloaks. In the thin light, the front door of Edwin Norwood's house was opened, and three figures appeared in the doorway. Edwin Norwood, his mother, the aunt.

Edwin Norwood was squarely in front of them, so that the two women's heads, with the hair on one slightly whiter and grayer than the other, peeked out from the sides of his shoulders.

The women's heads were uncovered. Winnie would have expected them to be wearing nightcaps; it was strange that they weren't. Their hair wasn't loose, but done up tightly, newly, in prim, English-lady knots. They did not look especially worried.

There was Norwood, with his sharpness and points and bird-of-prey expression. He was wearing his big wool English coat, with a long vest made from fox pelts on top of it, and they were not a coat and vest thrown over nightclothes. He did not look like a man who'd been roused in the middle of the night from sleep. For some reason he was fully dressed. He stepped forward; his mother and aunt were dressed to go out, too, in similar wool and furs. Norwood's hat was in his hands.

No one in the yard or in the road spoke a word. There was no wind, just the still, heavy, nighttime, salt-watery air, which seemed to take hold of the silence and deepen it, make it louder.

The aunt handed a lantern to Norwood. The flickering yellow light went up in a sort of draft to his face. He looked out at them with a wide, astonishing smile, with all his teeth showing; it was a smile that really seemed to begin at one ear and go all the way to the other. Every point, every harsh angle of Edwin Norwood was softened.

He called out, to the crowd in general, "We had learned the news of the delay to the south of our assistance, but we had trusted some help would arrive. But where are the wagons? We have need of, at the very least, four."

"Please, Edwin," said his mother, "allow these poor people inside to step outdoors. They have been waiting so long."

"I am certain these good people have come with arrangements for wagons," said the aunt.

Edwin Norwood nodded to his mother. He held out his lantern to his side and stepped down from the house, and the two women did, too.

"How marvelous you have come to be of aid," said Edwin Norwood. "It would not be necessary for any of you to accompany us all the way to our destination, in Rhode Island. But we would be most grateful for wagons."

He was taking the role of a commander, but no one could do anything about it, because they had no idea what he was talking about.

The internal network of the militia wasn't doing so well at this moment. Dumbfounded would be the best way to describe them. Winnie looked around from one to another, and felt as deflated and disappointed as she'd ever felt in her life. The current inside her had switched over to the same quiet meekness and surprise as her customers.

But shrewdly she wondered, like a hope she was trying to hold on to, is this a trick? A cunning English trick?

Then she knew it was not.

The front door of the house seemed to open wider, as if curtains were there instead of wood. Two men came out, then a woman, then two more men, then three women, then two more women, then seven men. All of them were in heavy coats and furs, and carried blanket-wrapped bundles. Some of the women had covered a part of their faces with hoods or scarves, and some of the men had pulled their hats down low. But there was no disguising the fact that these people weren't English.

A nervy tension entered into the silence, and made Winnie think of buzzing summer cicadas, if you could feel the buzz, but not hear it.

The woman beside Winnie was Mary Chambley, a spinner from just outside York, whose husband was in the militia. Winnie didn't know her well; she was not a regular customer. But she seized Winnie's arm like her closest friend, and whispered to her, as if Winnie couldn't see for herself, "Winnie, I do believe these people are Negroes."

A surge of new hope began building in Winnie. The Tory English Norwoods were part of the slave trade! That's what Edwin

Norwood was up to, and they had thought all he did was watch ships! He probably had connections to the southern plantations! He was doubly guilty! So was the mother and aunt! What a wonderful stroke of great luck! Running them out of town was exactly the right thing to do, no doubt about it!

"But why would all these Negroes be here?" said Mary Chambley.

"The Norwoods are slave traders, obviously, and we must stop them from taking these people to hell on a Carolina tobacco plantation, I would say," Winnie answered.

Mary Chambley thought about that and frowned. "If I were a slave trader, and bless God I have the right disposition, I would put my slaves in chains."

"There are all manner of chains, my dear Mary," said Winnie. "There may be chains hidden beneath their clothes."

"But Mr. Norwood said Rhode Island. They are going to Rhode Island."

"Rhode Island is on the way."

"I believe it would be Rhode Island they are actually going to, from the manner he spoke, Winnie, not passing through."

Edwin Norwood was talking to the militia. "We had a devil of a time of it farther up the coast, getting our guests by the troops. But my aunt had come up with a remarkable plan."

The aunt beamed in the light of the lantern. "We had put bandages on their faces," said Norwood, "as though they were victims of the pox. We had made it seem we would bring them to marooning on a quiet Maine island."

Winnie knew perfectly well, as everyone else did, that there were people in Maine and New Hampshire who had joined a secret system of hiding escaped slaves and arranging for journeys that were safe from the English, and from prowling, resilient, clever American bounty hunters.

Even though she'd been running the tavern at the center of York all these years, and had thought of herself as someone who knew everything that went on, she'd had no suspicion that something like this was taking place.

All her hopes collapsed, like a wave that folds without cresting. So much for action. So much for tonight.

She did not envy the Norwoods for being better than she was, and she didn't feel ashamed of herself, or diminished in any way. She felt slighted, though. How could the Norwoods not have asked her for help? Would they have thought she couldn't be trusted? Why were escaped slaves in this house, and not hers? Oh! How stupid and rude it had been of the Norwoods to not include her!

"Our guests are very tired, and have been through hardships you cannot imagine," said Edwin Norwood.

Winnie saw that the guests of the Norwoods, clustered here and there in the yard, were eyeing these night visitors with a lot more skepticism than their hosts. Maybe the Norwoods understood the reality of the situation, no matter how much of a different turn it had taken, but their skin was white, and they did not have bounties on their heads.

Mary Chambley left Winnie's side and went over to a Negro woman who was older than the others. "Where came you from?"

"Tibbetston," answered the woman. "From the hell of the place belonging to a man named Leyson."

Mary said, "How much have the Norwoods provisioned you with?" The woman held out her hands as if to answer, "Not a lot."

A few of the militia men began conversing with Norwood and some of his guests in quiet, energetic tones, like men conducting business.

"I have a wagon," said one, and the man beside him said, "So have I, and the loan of two oxen."

"I shall give you the loan of two horses," said another.

"I have two wagons to be spared for the present time," said someone else.

"God bless you," said the old aunt.

Mary Chambley was looking over her shoulder at Winnie, motioning for her to speak up, too. "My friend over there is the tavern keeper and I am sure she will want to make a donation," she said to the Negro woman.

Oh, fine. How much food was left from the long evening's revels in the tavern? Some salted pork, some bread, some cornmeal biscuits—perhaps enough to feed half of the travelers just a little. Rhode Island was a long way away.

Winnie ran a quick mental inventory of what she had in her

buttery and storerooms, and sighed heavily. She knew she'd end up stripping everything she had off her shelves and handing it all over. It was going to be hard to not count this as a loss, just as it was hard to stand there and be a good—no, a better person—and not keep saying to herself, "I am truly disappointed, but maybe they shall go after other Tories, and the next time, get it right."

CHAPTER XVI

ℋEADQUARTERS

THE MEN OF THE now-combined Tibbetston and Grilleyville militias met four times a week in the late afternoon for training exercises, the "training" being broadly defined. Gone was the outburst of optimism and cocky confidence they'd felt at the start of the year, as if 1775 would deliver war at their doorstep, and then boom, boom, boom, boom, that would be that.

They realized it would not be like a thunderstorm. A soberness and new sense of purpose took them over.

They gathered at the Grilleyville tavern to talk and eat supper together, but not drink. They'd established it as a rule that if any one of them desired to liquor up, it would have to take place in their own private homes on the Sabbath, the one day they never met.

They heard of a militia in Vermont that bragged of itself as so well disciplined, their men had lost the taste for anything stronger than chicory, and were living as ascetically as monks. It was not an option for people in Maine—not just the militia—to consider anyone in landlocked Vermont as their moral or physical superior, in any way.

Their gatherings became an end-of-the-day event in the daily routine of their chores. They'd go outside to someone's field, or just into the road by the tavern, and put in some target practice.

The eldest among them was sixty-one: a skinny, leather-faced bachelor fisherman named Dawlings, who always had to borrow someone else's gun, and never quite mastered loading it. He felt that Americans would fight better by using spears, nets, lines, and hooks, and never missed a chance to say so.

He never talked about what had happened to the Mowlans, but it was never far from his thoughts. They weren't actually his kin, but neither was anyone else; he had come to adopt them as his family.

One day about a dozen years ago, William Mowlan went to see him to talk about trading—corn for cod—and ended up bringing Dawlings home for a meal. Then it happened that every Sabbath, Dawlings trekked himself on foot up the hill to the farm for midday dinner. It was the one thing in his life that had drawn him to bring in his boat at an early hour, besides weather. He brought fish, and then he'd leave with double the amount in bread, cornmeal, jams.

He had loved the Mowlans. His body still felt the indentations of the children at play, climbing all over him; he still woke up on Sunday mornings wondering what Lavinia would be cooking. If it weren't for the militia, he would have set out to open sea on his own in his dory, in a fit of madness, hunting English with harpoons.

The youngest militia member was a fifteen-year-old boy called Squirrel, because he was small and fast and clever, with a chattery tone to his voice (before it had changed) and small, dark, excitable eyes.

Squirrel joined the militia because there were five children in his family younger than he was, and he never got enough to eat at home (but would never admit this). He ate in the tavern for free. His father kept pigs to be sold at market in Bath and Falmouth; he was sick of pigs. He wanted adventure, and he wanted to get out of Maine, too.

All four of the Wabanakis went regularly to the training exercises, but not John, who went once and never went back, because everyone kept calling him "Preacher," even though he asked them not to. They did not believe him when he told them he'd be as capable as anyone else when it came to shooting real shot at real Englishmen, and so what if he'd trained as a man of the church.

It was Dawlings who put forth the idea that maybe things were different down in Boston, but in Maine, the purpose of having religion was to have religious leaders who'd be counted on to keep the commandments, especially the one that went "Thou shalt not kill." Then everyone else could break any rule they had to, and if their conscience bothered them, they could go to the minister and be redeemed, which sounded Catholic, but the rest of the men agreed with him, and of course, so did Jacques and his sons, and Avens didn't put up an argument. They were all too polite and self-conscious around him anyway; he had known ahead of time that he'd never fit in.

There was never much by way of shooting, as they couldn't afford to waste shot. Someone would cry out, in the fog and twilight shadows, "Red devil ahead," or, from Dawlings and the other fishermen, "Red devil starboard!" They'd imagine the easy target of a phalanx of British soldiers coming up the road at them in daylight, wearing silly coats that were garishly, brightly red, like an army of man-sized boiled lobsters.

Sometimes they had to force themselves to go out at all, and sometimes they'd see themselves as thunderous, invincible. In the backs of their minds they knew it was ridiculous of them to be playing like children, as if their muskets were make-believe, as if they all had mothers who'd call them home for bedtime, not wives.

They couldn't complain about the winter because day by day it was the mildest one in anyone's memory. But everyone was getting restless. Springtime in Maine, with its slow, drawn-out thaw, was like a dream that would never come true.

It was beginning to feel that they were going around in circles, getting worked up for nothing, going nowhere. It was one thing to keep the knowledge of what happened to the Mowlans in the front of their minds, but it was a very different thing to keep themselves stirred up over what this war would be truly about.

What was it to be about, exactly? Oh, the English.

It was time to get a little more serious. They realized that they needed a place to use for a headquarters, somewhere big and secure, on high-raised land, ideally overlooking the Kennebec. After a quick exchange of ideas and the briefest of discussions, they decided unanimously to return, armed and in uniform, to Samuel Leyson's abandoned farm—or his estate, as he'd called it—not to ransack it this time, but to take it over.

Their uniforms were their own winter coats and breeches and fur caps, clothes they wore all the time, which only became uniforms when worn on militia business.

They knew where Leyson had gone, and they felt that he ought to be told of what was happening. Someone thought of asking Sarah Dudley for the address in Salem of her brother-in-law, and she gave it to Jacques and he passed it along—not of her family's house, but of her father's business office.

One of the men who could read and write was a cooper from just below Grilleyville. He made and sold all sorts of barrels, but his specialty was in containers for the transport of rum; he had not done badly with it. His name was actually Cooper, Hiram Cooper. He volunteered to write a letter. He had not written many of them in his life—it was always mostly invoices and threats to distillery people who owed him money, but he was satisfied with the result.

Hiram Cooper didn't bother with a standard form of address, but plunged right in.

He wrote, "We have constrewed our Selfs into Soljeers. What rights and privvliges would be gain'd for Americans, are not pertain'd to your self. Shood you think to come agin to this Tibbetston place & beg mercy we may dauble with the thawt to see it not o' cur it that you are kill'd. We took hold of your house, Samule Leyson, & your land. You Tory Pottage of Pus. You hav' surend'rd all prop'ty. You shall NOT HAVE IT BACK."

The letter was sent with the names at the bottom of every one of them, but no response came.

Once in custody of the Leyson farm, they regretted their hotheaded rush of before, and wished that the last time they'd been here, they'd had a little more foresight about leaving the main house wide open to the elements and wildlife.

It took a week to get the chimneys cleared and the fires going; it took almost two weeks to get the windows repaired and the place cleaned out. But now they had somewhere to go that felt official. They pictured phantom Englishmen everywhere around them. They told themselves it wouldn't be different from hunting, but they didn't actually believe it.

Some of them had been in the French and Indian War, but they had seen no actual battle, having joined up too late; some of the older ones had shot at Indians during the worst of the raids, but those Indians had been retreating, swiftly, with a hundred years of white-people experience in their minds, and it was the same as trying to put shot into a shadow.

The truth was, not counting the time a man named Dougalson, a Tibbetston farmer and lumberman, shot at, and missed widely, a dinghy containing three English sailors coming from their warship in search of fresh water, not one of them had ever aimed a gun at a living, breathing target, right in front of them, except as something to bring home for dinner, or to skin.

Once, when they were sitting around in the tavern, a man named Nashe, a trapper, had looked up in the middle of lighting his pipe to say something about this.

They'd been talking about the weather, and Nashe said, "Be a strange thing, war, to be shooting at something we leave there when it drops down dead to the ground, and what we cannot collect up, and boil for a stew."

That was all that was said, but it was definitely something to think about—for later. All the same, they didn't think of themselves any longer as farmers, tradesmen, and fishermen, who worked themselves to the bone on the hard Maine soil, the damp, cold shops, and the sea, and then dabbled at the end of the day in warplay, building up the nerve to go out and do it for real, even though, in their hearts (except for the excited boy, Squirrel), they knew how bad it could get, and they dreaded it.

They began to think of themselves as a unit, interlocked within themselves, and already functioning as part of something bigger. They felt like people getting ready for a journey, which was real and unreal, both together, like in a dream, with a definite sense of purpose, but no clue where they were going.

CHAPTER XVII

THE FOUNDRY

IT WAS MARCH. It was cold, wet, and bitterly windy. The tree-felling operation in the back woods of Tibbetston was taking place in earnest.

The general feeling was, "This is a very big thing, which we shall approach one step at a time, and not worry about the next, until we come to it." Up next would be the gathering of rock for the construction of the chimney-tower, which no one was looking forward to, not that anyone enjoyed what they were engaged in. It was time to stockpile wood. The furnace was going to need charcoal, a great deal of it.

Some farmers and fishermen along the coast, along with a few experienced lumbermen, had heard about the foundry, and came to help: they slept in the barns, at the inn, at the tavern, at Samuel Leyson's farm that was now a barracks and headquarters combined.

The kilns were almost ready, and were set in the lower field, near the road, but the first few loads of lumber were set aside to be smuggled down the coast as firewood for occupied, closed-up Boston.

First they took out most of the trees from Gun Ball Hill and, along the way, they cleared out the beaver dams and all the clogging debris from the pond and its stream. Then they pushed back off the hill into the woods.

There was no joy in the labor. Taking down trees was hard, brutal, tricky work, and the only time anyone felt a rise in their spirits was when they felled any giant, perfect pine with a trunk that was branded with the mark of the king.

Everyone who lived and grew up here remembered what it was like when English surveyors had arrived, roaming the woods with pistols, without guides, marking all the best trees to be saved and cut later for themselves, and they'd always known which ones were really best. The surveyors had looked at the trunks of those pines with calm, confident ownership, as if they were masts already, as if English sails and English flags were attached to them, instead of branches and cones and piney needles.

The surveyors had gone through the woods as if they were landlords of all they saw, as if everything was simply and naturally theirs, as if the people of Maine were either their tenants, or their servants.

It was not a likely thing that anyone English, on behalf of the king, would show up now and demand to be given what they'd staked out as theirs. No tree from Tibbetston would end up on an English warship; it was a sort of consolation.

People from here—just about everyone—became passionate when they thought about or talked about Englishmen getting off a ship from the other side of the world, and walking around on American land like it was theirs.

John Avens had something to say about that, too, and felt he had the right to, even though he was citified and educated, and grew up where you go to a shop to get food for your supper, not to the river or woods, or your own fields.

One day at the tavern, John interrupted a militia man who was formulating the idea that, if you looked for the one basic tangible reason why war with the English was about to happen, that reason would be this: "They had thought they would own what is ours, and would take from us, as masters, whatever they wanted to take."

John answered valiantly, soberly. "What you have in your lives and in your hearts, which Englishmen would take from you, by force or rule of their law, are the same things the Micmac, the Wabanaki, and all the other tribes had, too. Our feelings toward the English are the same as theirs."

And a hush fell over everything. He was talking about Indians? They were working like oxen and training for war, and he wanted to compare their feelings toward the enemy English with the feelings of *Indians?*

"Well," someone pointed out. "Respectfully, if you would not take offense at the observation, it wasn't Indians that came here murdering your sister and her family, Mr. Avens."

John was not involved in the tree-felling. He wasn't even allowed to venture into any trees beyond sight of the road, partly because, when you took one look at his smooth hands and fingers, and you saw no brownish-yellow hardness, no callouses, no grooves worn into the skin like tracks worn into a road, you'd get the idea you might not want to have him around with an ax.

And never mind the things he'd talk about. No one wanted a minister in the woods, who might only remind you of funerals and mortality, and could bring bad luck: with a man of God standing there conveniently to bless you on your way to heaven, a tree might have a greater chance of falling in a different direction from where it was aimed, and landing instead on top of you.

No one cared that John kept saying he was done with religion for forever. He was instead put in charge of the money, accounts, correspondence, orders for materials, and anything else for the foundry that had to do with words and paper.

For almost three weeks, dawn to dusk, the noise carried far, unrelentingly—chop, crack, chop, chop, crack, chop, bang, bang, hard, hard, chop, chop, crack—louder and louder as the day progressed. With the battering sound of the axes and the roar of falling trees, there were constant, harsh shouts, animal-like in their intensity. When the watery wind blew especially hard—with teeth in it, as they said—it seemed that there must have been a thousand of them out there—an army—instead of three dozen, plus the militia, who were helping, too.

The professional lumbermen tried gamely to establish their usual camp routines and their usual camp spirit, but it didn't last long; it was useless to pretend that anything was worth joking about, or even normal.

All those people needed to be fed. Winnie sent up as much as she could by way of provisions, along with money, but they were pretty much left to themselves to come up with an unstopping supply of meals.

The big hearth and its side brick ovens at the farmhouse were being worked full steam, and so was the small outdoor hot-stone pit Naomi's sons had put in for the big bean pot: there was bread, beans, more beans, chowder, corn cakes, corn mush, stewed nuts, boiled onions, rabbit stew, now and then ducks, now and then turkeys, now and then crabs, and anything else they could lay hands on.

Jossey and Little John and Vinny were up at the farmhouse every day, and Jossey had actually got to the point where she was telling herself—as if her milk had never stopped flowing—that the reason her baby was away from her was this: she could not be distracted from the cooking, and anyway, she had to keep an eye on her husband, in case he got it into his head to defy the Tibbetston men and go follow them into the woods, and that went for her children as well.

At least once an hour, Jossey was convinced that the terrible noise from the woods would either deafen her or drive her mad, but neither of those things happened; she just went on with it.

She realized that she wasn't any more sensitive, or any frailer, than Naomi or Sarah, and she had made up her mind to keep up with them. She felt she'd be damned, *damned,* if they thought she couldn't handle the extra laundry, or haul bean kettles, scrub pots, knead endless mounds of dough, and stay up on her feet in constant action for ten, twelve hours at a time, just like they could, even though they had advantages.

"Cooking all day beside a person, every day, if you wish to get a fair measure of what that person is like, the work will give it to you, fully," Naomi said one day. She was right.

But Naomi had the advantage of being older and more experienced, and her body was used to the work, and she'd never left Maine for years of being (relatively speaking) coddled in Boston.

And Sarah was younger, and, although no one mentioned this out loud, she also had some extra, internal energy, the kind that comes privately, with its own source of power: ninety-nine percent of Sarah's thoughts were not on cooking, Jossey realized, but on Patrick.

It was better to be chopping wood and cleaning and soaking small hills of beans, than to sit around like her former Salem lady self, wondering, "Where is he? What's going on with those cannons?"

"She could be my sister-in-law one day," Jossey told herself, and vowed to make this as easy on Sarah as she could. She really would. But she felt very strongly that, if Sarah for one second made the very large mistake of saying something like, "I am your sister, Jossey," she, Jossey, would spit. And never speak to her again. "I have a sister, and her name is Lavinia, in case you had forgotten," she would answer, bluntly.

She told herself to look the other way and pay no mind to the fact that Little John, her son, her own son, hardly minded her, hardly looked at her, if Sarah Dudley was around. So did Vinny— they were all used to calling her Vinny by now; they had dropped the "Pris" completely. Vinny acted as if Sarah Dudley had become, for her, the very model of the woman she'd grow up to be, instead of herself, Jossey, her own *mother*.

Maybe that was fair. It wasn't as if Little John were walking around saying how much he wanted to grow up to be just like his father. All he wanted to be was Patrick.

So if Vinny was a second Sarah, and Little John was a second Patrick, what did that leave Jossey? Was it strange, was it selfish, was it abnormal to want to try to make a little bit of effort to have something of yourself become replaced?

Who was going to be like her? It had never happened to Jossey before that she wished for someone to be like her.

The infant being suckled down at Winnegance was no doubt being imbibed every second with Naomi's clam-family ways, with the continuous smell going into his nose of mud and salt; maybe the milk of the woman who fed him was briney and tasted like clam juice.

That would not be the sort of thing a baby was likely to outgrow. He might even grow up to look like one of Naomi's sons— which would not be a bad thing—and, anyway, little Mowlan from the second he was born resembled John, not her; it was just like looking at a miniature, doughy, not-yet-baked version of his father. Jossey was putting dough in a pan as she thought this.

And the baby showed signs from the start of having the temperament of his father: he was quiet, he was often very solemn, as if the squint in his eyes and the furrowing of his brow were practice for later on, as if he already knew what it was like to be a thinker, and to always be willing to turn his eyes inward, to where a soul is. That was what John, her husband, was.

Her husband! It all of a sudden came to Jossey to remember she had a husband!

If Sarah thought she was the only one around with special inner energy, she was wrong—not that she was finding fault with Sarah. But Jossey felt a deep inner sympathy for her. If she, Jossey, wanted to see her man, all she had to do was take her hands out of the bread, wipe them, and say, "I shall be back in just several small minutes," and take off her apron and go out to the back room that John was calling his office.

And there he would be; there he was.

She went in quietly; her hands still felt a little sticky and she wiped them again on the sides of her skirt. She closed the door behind her. The candles on the table he used as a desk flickered lightly in the draft, but did not go out.

He turned and looked up at her, blinking with surprise, and she didn't give him a chance to ask her what she was thinking.

"I want to have another child, John," she said.

He'd been studying a drawing Tobe Firth had given him. There were dozens of them, of every aspect of a foundry, and this one, to Avens's eyes, looked just like a tower drawn by a clever child, as if drawn from a fantasy, or a dream. His brain had been having some difficulty with actual, technical details, but he'd been sitting there all morning, trying very hard to memorize the order of the layers of the outer and inner chimney, and the materials it would take to construct them, so that, the next time Tobe talked to him, he would at least have some small idea what he was saying.

"What is it you are saying, Jossey?"

"I want to have a child," said Jossey. It was taking him what felt like a long time to understand what she was telling him, and she was just about to say, "Like the Night of the Tea, John," when he got it.

"What, Jossey," he said. "Now? In daylight? You mean, *here?*"

CHAPTER XVIII

WAR

THEN SUDDENLY, with four words from a messenger, it started. "We are at war." Everyone knew that the things that lay ahead were going to be worse—much, much worse—than any one of them, in the worst of their visions, had imagined, or prepared for.

"We are at war."

It was the difference between preparing for a storm, while half-expecting that it will die as a squall out at sea, and never hit you, or it would hit only slightly. And then it hits, and it's a hurricane and blizzard combined, making a mockery of your designs to be ready for it.

It became known to General Thomas Gage, commander of Massachusetts, that under his nose, ammunition consisting of shot, powder, and gun balls, was being smuggled to storehouses in Concord. A population under military occupation was not supposed to be able to confound its occupiers in quite the way Boston was doing. It was decided that enough was enough.

By early April the number of soldiers in and near Boston, under General Gage, numbered nearly 5,000. At 10:00 on the night of April 18, 1775, with a two- days-past-full moon on the rise, 800 of them, in two battalions, left Boston for a night march to Lexington, seventeen miles away, and then Concord just beyond it.

The first 400 met up with a militia in Lexington that numbered fewer than forty. In less than half an hour those forty were dispersed: it was believed ten of them were killed. By the time the British reached Concord, militia men had gathered—in the town and on the route—from twenty Massachusetts towns. The number of slain British climbed past one hundred.

They had not expected to meet any sort of resistance at all. If, on the morning of April 19, Gage had not sent reinforcements, under the command of an English officer named Percy, things would have gone very, very differently. But the reinforcements had arrived.

A letter had arrived in Tibbetston.

John read the letter out loud to everyone who'd come down to the village and were crowded into the big main room of the Wabanakis' house, where nearly everything that had belonged to Jacques and Naomi was gone; it was fully now the home of the Avenses. The shiftings and transfers of their daily lives were no longer things to remark on, or feel strange about.

Jacques was there, and Naomi and their sons, and Sarah, and two men from the militia, and Tobe Firth, and Jacques's nervous teenage helper James, who was doing an all-right job managing the work of the smithy, not that there was much by way of normal smithy jobs, as everything was revolving around the foundry.

The children were asleep—John had waited for that—and Jossey was beside him. The letter had been delivered by an exhausted man from Cambridge named Roland Lawler, who until the occupation had been a well-off clerk in a Boston waterfront warehouse. Forced out of his job, as he had refused to work for the English, he had become a Son of Liberty, and in fact, had taken charge of the secret provisions coming into Boston from all the colonies. He'd ridden hard, with only a few stops to rest and change horses, and tell people he met what had happened.

This man had only stopped in Tibbetston because the pastor of his church had asked him to. His pastor, and the writer of the letter, was John's friend Jonas Emerson. Otherwise it might have been weeks before they knew.

"We are at war. Your friend Reverend Emerson is most anxious, and most fearful, and most cast into gloom and dread, as are the rest of us. He bade me tell you, though he wrote to you before he would wish for his family to come to you for safety, in this dangerous, wretched time, his wife and children said a resounding nay to that, and would not quit his side, not with him having been wounded," the messenger told John.

"Wounded! In what way?"

"Mr. Emerson was set upon with the blunt end of a British gun, which he took in the shoulder, and had the joint of it somewhat crushed, but it would not be the arm he writes with, and we are thankful it was no worse, as what happened to many others."

"How came my friend to be at Lexington?"

"He was not. He was not out of Cambridge. The British on the retreat back to Boston caused hellish damage to houses along the way, and to people at large in the street, as what he would tell you in the letter." Roland Lawler warmed himself in the smithy, ate some food and took more for the rest of the way, and was off again.

The letter was several pages long, with cross-outs and under-lining. It looked like the text of a sermon. John wondered if had been actually delivered from the pulpit. He hoped so.

"The Lexington men were said to be the finest, and best-trained," said Jacques. He was saying what was on everyone's mind.

The pages shook in John's hands, as if wind had started blowing inside, but there wasn't any wind. The moon wasn't up yet. The night was lightly foggy, and completely still. John realized the intensity with which, all along, privately, he had fixed his mind on what had come to seem to him a fact: he had believed there would not be a war.

"My dear John, I shall lay aside my emotions to describe as plainly as I am able, the events that took place on this hideous, baleful night in Massachusetts," he read. "I cannot furnish as many particulars as you would want, at this time, as no more than what I have stated is known to me. But I must make known to you what I had witnessed."

It was not the same voice John had used the day of the funerals when he'd recited the new declaration of rights, from the first-ever meeting of the Congress, in place of prayers.

It wasn't just a matter of being stirred, or uplifted. He had stood in the field that day and, as he spoke, he believed that what he'd said contained something of hope. It was not idle rhetoric; the ringing sound those words gave off had not been hollow or artificial, but as deep and real as good, big bells.

Hadn't there been a glimmer of consolation that day, like hope itself, pure and clarified, rising up in spite of themselves at the edge of their sorrow, like a sliver of light at the edge of the sky, when they'd thought that the clouds were too thick, too black, to let anything through? There must have been some hope, some consolation, or at least a little relief that day, he now felt. Yes.

Or so he thought now because he realized that, on the day of the funerals, the thing they could go home and look forward to was a *future*.

And now it was here. John pictured his old friend: a just-minded, honorable, gentle, good-humored man with pale brown eyes and a high, broad forehead, who would never put on an English wig, in spite of the fashion for men of his rank, and who never mentioned hell or damnation in a sermon, preferring a rational God, of even-handedness and calmness. If there was ever a man who could be counted on to be a pillar of steadfastness in a tempest, it was Jonas Emerson.

The letter was clear, without the slightest rhetorical flourish. The quiet, somber sentences had the gravity and power of a drum being steadily, quietly pounded.

"We are at war," repeated John.

Then he continued to read. "The Concord stores of gunpowder and weaponry which the English were in pursuit of were hidden in cornfields and woodlands before the English fired a gun at Lexington, there having been alarms put out well before, by courageous riders who galloped from Boston with the news.

"One of those riders was a man named Dawes and the other was Mr. Paul Revere, who arrived at Lexington, but was taken captive before succeeding the eight miles to Concord. I have learned he was able to escape captivity, and bless God for that, as he is a man of rare character, and embodies in his person not the soldierly value of an officer (or a gentleman), but the reckless, rapscallion nature of a rogue, who loves his country and his own career with equal passion, and is thus heroic.

"There are parishioners of mine who having learned of his capture, but not yet his escape, vowed to take hold of the silver bowl of our baptism font, and bury it, for they would want to not set eyes on it, should fatal harm come to that man. The bowl was made by his hands.

"Yet I digress, for I full dread the telling of what comes, and would wish to postpone it, as a portion of my mind would nag at me with the persistence of a child, wishing to see myself having slept, and having only known what took place in a dream. Were it so. My own wound, which good Mr. Lawler must have described to you, is as no account, in comparison to what others have suffered.

"Our losses loom greatly. I fear there are many parishioners who are stunned into radical thought upon perceiving that their minister was struck by an English soldier, when they would, in their innocence, have considered a minister taboo from acts of war.

"The march to our beautiful Lexington, and then, following it, Concord, yielded no tangible gain for the English except this: the unspeakable gain of corpses, on both sides, and wounds that may never be healed in the bodies of men, some of them so young, the hairs have not grown on their cheeks. The very name of the place, Concord, with its implicit meaning of peacefulness, resounds in my mind with grievous hurt.

"I know not how many fell at Concord, or all together on this day. Militias of our colonials raced breakneck from all towns north, south, east, and as far to the west as Worcester.

"Our colonials once learning of the massacre on Lexington Green—and I have chosen the word with deliberation, massacre, for that was as it was—were roused most strenuously in body and soul, and stood valiantly at Concord, with resolution. In keeping with the strictures of their honor and resolve, they would not fire until fired upon.

"When firing had started, the American men showed their intelligence, cunning, and mettle. Many British fell, to the stupefaction of the officers, who had not had the inkling of the state of armed resistance they would meet, until they met it.

"The plan of General Gage had been to intimidate, subdue, and secure the towns surrounding Boston and I assure you, the plan had made no provision for a virtual army of opposition. And one must bear in mind the condition of the British who had marched near twenty miles all night without rest, and had been forced to fight all day, against a force that had proved stronger.

"Many an American militia man saw fit to act with stealth, and to shoot with fixated aggression while concealing himself behind a tree or bush, or whatever would offer hiding, in the manner of Indians.

"It had seemed to the British the very shadows were shooting at them, and they knew not how to manage, and were thwarted out of their wits, being accustomed to ranks, in the open. They had no feel for the countryside. The rage and exhaustion of their troops, together with their dying and injured, and the totality of the grim events of the Concord resistance, put the British at a sore disadvantage.

"Yet the British who should have been defeated at Concord were not. Reinforcements had arrived, supervised by a British lord by the name of Percy Hugh, Lord Percy: a man who had come to America to establish a military renown for himself, whilst waiting to inherit baronial lands in England.

"Until this April week the man Percy had no cause to write to home in boasting of his success in America, for of accomplishment, there had been none. He and his troops which numbered in the hundreds mustered readily and came through Cambridge, and with them they brought a cannon, which they set up on Lexington Green in the very place of the massacre of hours earlier.

"Thus the retreating English on their return from Concord were spurred in Lexington from fatigue and defeat by sight of a cannon, and all those men, and Percy, prepared to wield the fullness of might. It had enraged the man to have learned of the numbers of dead and wounded English. It became his personal mission to cause as much damage as possible. Had the man Percy not arrived in Lexington, I believe the British would have surrendered.

"My dear John, I speak of the hours of only two days. Two days that shall forever have changed us all, for no matter the type of person any of us is, whether peaceable or pugnacious, we cannot turn away from the knowledge that the war we must wage is a war of necessity. It has come.

"I must tell you now my part in this. This is a thing which shall torment me all the days of my life, and I speak not of my wound. It was I who had pointed the way to Lexington to Hugh, Lord Percy.

"'What way to Lexington?' he had asked of me. I knew not of

what took place. I knew not who the man was. That he was English was plain to me: an officer in full uniform, a common sight. When he spoke to me he was alone. Had I turned the corner I would have realized the troops, silent in the Cambridge road. It was after I had pointed the way that they marched by, with four horses pulling the wagon which carried the cannon. In asking me for the way, Hugh, Lord Percy, had been civil and most mannered and, having noted my calling, had addressed me as Reverend Sir.

"I had been called to the sickbed of a man in my parish who was dying of stomach disease at a young age, only forty-one, with a wife and three small ones who were sorely in distress. It was not the man I had come to be in aid of. He was accepting and peaceful of his state, having become so feeble and pain-wracked, death for him was a boon. For some eleven hours I was within the house. As you know yourself, a house of death is a house closed off to all outside its doors.

"Upon quitting the house of my parishioner, with the lament of his wife resounding in my ears, and with the sight fixed into my mind of their children's expressions, once they had it lodged into their brains their father, who lay before them, would stir no more, I scarcely knew the time of day, nor where I was, nor which path my feet must embark on to fetch me to home.

"There came alongside me a French fellow I had met only briefly days before, a man whom you would know not, as he had only last week arrived at Harvard as tutor.

"He greeted me in French. Though we had conversed in his language when we had met I could not for the life of me summon memory of even one word. This man's command of English being scanty, we had no means of address. Would only it have happened that Hugh, Lord Percy, encountered this fellow in place of myself. There was no other person about.

"As I write this—and I must soon draw to a close, as the pain in my shoulder requires attention—I am wracked with the wonder of an English officer setting out through our Cambridge with several hundreds of men, and horses and that wagonned cannon, to serve as reinforcements to a near-defeated army to the north (bearing in mind, which fact I knew not). And the man *had no map*.

"The man knew not Lexington and Concord from the way to

the moon. Had I pointed just several degrees differently, Hugh, Lord Percy, would have embarked on a course that would have brought him to Newton in the west, where he would have met up with the combined militias of four or five towns. I would take it for granted the English officer would not have supposed a man of God would have lied to him concerning the correct route. I could have sent them all in circles which would have ended with putting them at the bank of the Charles.

"Yet I pointed the way to Lexington, bade my French acquaintance good day, and turning the corner, encountered Percy's troops. My dazed mind could not comprehend the enormity of this. It was then that my wife with our two elder boys came upon me, having come looking for me, and having learned at home of, first, the massacre in Lexington, then the battles of Concord.

"I was brought to home to rest, but rest did not come. Everywhere people were frenzied, fearing great harm.

"The hours that passed this way were most difficult and at length, while my wife remained at home with our little ones, my two elder boys, who would not be kept out of public life, came with me to Harvard Yard to observe the re-entry into Cambridge of the English, bearing on their persons the terrible memories of Lexington and Concord. And bearing also the inconvenience of the incessant attacks along the near-twenty-mile return march, from the militia men who had followed them.

"Yet our militia men were sadly outnumbered. Leading all of the troops was Hugh, Lord Percy. The cannon he had brought was not fired. There had been no need of firing. Its very presence was sufficient.

"Percy had given to his men the dishonorable, cowardly permission to pillage, loot, and set fire to any residence along the way they felt inclined to.

"Many of the English soldiers, forgetting their exhaustion, empty stomachs, and parched throats, had arms filled with what they had robbed; one young man had a chicken tucked into the chest of his coat, with its head protruding out between buttons. Another had an armful of silk ladies' dresses. Another had a man's coat made of beaver pelts, which he had put on, on top of his own, and which I recognized as belonging to the French man I had not been able to speak with.

"As for the French man himself, he had been stripped of it, and of whatever belongings were on his person. I saw him once more, just minutes after having been wounded. Strangely, I was then of the wits to converse with him, and said to him in French, absurdly, as though this were the worst event to have befallen any one of us, 'I am sorry your handsome coat was stolen from you.'

"I know not the exact count of how many Cambridge residents were killed in their own homes by these savage, unconscionable men. I have news two small children were put to death, and one old man of eighty who had barred the way at his gate, and was driven through with a sword.

"Even now the smoke of the fires has not left the air of our beloved Cambridge.

"My sons were uninjured. I had received my wound with no opportunity to observe from whence it came. The crowd was thick, the mayhem and chaos was as a nightmare. I had turned my back to the street, having noticed, in a house nearby, that a British soldier was shattering the windows.

"My sons were in front of me (I had had them behind me as I had faced the road). Calling out to the officer to stop his heinous activity—for he was breaking the windows because the citizens of the house had barred the door, and his plan, I had seen, was to fire into the house through the openings—I was struck by another soldier from behind, with a blow such as one would employ with an axe for the splitting of wood.

"At the time I fell forward, stumbling into the arms of my sons, the soldier who had broken the glass had fired his gun into the house.

"I heard a man's scream of agony from within, and it had seemed to me it must have issued from myself. My sons had the compulsion to set me down beneath a tree and seize weapons and join in with the militia, but I prevailed upon them to see me to home.

"I shall say no more, being anxious to put this letter into the hands of the good man I have prevailed upon to stop with you on his way to Augusta.

"Throughout this ordeal I had found myself more than once with the thought weighing much on my mind of what was done to your sister-in-law and her family and, I must confess, as much as that knowledge grieved me, my friend, it was as if the province of Maine were a world apart from us here. I had grieved remotely, for you and your wife especially, having had no close experience until now in acts of war.

"What my eyes have seen, what my ears have heard, what my soul was made to tremble from, have lodged with me deeply. I am told I am not to venture from home until which time my wound has had some healing.

"However, my friend, as soon as I am able, I shall present myself to serve with the army as chaplain, or, should they find it unnecessary to have one, then as soldier.

"I thank God my sons are of an age too young to accompany me.

"My family would wish to stay in Cambridge. I bow to their desire. I shall close with my word to you, my friend, I am sorely unhappy to not have you here beside me at this moment, for perhaps between the two of us, we might have found the means to bow our heads together in prayer, as though we remembered how to do so, and why."

John had reached the end of the letter. The fire in the hearth was nearly out, but no one seemed to notice. The silence that deepened in the room was the silence of people who know that there is nothing to be said.

Jossey took hold of her husband's hand. Inside herself she was talking to her sister. "Lavinia! Do *not* let my husband join any army! Should he think of it, crush the thought in his brain at once! He is staying right here! Lavinia! If you let him go to war I shall never speak to you again!"

Jacques broke the stillness after what felt like a long time. "We are at war," he said.

CHAPTER XIX

PATRIOT

T HE CONGRESS, in Philadelphia, appointed George Washington commander in chief of the Continental Army. What was
needed most of all were men to enlist. Winnie put up a recruitment poster in the tavern, and the very afternoon she did, Iron
Man Tobe Firth came down from Tibbetston to see her on foundry business.

There were not many customers in the tavern, but everyone
looked twice at him, and would have shifted out of his way, suspi-
ciously, if it had not been obvious he was Winnie's old friend.

He was not especially large or tall. He was shorter by several
inches than Jacques Wabanaki, and had the same stocky bow-turned
legs as Jacques. When he stood beside little Winnie, she didn't
look so little.

He was rougher than Jacques but equally strong, perhaps more
so. His eyes were small and set in deeply, with a pale gray color, and
seemed always to be in the state of alert; his thin hair was almost
the same gray, and was very sparse.

He told people he kept his hair nearly shorn on purpose, so that,
in the event he met up with hostile Indians, he could afford them
no reason to want to scalp him; but in truth he was aging, and
going bald, and refused on principle to wear a wig. He was thick-
necked, big-handed, quick-tempered: he was the type of man in
appearance who gives any stranger pause, with the feeling you
would not want to find yourself distressing him, or rubbing at him
the wrong way, even innocently.

Mr. Firth took one look at the new army recruitment sign, then tore it down and threw it into the fire. He sat down with Winnie at her table, and made a new one himself, to replace it.

PATRIOTS! DEFENDERS OF AMERICA! FIGHT ENGLISH & NEVER LEAVE MAINE! MOST EXCELLENT ENDEAVOR! ABLE BODIED MAINE MEN WANTED FOR FORGE WORK IN NEW CANNON & GUN BALL FOUNDRY, LOCATED ON KENNEBEC SHORE. MEALS AND LODGING PROVIDED. MUST BE OF SOUND HEALTH. APPRENTICES WELCOME ABOVE AGE TWELVE. INQUIRE FOR PARTICULARS OF MRS. WINIFRED GOODRIDGE.

At the bottom of the notice, Mr. Firth made a sketch of what he said was a cannon, with, beside it, a wooden shot gauge, which was a slab of board with different-sized holes, for sorting balls; and he also drew a dozen balls for a four-pounder, and another dozen for a six.

It was not difficult to make out the meaning of the gun balls, but his cannon looked like a puny little slightly bloated spyglass, and his gauge was out of proportion, and looked like the hateful arm-hold of a Puritan stock, as if he'd copied it from an old New England town green.

"It would seem some poor wretch's arms had just been secured with chains in those holes of yours," said Winnie. She was careful to conceal the fondness she had for him, and teased him instead.

"Had I thought you make iron with the level of skill you would draw, I should have to raise an advertisement to find myself a new manager."

She took his poster—he had used the long parchment she wrote accounts and inventories on—and folded it so that only the words would show. Then he nailed it to the wall. None of Winnie's customers would ever heed it, thinking it was a joke, even when Winnie said it was real. Who had heard of raw iron in Maine?

Winnie poured him some cider and put a plate of good Maine crabmeat, already picked by the maid, in front of him, with a bowl of potatoes and a plate of corn cakes, and they got down to business, talking while Tobe ate and she whittled. She was making a stick doll for Mr. Firth to bring back to Vinny-Pris, which Mr. Firth could have found fault with, for being more of a stick than a doll, but did not.

Winnie had already finished an oak model of a dory for Little

John. It looked like a hollow whale, without flippers and tail, not a boat, but Mr. Firth did not mention that. He was grateful to Winnie for not requiring him to pick his own crabs, which were singularly large that season; there had been no such thing in Pennsylvania. He had only just started learning what to do with a lobster. He liked Maine. Very much.

He had brought a pile of bills Winnie needed to pay, and a headful of reporting.

The kilns had leaked miserably but were better now, he reported. The stream on Gun Ball Hill was more trouble than anticipated, there being more by way of water than they had thought, but the surge of power might be blamed on the thaw, and could anyway be managed.

Fleep Wabanaki was up at Moosehead working out a deal with some Indians he knew to cart down ore.

The stone tower for the foundry furnace was halfway up, and would have been done by now, had it not been pouring with rain all last week.

But they were not going to have to build their own waterwheel, because one of the militia men had remembered an abandoned grist mill outside Grilleyville. They had lashed four wagons together, with someone else's borrowed oxen; and they had brought up the wheel (with a great deal of trouble) to Tibbetston.

There were sixteen men in total working on the Mowlan farm nearly all the hours of day and evening. They could use twenty men more, even thirty, and if truth be told, the militia men were becoming disenchanted with the notion that their labors—especially the work of building the chimney—were serving a second purpose, of making them fitter and more vigorous as soldiers. All they were getting was tired and pained.

But they were also getting fed, and so were their wives and children who needed it. Mr. Firth was generally not pessimistic about their chances for getting the operation running before long.

Jacques was building the forge himself, and he was particular about it. For the gun balls, they could ladle the hot liquid iron into molds directly from the furnace hearth, but for cannons they needed Jacques, who would insist that what he did was the highest, most exalted endeavor a human being could embark upon.

Smithing, in the eyes of Jacques, was simply of a higher order than anything else, including everything ever made by masterful painters, makers of statues, composers of music, and perhaps by God himself, who had built the world, and many people in it, with far less care and skill, it would seem, than Jacques carried out in his shop.

God, Jacques would say, was good at being God, but he should have had someone with the mind of a blacksmith to take care of creation.

Jacques had acquired a suitable hammer from a smith he knew near Falmouth. He had removed his picture of the Virgin from his smithy in town, and had it with him in his new shop, as if the mother of Christ was the patron saint of cannons.

He'd ordered bellows from Connecticut, and would not accept the same type as Mr. Firth's, from Pennsylvania, which would do for the furnace but not the forge. Jacques would have a smaller waterwheel, for driving his bellows. This wheel would be constructed, he had promised, within the month, which was doubtful.

Jacques held to having everything in the forge just so, and was indeed *most very* particular about it. If Jacques were Noah, Mr. Firth felt, the ark would have never gotten finished before the flood. He would still have been fussing with some part of it.

"He would sound as my husband. I believe you once said the very same things to me about Hobe," said Winnie, with a catch in her voice, like an almost-swallowed cough, which was always there when she mentioned Hobe Goodridge.

"You said once, as I recall, that Hobe in the part of Noah would have drowned, rather than sail on a boat that was anything less than perfect."

"I might have said so," he answered. "But there would not be much of a comparison. Hobe Goodridge was not Indian. And Jacques is. The Indian, I believe, constitutes more of him than what is French, blessedly."

"That would mean," said Winnie slowly, "Jacques would not hold a gun to himself because Englishmen in London had told him he could not craft iron."

"That may be true, but it was not the thought I had come to. I would mean instead, Jacques had compared himself to God. Your husband would have compared himself to the devil."

"My husband would not think the forge a hell."

"No. He had loved the forge," said Mr. Firth. "It was the world he had trouble with."

Winnie's fingers shook as she held her whittling knife, and she had to put it down. It was impossible for her to sit with Mr. Firth and not have the feeling that all those years she had had to live without Hobe were pressing down on her with a terrible weight: Mr. Firth had brought it all back.

She remembered everything of her old Plymouth life at Hobe and Tobe's foundry. When it had closed, everyone had said there would never be another one like it.

But there would.

She would spend every cent she had to make it so; if she had to sell the tavern, she would do it. Last night there was a customer, a worldly, friendly merchant from New York on his way to Augusta, who had traveled to somewhere in the Alps, and told Winnie a remarkable story about a man who went up a mountain to shoot some food, and was killed in an avalanche, at the age of twenty-nine, and for forty-some years, his body was thought to be lost forever.

One day he was found, frozen and intact, in an ice slab, and the body was carried down to his widow, who had never married again. She bent over him with her old woman's back, and beheld, with her aged eyes, the astonishing, young face of her husband. She begged the villagers to allow him one night in her hut before they buried him, and they let her.

When Winnie heard this, she had felt as if a kind of avalanche had hit her, too: but it was emotional. It was envy, of a powerful thrust. She felt that the woman in the Alps had been lucky. There had not been a tomb of ice in Plymouth to hold Hobe.

She picked up the knife and carried on, and used the blade to smooth some rough spots in the wood, as she did not trust herself with the point. Mr. Firth said quietly, "We shall never stop speaking of Hobe."

"Thank you. I am sure you find Jacques similar to him, then, in certain ways."

"That I would do. I shall have hope for his wheel to be done, as his Nantucket sons are helping with it, and would speed him along."

"And what of John Avens?" said Winnie.

Mr. Firth sighed. "He is managing," he acknowledged, "and he has asked most intricate questions on the workings of the furnace, and has sent to Cambridge for books on chemistry and all manner of studies on minerals."

"What of Patrick?"

"At sea."

"And the children, that I make these toys for?"

"They are busy bringing up buckets of sand for us. We call them buckets but they are bowls, and the two of them sleep well at night, being run off their feet with the effort."

"And Naomi, and Sarah, and Jossey?"

"Cooking," said Mr. Firth.

"And the babe sent out to be suckled?"

"Still sent out," said Mr. Firth. He wanted to take up the thread of his report that had to do with the furnace, and was next on his way to describing to Winnie the mixture of raw materials he had designed for the ore extraction, when a man, a stranger, came into the tavern, and headed straight for their table.

Winnie nearly jumped out of her chair. Down went the knife to the table. She held a hand to her chest and patted herself lightly, as if that would make her heart stop pounding so fast. She had been spooked; she had not seen the man until he was near her, and she had not heard him approach.

"Would I be having the pleasure of speaking to Mrs. Winifred Goodridge?"

"You would," said Mr. Firth, before Winnie could answer for herself. He seemed to think Winnie needed his protection and, collecting herself, she gave him a look that meant, "it would be a good idea were you not to do that again."

The man was Jackson Prout. He was covered with dust from head to toe, and could barely stand upright, but those were the least of his problems. He wore a three cornered hat, and removed it with a gracious, gallant gesture, which was all the more impressive considering the condition he was in.

"I am someone that has a friendship with a man that was born from these parts, that I believe you hold highly, by the name of Patrick Rouse. I am told you have pressing need of men, to work iron for you. That man I would be. Jackson Prout, I would be, come from Lexington."

The events of Lexington were not far from anyone's thoughts. Had Jackson Prout not so quickly established himself with that connection, he would have frightened Winnie more than he did, and Mr. Firth as well, and anyone else who saw him.

It seemed a ghoul, in the disguise of a badly wounded man, had appeared among them, with strange, unearthly pallor, and a face contorted with groaning, although no groans were issued.

His coat was torn and filthy, and it was hard to tell the blood-stains from the caked-on dirt; same with his breeches. There was a slash on the right-hand side of his coat that ran at a diagonal, like one-half of the letter X, from just under the shoulder to the opposite side; it stopped just under the place in the chest where a heart is.

Even to someone who had never seen what the blade of a sword could do, when lashed at a man—from the angle of someone striking while sitting on horseback—it would at once be apparent that Prout, at Lexington, had been so attacked. His face was so pale, the blood seemed to have left it completely.

"If you would please," said Prout, "my horse is near meeting his Maker, and I would enter myself in your debt if you would see he was stabled with warmth and care, and allowed to lie down and heal, in clean hay, with soothing words, and a rug laid onto his flesh."

Prout spoke as if the horse were more important to him than himself. Winnie called for her assistants, the Churches, and they scurried out to the horse as quickly as they could, more to flee the disturbance of Prout's appearance than to rush to be of aid to the animal.

"I am told," Prout said to Winnie, "you were in aid some months ago on New Year's Day to Negroes that were sorely in need of it. Some of those good people are known to me, two being cousins to my wife. You shall be glad to know all are safe, and by way of being settled most freely in Rhode Island."

He tried to smile at Winnie, as if thanking her. He held up his hand to his head as if he wanted to tip his hat to her, but the hat was in his other hand. He had forgotten that, and looked about wildly, as if the hat were just blown off his head by a wind.

"Sit down, man," said Mr. Firth, and took hold of Prout, who was listing and swaying on his feet. Winnie called for the maid to bring out a bottle of her good Spanish wine, and Prout said, as he sank into a chair at Winnie's table, "Not wine. Rum."

"Rum," called out Winnie.

"You were at Lexington Green?" said Mr. Firth.

"Aye. With the militia."

"We are told the losses were heinous."

"Aye. Two of my boys shot but not killed, and two men that had trained with me, killed."

"You are the man of the farm, who had ministered to Patrick Rouse?" said Winnie.

"Aye."

"You are friends, too, with John Avens and his wife?"

"Aye. I was often to their house in Boston."

"Then all of what I have is open to you."

The few customers in the tavern had suddenly found reason to need to leave, with expressions on their faces that meant, "Perhaps this fellow brings ill luck or worse, and I shall not give him chance to affect me."

But one man inquired of Winnie if she wanted him to fetch the physician; there was a man who called himself one, just a short way from the tavern, but he'd been drinking very heavily the night before—in fact, with the traveler who'd told the tale of the Alps. Winnie knew what condition he must be in, and felt she could better tend to Prout on her own.

As soon as he had quaffed down some rum, Prout tried to stand up again, saying, "Kindly tell me which direction I must go to reach this foundry I heard tell of, as I am unfit for battle, and must apply myself to other work. I am told John Avens is there, and his family, and I would do well to be among them. As I cannot blow the heads off English on my own, I shall satisfy myself with making the gun balls for others to do it."

"In good time, in good time, but first you must eat, and bathe, and rest," said Winnie. She reached for the rum bottle, not to replenish Prout's cup, but to gulp some herself.

It was one thing to learn about a battle of war from the description of others, and to shudder at it, and feel moved; but it was something altogether different to sit at a table with a man who had been there, when you knew the man might not have many days left to him, because of it.

"I fear I had left Lexington without paying mind to bringing with me any goods or belongings," said Prout. His voice was low, mumbled, like a man who is talking to himself. "I had but the one thought only, and fear I was partially separated from all my wits. It had seemed most expedient for me to quit my home at once. For four of these last nights, the horse and I slept in woodlands, having rode hard, and I am astonished we two are not perished already."

"I have a change of clothes with me, not used, which I shall give you the loan of," said Mr. Firth, and Winnie shook her head, and said there was no need for that. In two trunks in her bedroom, she had kept every wearable piece of clothing that had belonged to Hobe, and as she had checked it all, through the years, and aired it all out now and then, she knew that the wools were not worm-wrecked, and the muslins and weaves were as intact as the last time Hobe wore them, even though all those years had gone by.

She had been thinking of giving the clothes to Mr. Firth, as strange as it would have been to see him wear them, and she was not reluctant to have changed her mind. Mr. Firth was much smaller than Hobe had been, anyway, so it was just as well, she felt.

She called for the maid to prepare plates of bread and meats for her new guest, and found herself deciding that Prout should have his wish to go to Tibbetston, as soon as he was able to be put into a carriage. If he wanted to hold to the belief he was on his way to new employment, so be it. She would go along with him; the Churches could manage the tavern without her just fine. She would sit up front in the carriage alongside Mr. Firth.

She found herself wanting very badly to not be separated, at least for now, from Mr. Firth, and she told herself the only reason she felt this way, besides a sense of responsibility for her new guest, was this: she wanted to make sure her investment in the foundry, in Mr. Firth's care, was safe, and well, and flourishing.

It was not, she told herself, personal, as though there must be nothing of personal feeling in wartime. "I shall see you to Tibbetston myself, along with Mr. Firth, and rest assured you are well looked after," said Winnie, and she was careful not to meet the eyes of the Iron Man as she said so.

Edwin Church came to the doorway and motioned for Winnie. She went to him quietly. "The horse he came in on, is no more," he whispered, and Winnie answered to have it buried.

She put on a cheerful face when she returned to her table, telling Prout that the news of the horse was most excellent, in spite of its weakness and exhaustion, and had been brought to a stable on the other side of town. Could Prout go and see it? No, he could not, said Winnie, as the man whose stable it was, was most particular about intrusions. Could Prout return to get it back, then, once he'd settled into his foundry work? He most absolutely could, said Winnie.

It was three days later when they arrived with him at the farm. Jacques and Naomi moved out to the barn to accommodate him. John and Jossey and the children were there too, but it was Sarah who nursed him mostly, and who never left his side.

When he died, on the fourth day after he'd arrived, no one could do with the children, especially with Little John, what Winnie had done about the horse, as much as everyone wanted to.

Jossey commanded John to speak to their children of death in a general way; she herself had no words. "Death," John said to them, "comes when God says so, and there is nothing we may do but accept that God has a reason."

His little daughter raised no objections to that, but she had not known Prout well. He was first a friend of her parents in long-ago, faraway Boston, and then he was a stranger on a sickbed, who was weak with fever and could no longer speak, and was dominating Sarah's time and attention, which Vinny missed.

She was a practical girl, and at this, her first witnessed death, she was simply relieved.

Having thought about Death very strenuously, she had finally made up her mind that Death was like a large dark shadowy thing, just about completely invisible, which, as a principle of its nature, only went twice to the same group of people, to kill someone.

Vinny counted in "the same group of people" everyone she knew, especially everyone she knew in Maine, her home, right now. After the second time Death took someone, it had to go somewhere else, to someone else's group, like a bear that ate all of the berries in one large part of the woods, and must leave for a different part.

First went her cousins and uncle and aunt, she reasoned. Then this man who everyone was crying about.

Where should the man from Lexington be buried?

Jossey had strong feelings about that. "Not with my sister!" cried Jossey, bluntly. "He was our friend, and I was fond of him, and I *know* he has no family, and I *know* he was a patriot at Lexington, and that is *noble,* but we shall *not* turn that burial ground into a *general cemetery.*"

As she listened to her father and all those grownups surrounding her, the little girl felt a weight lifted off her shoulders. Twice!

Death had been here twice already. It was gone. She was safe. Everyone was safe. All the berries in this part of the woods had been eaten. No more death, she decided.

But her brother had other things on his mind, and insisted on speaking to his father alone.

"Papa, I want to go to Lexington again. I shall remember the way myself if no one brings me. I want to go back to Mr. Prout's farm. I want to be trained. I want to go to the war."

"What shall Uncle Patrick feel, when he comes back here, and shall be looking for you?"

"You must tell him where I am, and he may come and find me there."

"Your mother would be most unhappy to be without you, fearing for you, as one does for all soldiers, especially very young ones," said John. "So Mama would have to go with you, and you would have to bring Vinny as well, and then I shall have to go also, or I would become too lonely, and we should have to bring your brother, for he is only a babe, and we could not leave him behind."

Little John thought about that. He was working out the details in his head, and reached a snag. "Mama said she has no milk inside her. That is why he is away, to where milk is, and cannot come back until his teeth grow."

"I know that. There is no milk in war. A baby must be nourished."

"How long would teeth be in growing?"

"Oh," said John, gravely. "Years."

"Then we shall bring along a lady with milk."

"She would not choose to come. She would not be part of our family. But I believe we should consider what you suggest. If it would be all right with you that your brother dies, as shall happen, as Mr. Prout died, and your aunt, your uncle, and your cousins, then I promise to agree we shall all leave at once for Massachusetts. I would begin to start packing our belongings right now."

"If my brother dies, Mama shall talk to him, as she talks to Aunt Lavinia."

"Mama does not talk with Aunt Lavinia, John."

"She does!"

"But Aunt Lavinia does not answer her."

Little John knew his father was right about that, but pressed on with one last try. "Perhaps my brother when he is dead will answer her."

"But how would that become a possibility, when your brother is only a babe, and does not know how to talk?"

"How long does it take to start talking?"

"First you have to have teeth."

"Oh."

After a long moment of careful thought, not particularly about his brother, who he had never felt very attached to, and whose face he barely remembered, Little John shrugged his shoulders. "Perhaps we shall have to stay here," he said, "as Mama was sad enough already, to last for forever."

"I admire your reasoning," said John.

"Thank you, Papa. Are you going to bury Mr. Prout below the foundry?"

"We are, as the ground is broken already, and that is where he was headed."

"Why did Mama say he must not have a grave with my cousins and uncle and aunt?"

"Mama is very protective."

"What is the difference between a burial ground and a cemetery, Papa?"

"A burial ground is only for family."

"Can dead people come out of the ground?"

"No. Had you wondered if they would?"

"Sometimes," acknowledged Little John.

"But they cannot get out of their coffins."

"That is what I had supposed. When Mr. Prout is under the foundry, shall the furnace burn his coffin?"

"Fire cannot enter the earth that deeply."

"But what about hell?"

"Hell is not in this world."

"How do you know that, Papa?"

"Because," said John, "I went to Harvard College, and that was one of the things I had studied."

"But I shall go to sea."

"I know," said John. "You would not take well to studies. You would not care to wonder on things such as hell."

"That is correct, Papa. Did Mr. Prout go to heaven?"

"Yes. He was a patriot, and a good, brave man."

"Shall the man who struck him at Lexington go to hell?"

"We shall hope so," said John.

"Good," said Little John, and breathed a huge sigh of relief. Everything was all right. Sad, but all right.

And now this! Just a few days after they had buried Jackson Prout, on a fine, clear day in early June, Fleep Wabanaki came back to Tibbetston with six heavy, dirty wagons of iron ore, eleven Indians who were aiding him (who stayed for dinner! Indians!), and deer skin for making vests, furs for extra bedding, and food they had hunted: a brace of ducks, a dozen quail, four turkeys, six hares, and the meat of two pigs they'd encountered on the way, which had escaped from someone's farm.

The Indians were not wearing feathers and paint, which was something of a disappointment, but the disappointment was more than compensated for.

Fleep brought the news of something wonderful, from hundreds of miles away (but still in Maine). Far up the coast, and to the east, at a place called Machias, the militia had gone to battle with the English, and they had boarded an enemy ship, and *captured it.*

There was a battle! The name of the ship was the HMS *Margaretta,* and the Americans had *won.*

Up at Machias, the English ship was meant to be protection for an American Tory who was brokering lumber, firewood, and food to be sent down to Boston, not for colonists, but for English troops. This man had slipped away from the militia but that didn't matter.

The Americans gathered up whatever ammunition they could find, and sailed out to engage with the astonished British, who stood wonderingly on deck and watched them approach, saying to themselves, at first, "We are the finest naval power in the world, and no one who fires on us shall defeat us." Then, "Oh no, since when have these clumsy, inept Americans got themselves a navy?"

Little John was not sorry to learn that the English captain of the enemy ship was killed, and he scarcely paid attention to the talk of the grownups, which was grim and full of worry, instead of jubilance. The two other English ships that had been at Machias with the *Margaretta* had escaped, and were sailing down the coast. How many warships were now along the coastline? Two dozen? Perhaps thirty, they estimated, perhaps more. How many English troops were in New England? Twenty thousand, perhaps thirty, perhaps more.

What shall the English do by way of retribution? Where shall they strike as punishment? That was all his father and the Wabanakis and all the rest of them were talking about.

Not Little John. Until now, he had not given a name to the round little rowing boat that Winnie had made him, which could not be put into the river, but did fine in the pond behind the Wabanakis' house. Every afternoon when he had finished his chores for the foundry, he ran down the hill to the pond.

He had gotten his mother to give him some cloth for a sail, and he had put it on the boat himself, with a stick for a mast; he'd gotten Jacques to put a hole in the boat to secure it. He had learned from Fleep that there were four guns on the enemy ship—a sloop—so he decked his boat with acorns, to represent the cannons, and called it *Margaretta.*

And he fired at it and captured it, fired at it and captured it, over and over. He put a twig near the bow to stand for the enemy leader. He was careful not to call him a "captain," as that was a sacred word, to be used in reference only to Americans. Sometimes he hit the enemy leader with pebbles. Sometimes he knocked him over the side and let him drown.

The militia in Machias had soared to greatness, he felt, because they had left dry land. Everything great that could happen could only happen at sea.

He was glad he did not have to join up with the war in Lexington. He had got it in his head, when Prout died, that it must be his own duty to go back there and replace him, as if that were a rule of the war.

When someone dies in it, you have to have the person replaced, he had felt. He had felt sure that volunteering to join was the right thing to do and, for the first time in his life, he was happy to realize he may have been wrong about something he had given careful thought to. Perhaps they would not have accepted him. Perhaps you had to be eleven, or even twelve, for the militia.

By then, he'd be tall enough to go onto the sloop—the *York Sawyer.* He said the words over and over to himself, Uncle Patrick, York Sawyer, Uncle Patrick, York Sawyer.

If things went his way, he would not have to be stuck as just a plain old foot soldier with any boring, dirty, land-based, landlocked army, that marched and marched and had to sleep on the ground, which would be terrible. It was just like chess, which his father had just started to teach him.

Soldiers were *pawns.* If you went to sea, it was the same as a knight, or even a bishop, and if you captained your own boat, that was *king.* And if you went to Harvard like your father and studied, he felt, that was not even in the game. That was just a man playing chess, not a figure.

"King" was what Little John planned for himself. He would wait if he had to. He would try to be patient about how long it was taking him to grow up. He just wanted to be out at sea, in the wind, with his uncle. It was all he thought about. "I shall shoot real cannons. I shall put up real sails. I shall kill real enemy leaders. Soon."

CHAPTER XX

CHARLESTOWN

IT BECAME KNOWN to militias in and around Boston that the British, having amassed a fleet of warships in the harbor of Charlestown, next to Boston, would storm the town very soon and call it theirs. First they would take Charlestown, it was planned, and next, they would occupy Dorchester Heights on the other side, to the south, and thus establish Boston as locked-in as a prisoner in a cell.

What had not been successful with the closing of Boston Port, it was felt, would come to fruition by military strategies and sheer force. They felt smug about their chances to quickly subdue opposition.

The provisions being smuggled into Boston and its surrounding towns were nowhere near enough to sustain people: people were taking down fences to use as firewood; clothes were getting ragged; there was a terrible shortage of food. At first, the deprivations were felt most keenly in terms of annoyance. It had been a long time since people in Massachusetts knew what it was like to not have an abundance of everything they wanted. By the summer of 1775, the annoyance became something very different. People were hungry.

And there was no central leadership as of yet in New England: instead, the various militia groups, from the English point of view, were much like gangs of ill-tempered chickens, without the controlling dominance of a rooster.

"Finish up in Boston by taking the hills of Charlestown and

Dorchester, then the rebels shall be as our chickens, caught in our hands for the pot," was their idea.

It was only June, but already, the year 1775 was slipping away without a single significant show of English might, after Lexington and Concord. English forces in New England were most anxious to set things in motion to get out of New England before another winter was at hand.

They were in a hurry to transfer themselves to the warm southern colonies—not just to take occupation of the South, and sever the newly-made unity of colonies distanced so greatly from each other—but to secure the financial situation of the tobacco plantations, for themselves. American tobacco, exported to Europe, was like a fountain of money; the English plan was to move as many troops as possible to seize that fountain, and own it.

It was with a sense of predetermined victory that the English sent more than 1,000 soldiers to take Charlestown on foot, with the warships prepared to back them up with bombardment.

There was nothing by way of defenses in Charlestown to meet any sort of attack: the two prominent hills, Breed and Bunker, stood vulnerable and passive in the early summer light.

On the afternoon of June 15, aware that there would soon be British action, Patrick left the *York Sawyer* in a cove near Nahant, well hidden from English knowledge.

Staying with the sloop were the two older crew men, Enoch Lister and George Huggins. Patrick took the younger men, Asa Patch and the new boy who was no longer new, Otis Rawley, into Charlestown with him. They came on horseback and had English muskets and shot for the Charlestown militia, taken from a British ketch by the Hammerheads in Nahant. The guns were of the type called Brown Bess, which were heavy and awkward, and weighed, each one, nearly ten pounds. They were delivered to Asa Patch's uncle, at his house on a pleasant street in the Charlestown flats.

A letter had been waiting for Patrick in Nahant, but it put him in no good humor. In writing to him, Sarah had made the decision to not speak of Jackson Prout, not even that he had left Lexington for Maine.

Sarah described instead the situation of the foundry, and the placement and filling of the kilns, and the building of the chimney, and the arrival of Winnie, who had turned over the tavern to her assistants; and she alluded to the building of a cabin on the leeward side of Gun Ball Hill, for herself: a simple log house with a main room, a buttery, and one bedroom; she would share it, she said, "for the time present, with Mrs. Goodridge."

What did that mean, "the time present," Patrick wondered, but had no answer. He found the letter disturbingly frosty in tone, containing nothing but information. Even the information of a personal nature did not convey a spirit of the personal.

"There was a man sent from Salem," she wrote, "to my maid Sarah Pease, still stopping in Falmouth with her mother, who is not recovered from illness. The man is in the employ of my family and, as Sarah Pease pleaded ignorance for my whereabouts, except that she felt the conviction I had sailed for London, the man turned face and went south, quitting Maine altogether. Thus I would lay aside for the present the fear of my discovery. I confess in moments of agitation, having known of the history of Mr. Mowlan, whose footsteps I walk in daily, here on their farm, I have been badly aroused to fabulations that I, too, may be kidnapped, not by English but by Dudleys. Yet I am cheered by the children, for Little John and Vinny have appointed themselves my guardians, and have each of them assured me, should any person loom up to cause me harm, they will hold themselves stalwart with courage, and defend me. Having them close to me is regularly a joy, and I am able, in moments stolen from the many chores I am occupied with, to instruct them on their grammar and reading, and other lessons as well. Your sister Jossey is well, as are we all, as most we can be in these dubious times. Yours most truly, Sarah Dudley."

"What a miserable letter," was Patrick's reaction. It could have been written for a most casual, almost meaningless acquaintance.

Patrick felt tempted to answer it in a vigorous voice, protesting the lack of—of affection. Yes, affection. He was forced to admit to himself he had considered his place in Sarah's heart a large place indeed, if not occupying the whole of it. Affection, he had expected, and at least some hint of longing. She had not said she suffered from his absence, had not left room for the smallest hint of attachment to him.

But there was no time to write letters to Tibbetston. There was something stirring in Charlestown: something enormous.

Asa Patch's uncle, Mattias Patch, who before the occupation of Boston had been a clerk of the Massachusetts court, welcomed the *Sawyer* men with a small meal and plenty of Dutch tea, and what warmth of a fire he could muster, and also with a state of nervous, grim excitement.

He didn't know exactly what form the militia would take by way of a stand against the oncoming English offensive: but a stand was about to be taken.

The guns Patrick brought to Charlestown were concealed in Patch's root cellar, as there were British soldiers nearly always gathered near his house. The method by which the guns were smuggled in had been used before, by others, and it served Patrick well.

A pine coffin, not full-size, but a coffin for a large child, was carried on the back of a fine bay mare, whose reins Patrick held on to. Should a British sentry take worry and demand to be shown the inside of the coffin (they never did), they would have been overwhelmed (as soon as they neared it, before the lid came off) by the malodorous air.

Beneath the lid of the coffin was a regular wrapping sheet and under the sheet, and on top of the guns, was the putrefying body of a Nahant raccoon, whose skin had been removed. For good measure, a sign was attached to the coffin that said, like a notice for business, MR. HAMMER, COFFIN MAKER OF NAHANT, MOST EXPERT & RELIABLE. It was a Hammerhead joke; but Patrick had a most unpleasant ordeal with the smell of the rotting animal.

There was nothing to be done with the raccoon but bury it in Mattias Patch's cellar. The smell would linger on the guns afterward, but would be joined with much worse.

Patch's wife and children had fled Charlestown to the home of a cousin in New Hampshire.

But at the Patch home were young Asa's twenty-year-old cousin, Olivia Sunderson, who wrote poetry in what she called "pretty rhymes," for all manner of public and private occasions, and two of her friends. They were visiting from Hingham, a town to the south of Boston: singularly pretty, well-established, and placid, Hingham was a town of quiet, educated, careful-mannered people, who'd had no experience of strife beyond their own personal affairs.

Olivia Sunderson and her girlfriends considered themselves highly patriotic, and had traveled by carriage to see the places in Lexington and Concord that everyone was talking about. They stood wondrously in spots where they were told deaths had happened. Olivia had written a poem about it, enraptured, while riding in the carriage back home, and the newspaper in Hingham had printed it.

> O men of Lexington Green!
> Fall'n, the angels in heav'n you have seen.
> O men of Concord Brave!
> We make hallow'd the lives which you gave!
> You stood of courage strong,
> And the flood of your blood shall move on.
> Hark to the sacrifice noble!
> Hark to the sacrifice noble!

Olivia and her friends had come to Charlestown not just to pay a visit to Mattias. Olivia had learned from an old Irishwoman-fortuneteller near Hingham Green (Olivia was a mystic-minded girl, and was always consulting this fortuneteller) that there was going to be a terrible, magnificent confrontation on the Charlestown Peninsula, very soon.

This was only partly a soothsaying premonition; the warships by then were well in place, and the plans of the British well known in many circles.

Of course, having been given the prediction of what sounded like a battle, Olivia would be told of its outcome, for an extra few coins, and the stupid old woman had spoken with glee: "If you are there to witness the splendor, my dear girl, you shall see with your own eyes a marvelous enemy defeat, and you shall have a great story to be able to tell to your children, and theirs, and theirs as well."

So off went the Hingham young ladies to Charlestown with

their parasols and canvas valises and, for Olivia, the keen desire to gather ideas for a poem, this time from first-hand observation. It had seemed such a wonderful adventure, which grew more and more interesting, especially after Patrick and his two young men had arrived.

Three men, three ladies! What fate! One of the girls, upon meeting Asa Patch, felt immediately moved to consider him as a beau. The other stared at Patrick with doe-eyes (which Patrick failed to notice). Olivia was pleased to find in Otis Rawley a seriousness, intelligence, and sensitivity that seemed to be well matched, she felt, with her own.

How pleasant it was to be in the company of privateers, actual privateers! How adventurous to be so close to warships! And soldiers everywhere in the street! How thrilling the war was! How inspiring!

And Patrick Rouse! *Everyone* had heard of Patrick Rouse! The very man whose sister and all her family were *slaughtered*, by hateful English, in the *wild* frontier of Maine!

And he captained a boat that attacked British frigates! And he was handsome! And free of arrogance! And he had traveled to Canada to try for the rescue of his brother-in-law of Maine, who was famously taken captive, and who'd returned alive, but with a foot *cut off.*

And then, that brother-in-law was in the slaughtered family! Everyone knew all about the murdered Mowlans! Oh! To be close to such things!

Olivia Sunderson, less than one week after the day in her uncle's drawing room when she poured out Dutch tea in a fine pewter pot for the men of the *Sawyer,* and giggled with her friends, and considered herself on a splendid, romantic outing, would be back in Hingham in shock, and would hang herself from a beam in her mother's spinning room, leaving behind, without explanation, just these three lines:

My eyes that saw War,
Are not eyes,
Allowed to ever look more.

Olivia Sunderson was not listed in the meticulous records of those who died because of what happened in Charlestown. The lists are all of men.

Olivia Sunderson had stood by a window of her uncle's house, with Breed's Hill, and Bunker next to it, in plain sight. There were many, many people out watching those events of June 17, and many of them were forced through sheer horror to stop watching, but Olivia would not come away from the window when her friends begged her to.

In the first round of cannon fire from the harbor, a militia man named Harry Greenough, from Charlestown, thirty-two years old and a schoolteacher (the schools were closed down) was hit as he crouched with his musket at the top of Breed's Hill. He'd been prepared to fire the musket. After he was hit, he remained crouched in exactly the same position, but his head had been removed, and lay on the ground beside him, in full view. And that was only in the first few minutes of the fight.

The girl had watched that happen; she watched everything that came after it, unflinching, and had concluded on her own that she would not be part of a world in which such things took place.

She could not unlearn what she had learned.

Olivia Sunderson. Age twenty. Certainly, if she had written a poem about the events on the two hills of Charlestown, it would not have been a poem of pretty rhymes. She would have found no glory, unless she told a lie. It would have to be a poem of the harshest, most dirge-full, most baleful, most appalled and sickened words that could ever be placed on a page.

Patrick, having delivered the guns, would not agree with his heady young men that they should linger in Charlestown, to be of aid to the militia, especially as Mattias Patch—who suffered from gout, and had been ill and confined to home—was not able to do so himself. Patrick wanted to get back to Nahant (and back to Maine). He convinced Asa and Otis that they would be of better service on the sloop: he told them he would consider a run from Nahant down the coast, as risky as that would have been.

But just as they were preparing to bid farewell and good fortunes to Mattias Patch and his visitors, on the evening of June

16—just as Patch saw them to the door, with a request to please try to smuggle in, next time, somehow, a few cannons, or at least some American smooth-bore muskets—a messenger arrived, sent from Patch's friend Joseph Warren, the beloved physician, officer, and Son of Liberty, who had a house nearby.

There was not a person in Charlestown or Boston who didn't know the doctor personally, or at least had heard of him. He was aging, he was not of strong health, he was exhausted to begin with, but on the afternoon of June 17, realizing the extent of the horrors, Dr. Warren went up Breed's Hill and announced himself as ready to join the fighting.

William Prescott was the name of the man who had command of the American militia men. This band of men could not yet be called an army.

Dr. Warren was of higher rank than William Prescott. As soon as the doctor arrived at the redoubt, the officer stated his desire to have him take charge, but the doctor would not hear of it: he could not allow a man in authority to lose face in front of his men. But the outcome would have been the same, whichever of them had commanded. Dr. Warren would be shot, and would die on the top of the hill, along with very many others.

The dead would lie everywhere on the acres of Breed's: down its slopes, at its crest, in its trenches. Over their heads, fires would rage in Charlestown, with thick black smoke that joined with the gritty black smoke from explosions of muskets, and rose up into the pure, limpid blue air.

Soon, the smoke would grow so vast, for all of four days, it would obscure the sky completely, as if the sun had gone out, like one candle.

The messenger who came to the Patch home brought astonishing news. Everyone knew—and was waiting for—some word of what sort of defense the militias would take. But no one expected what came.

In secrecy, the militia was going to do what seemed impossible: under cover of darkness, while the English on the warships slept, and while the English in Boston slept, too, the Americans would build themselves a redoubt at the top of Charlestown.

Most of the militia men were farmers, accustomed to digging hard soil: why not an earthen fort?

There were some 800 men who began the work on the hill, just after midnight, and in the course of the night and the following morning, more men would come, from militias all over Massachusetts and two from New Hampshire.

There were double as many British. But more than 1,000 of those Englishmen would die, when their officers had expected losing ten, perhaps twenty.

"There is to be a redoubt put up. Tonight. Be silent, as the English ships are so close, they shall hear our shovels clinking rock, if we are not careful." Those were the messenger's words.

Before Patrick had the chance to comprehend what was happening, shovels appeared; a shovel was put into his hands. Asa Patch and Otis Rawley had no intention of going anywhere but up to Bunker's Hill, which was the site first chosen for the redoubt; this was hours later switched to Breed's. Breed's Hill was closer to Boston.

In the morning, the English woke rubbing their eyes with disbelief at the sight of a fortress, brazen and amazing on its peak overlooking their warships.

Many English soldiers admired the new fort on Breed's Hill, and even as they said, "We must seize it, else quit New England in disgrace, for if we lose Charlestown, we shall lose Boston," they marveled at it, and felt it had to be God who had caused it. The lazy, undisciplined, un-organized, cowardly rebels, it was felt, could never have pulled off something like this by themselves.

What those militia men did on the hill that night was closely similar to games they had played as boys, building play-fortresses, sometimes out of snow and ice blocks, sometimes, like this, out of dirt.

The redoubt would be sixteen feet long and eight feet wide, with walls six feet high and one foot in thickness. A small breastwork would be added in the early hours of morning. This was how they defended their town. There was no time before morning light to have a second fort completed on Bunker's Hill.

What they had not considered was that, in choosing the other hill, for its better defense of the city, they had allowed the British an excellent means to storm them. Breed's Hill went down directly to a beach of the harbor.

The masses of British soldiers who came to Charlestown, in longboats from lower down the Boston waterfront, could beach their boats easily, and simply proceed.

When all those English soldiers arrived in their longboats, and stepped to the base of the hill, it was much like what happens when birds are nesting in a tree, and the tree is being felled by axes.

Every American man who was there knew exactly how much was available to them for ammunition. Very little. When they ran out of shot, they had nothing to use in their guns but rocks. When they ran out of rocks, some of them were able to retreat off the hill into houses of neighbors—whichever houses had not been burned—and some were not so fortunate.

What Americans were left could not have defended themselves with bayonets. Their guns were mostly fowling guns, or simple muskets unfitted with blades. The guns from Nahant were taken out of Mattias Patch's root cellar, but they were no more useful in the fight, as it happened, than a pile of spoons.

Asa Patch and Otis Rawley, between them, managed to carry the guns up Breed's Hill—in their arms, not choosing to enter what would soon be a battlefield with a coffin, even though it was a small one and, at closer inspection, a fake; they had felt it would demoralize everyone. But in their haste, they had left behind the lead shot. It was still in the coffin. By the time they realized their mistake, it was too late to go off the hill; the English were advancing, and the road between the hill and the town was thick with soldiers on horse and on foot.

Those guns lay stacked in a heap at the top of Breed's Hill and, at the finish, the Americans who were still standing did not have the power in their bodies to lift a single Brown Bess, and bring its weight on the heads of English soldiers who were bearing upon them.

Patrick's gun delivery went back into the hands of the British.

The dead on both sides numbered some 2,000. When the firing stopped at last, the hush was the same as if all of humanity and all of living, breathing Nature had suddenly pulled in a breath, which might never be let out again, as if all of the world had stopped dead. Many of the bodies looked slight, and lightweight, having fallen on the hill at odd angles, and it seemed that, if large birds should swoop low—eagles, perhaps even crows—they would be able to pick them all up, with talons or beaks, and carry them off, as if those men, with life all stopped, were no more substantial than sparrows.

There was no aspect of Breed's Hill that did not hold earth that was not stained dark red. Asa Patch was shot in the lower right arm, then again, half an hour later, in the shoulder of the same arm, then again, ten minutes after that, just over the heart, which killed him. Otis Rawley was killed the instant a warship gun ball came into the east side of the redoubt: he had run out of shot, and was squatting down, with his head ducked low, trying to dislodge the loaded musket from the hand of a militia man who was dead. Patrick saw neither of these things take place, and had to be told later on.

Having gone up the hill at midnight to help with the building, he had resigned himself to doing what was necessary, however long it would take.

He admired William Prescott. He admired the idea of the fort for its daring, its cunning, its surprise. He actually said to himself, "We have very much of a strong, good chance to withstand attack," and he truly believed it. "I shall leave with Asa and Otis as soon as we are able, and we shall turn the sloop north to Maine." He believed that, too.

Up on the hill he felt very much out of his element, but he'd made up his mind to hold his own in terms of the digging, which he'd had no experience of, unlike most of the others. And he would not allow himself to be outshone by his younger men.

At sometime near 3:00 in the morning, while striking the flat of a shovel against loose dirt at a corner of the redoubt, to pack it down, Patrick suddenly sank to his knees with a cramping in his stomach that set in so swiftly, so violently, he would have thought himself kicked—kicked hard, in the center of his stomach, as if by the foot of a shod, rearing, angry horse. He began to retch, with shuddering spasms through his body, and though he muffled himself as best as he could, he could not silence the sound of the retching. Colonel Prescott came over to him and ordered him off the hill, at once.

But as he knew of Patrick's reputation, he made light of it. "Rouse," he told him, "I have heard of sickness at sea, brought on to suffering souls that are lovers of land, and find themselves, at sea, unable to abide the moving ocean. But you are the first man I heard of to be struck with the sickness from finding yourself off the ocean, on dry land."

Asa Patch had been with Patrick when he took sick on the sloop. In fact, the wagon that had conveyed Patrick into Boston from the sloop that day (Mattias Patch's wagon), was used to bring down bodies from Breed's Hill.

When Asa first heard Patrick sickening, and saw him doubled over, he called out to him, "Again, Sir? Again? How can it be twice the same manner?" Asa laughed at Colonel Prescott's joke. It was not often that anyone made fun of Patrick Rouse, that is, anyone who was not in his family.

Asa consulted with Otis. They decided that their captain was ill because there must have been poisons emanating from the odors of the raccoon, in the coffin of guns: all along, on the ride from Nahant, Patrick had been sniffing the poisons unawares, and now, thankfully, the awful things were escaping from his body.

This was Otis's idea: he had learned from his midwife mother that the body has a way of discharging foul things without help of plants and medicines. But he was also prepared, if his captain took long to get well, to go and find some plants and medicines.

"It shall pass with the puking, certainly, and he shall be back to himself in no time," they had decided.

When Patrick left Breed's Hill, confused, barely able to walk, and reeling and retching, he had no means of judging the correct way back to the Patch house. He did not know the Charlestown roads. He was out in the blackness of night. He collapsed on a narrow, dusty lane, two hours before sunrise.

He had discovered himself unable to support his own weight, as if his knees had turned to jam. He did not lose consciousness, although he wished to, as the heaving kept coming over him again, racking him. He happened to have fallen in front of a house belonging to one of the militia men.

No sooner had he slipped to the ground than the door of the house opened, and there, in the darkness—they would not have dared light a candle—were the militia man's wife and several children, reaching out to pull him inside; they grabbed hold of his collar as if it were the rim of a sack.

They could not manage to get him into a bed, for he lay on the floor in their front room, dryly retching and shaking, and was too much for them. They had no wood for a fire, but brought him blankets; and there he stayed, until evening of the next day, when one of the teenagers of the house took him by the hand and led him to the Patch house, which was far enough from the waterfront to not have been struck or set fire to.

Patrick never saw the fort on the hill in daylight, or completed, or defended, or seized, or destroyed. He remained at the Patch house until, in the next week, on June 21, he heard the news that General Washington had decided to hold the center of his new Continental Army in Boston—not in the city itself, but in Cambridge. He would take over Cambridge Common as his camp.

"The army shall be here by early July, and there shall be no further damage to Charlestown," Patrick said to Mattias Patch.

Patch answered, "There is not much, by way of being left, to give harm to. I would have my house burned down and everything in it, and myself as well, to bring back to the living my good boy Asa and his mate, your Otis."

"Go to Cambridge Common and tell Washington himself what took place here," Patrick answered.

"He would know."

"Then allow him to hear it again, and say, though the English would call this their victory, a thousand of their dead are in tombs on American soil, or the waves of American water, and Boston, my friend, is not theirs."

"You are not well enough to travel, Patrick."

"I am."

"Our boy Asa had fairly worshipped you. And considered himself blessed to have been aboard with you, these six years."

"And I him."

"And the boy Otis, from Lexington, a good boy. He sat in my chair and drank tea, and had towelled his hair with one of my wife's linen tea cloths, for the sweat had built up most intensely."

"And the messenger arrived, and we took shovels and went up that hill."

"Yes. Then you went up that hill. How came you to be spared injury, Patrick?"

"I do not know."

"You must never forget my nephew Asa, and the other boy as well. You must go. God speed, then."

"And to you."

He returned by himself to Nahant, to the sloop. His other two men, Enoch and Huggins, had set out in a slightly different direction, looking for him; Patrick arrived back before they did. For a few very terrible moments, he considered setting off alone with the *Sawyer*.

He could picture himself stripping off his clothes at the bow, and climbing up, with the good strong wood of his ship at his feet. And then he would leap in the sea. Perhaps, he thought, the sound of the ocean inside his ears would drown out the other sounds that kept echoing in him, as if his brain were as hollow as a drum. The sound of every cannon and gun that was shot on June 17 was resounding inside that drum. He had not seen any part of the battle, but he had heard it.

He imagined himself sinking feet first straight down, like an arrow, down toward the bottom of the sea. He imagined silence.

"Weight myself, then be done with it quickly," he thought. He wondered if he would be able to manage tying on an anchor, or some other heavy weight, with a rope attached to his foot, or around his waist. That way he would assure himself of repelling any effort of his body to stay buoyant. He pictured himself tying a knot, not for a sail, but for its opposite.

And he thought, more soberly, "It would likely be exactly my fate that, should I attempt to drown myself, weighted or not, I shall puke out as much ocean as I would swallow, and find myself bobbing about on a wave, for a shark to find and devour." He thought of Little John. He saw the boy's face in front of him. He did not want his nephew to have to be told that he had died by the teeth of a shark.

Died by an English gun ball would have been all right, but not by a shark of New England waters.

Enoch and Huggins returned while Patrick was in the middle of these thoughts. They found him on the *Sawyer* alone, down on his knees near the stern, retching the bread and water he had thought he would be able to hold down.

They already knew what had happened to the two boys, but if they hadn't, they would have known it at once, by their absence. No living crewmen of Patrick Rouse would let their captain be weakened alone; they would have been at his side if they had lived. Enoch and Huggins positioned themselves at either side of Patrick, like posts holding a wobbly, unsound gate.

"Praise God you are alive, Sir," Enoch said quietly.

Huggins said, "We shall like to go out, Sir, to make some damage to frigates. There shall not be point in setting down for Boston. But warships are collecting more and more in Maine, toward Falmouth."

Enoch said, "Should you have the need to stay shore-side, Sir, it would be well for I and Huggins, together with what Hammerheads would join us, to make sail without you, temporary-like, should you ascertain yourself unwell for the rigor."

That brought Patrick to his feet, and fully back to his wits. "I want no one on board this ship but you two, as I have with me now. We shall manage the same way, somehow, as if Asa and Otis were with us."

So it was decided to set off north, but before they left Nahant, Patrick wrote to Sarah. He tried to make his tone impersonal and aloof, as hers had been. But his feelings crept into his sentences anyway. He said nothing of what happened on the night of June 16, or the day that followed, or the days that followed after.

"I shall not come to Tibbetston for the near future. I am unable to offer speculation as to when I shall. I am much engaged. There are English frigates that await, unawares, what shall hit them from out of my cannons. You must tell Mrs. Goodridge, and Jacques, and all, for the production of gun balls, *be of haste.* Tell my nephew, and my niece, give care to their lessons, do not be unkind, and think not of warfull subjects. Tell my sister Jossey I am well, and much alive, although in truth there are minutes of each day, and each night, when I have knowledge that the fact I am alive is something to shame and appall me. From, Patrick."

CHAPTER XXI

THE EXPEDITION

BENEDICT ARNOLD, with his already-made reputation for daring and courage and audacity, had been made an officer of the new Continental Army. Under sanction of Washington, he was on his way through Maine to storm Quebec and conquer Canada. He planned to just simply go up there and take all of it from the English, as the English had done to the French.

It had seemed such an excellent idea back in Cambridge, and in Philadelphia as well, where the Congress was rubbing its hands with impatience at the desire for large, dramatic action. Surely there could not be many British troops in Quebec, not with the numbers of them in New England.

So the plan was set up to be this: Take a section of the army, go up there, drive the English out, and take Canada as a fourteenth American colony. Why not?

In the dashing role of a potentially conquering hero, Benedict Arnold was coming up the Kennebec River with 1,100 Continental Army soldiers, in newly-made batteaux. Those boats had been put together for the expedition very quickly, in a town to the north of the mouth of the Kennebec.

They had started from Cambridge, and had marched to Newburyport with great pomp, to the constant cheers of colonists along the way. From Newburyport they were taken to Maine by whatever American boats they could get their hands on—fishing boats, merchant frigates, a couple of schooners, and sloops that belonged to the Hammerheads of Nahant.

George Washington himself had commissioned the transport boats for the expedition to Canada.

Benedict Arnold would choose to be conveyed up the Kennebec in a large, handsome, sturdy birch canoe, but for the others, there were those twenty enormous batteaux, all built of green wood, which was something like picking corn off the stalk before it ripened, with the delusion in your mind that, when you put it to roast on a fire, it would turn out just fine. In the hasty construction of the boats, which were not very different from the longboats of the British in Boston, no one had stopped to think that something might not go well with them in the tidal, salty Kennebec maelstroms.

The boats never had the chance to withstand any watery danger. It did not take long, once past Augusta, for the boats to simply fail. It seemed to be an impossibility that coastal Maine men would build boats in a shoddy way, with unseasoned wood; but that was what happened.

Benedict Arnold would find himself farther up the river with the need to buy a whole new fleet of boats, which would hold him up considerably. His troops would run out of provisions long before they ever reached Canada. No one had stopped to wonder if perhaps the expedition had been put together with elements of the fantastical, which had disguised themselves as reality.

The green-wood boat builders were like builders under a spell, thinking only of action. Action now! An expedition into Canada! Hurry! They would have to reach Quebec before winter!

General Washington had promised good money. It had never happened before that boat men in Maine were given a paid commission from the army.

There had never been an army before. Mostly, those boat builders were thinking about how good it would be to have money in their hands, even though what they were paid was one-sixth of what they expected, and the rest would never come.

George Washington had wanted boats for those troops by the mouth of the river, and boats by the mouth of the river he would have: no one said anything about the need to have seasoned wood. No one said anything about the fact that no Maine person would ever commit themselves to a trip on the river of even one mile, in any one of those batteaux.

So into the roasting pan on the fire, so to speak, went unripe corn. No matter the strength of your delusion, no matter how wrongly you have planned, you are never going to be able to eat that corn.

This was what no one was thinking about when the expedition of Arnold came through Augusta.

The fort on the river at Augusta—Fort Western, it was called—was originally established more than one hundred years ago, when Augusta was all rough, unknown frontier. It was built with English merchant money for English traders, as protection against Indians.

It was now completely American. There had not been an English ship or English soldier at Fort Western for a long time.

It had turned itself into a sleepy, quiet place, but today, Fort Western was so crowded with excited, good-humored, noisy people, dressed in their best clothes, and joking and laughing and gossiping, it seemed as if there was no such thing as a war in America. It seemed as if a fair was going on, or the Olympics, like in ancient Greece, which Vinny Avens had just been learning about.

It was a rowdy Maine gathering, and to Vinny, it was as far from Boston as anything could possibly be. What was happening here was nothing like the small, polite gatherings with church people in Boston, where you couldn't laugh out loud with your mouth wide open. In Boston, even during games on the Common, there was a strict decorum, especially for children who were the children of the pastor of the church.

In Boston, no one was allowed to shout, cuss, spit, ignore grown-ups, get your clothes mussed, tumble like a puppy in the grass, and tussle with your brother (and hold your own, even though he was bigger).

In Boston, even on holidays, you could not run freely about in circles, or spin yourself silly with your arms stretched into the air, just to do it, just because it felt wonderful to be a wonderful little girl on a marvelous excursion.

On the grassy bank near the fort, waiting to see Benedict Arnold and his army come into view, Vinny reached out her arms on either side of herself, and spun herself silly, around and around, into a dazed, wild stupor, so that everything she looked at was running all together—trees, sky, water, light—into one single blurred, bright thing, like a wide-awake dream, all liquid and vivid and remarkable.

It was important—and wonderful—that no one was crying today.

No one was saying, "Our family must still be in mourning for our Mowlans who are dead in the ground." No one was dead today. No one was dressed in black. No one was grim. All the world was spinning, spinning, spinning.

"Lavinia Priscilla Avens!" cried Jossey. "You would make me dizzy just to watch you! How shall you see the spectacle which is coming, if you are cross-eyed with spinning! You shall hurt your poor brain!"

The little girl spun harder. She knew she wasn't hurting her brain, which she valued very highly. She did not care about any spectacle that was promised her.

She had spectacle enough on her own. She did not care that in two of the wagons from Tibbetston, under cover of hay, there were gun balls, the very first balls from the foundry, waiting to be given over to Benedict Arnold, to be shot by Americans at Quebec. Why should she share in the pleasures of the grownups, and her brother, too? It was not a particularly important thing, she felt, that the foundry had actually produced cannon shot.

In fact, it annoyed her to have to part with the gun balls. She had considered them her own property, as if the foundry had been established to amuse her. She had just begun to have some real skill in the game she had invented herself, back at the farm.

There was a section of land in the cornfields that sloped down, in a gentle way, and it was perfect for setting up her dolls—not her wax ones, which were fragile and uninteresting, but the five wood ones that Mrs. Goodridge had made her. Sometimes the dolls were dressed in strips of cloth, but they were usually naked to the elements. They were supposed to represent her family, Mrs. Goodridge had said, but they were all the same size, and they all looked exactly the same, with tiny pine-heart eyes, and hands that had no fingers, and feet that had no toes: it wasn't as though they could be thought of as shapes of actual humans.

At the bottom of the slope, in her game, would stand the dolls, each one propped up with small stones or dirt mounds.

It took hours of practice before Vinny mastered the work of rolling gun balls from the shed near the foundry to the top of the slope, but when she had done so, she took huge delight in pushing them off, aimed just so. Her father and mother, and Sarah, too, who was always somewhere nearby (except now) considered it harmless play.

Sarah had gone to Falmouth to see her maid, who was also named Sarah.

She had gone on her own. Vinny had pleaded with her to be taken along.

Everyone was saying "no" to her. *Everyone.* Sarah had said, "While I am away in the city, you must look after your mother, and help with your little brother when he comes back."

"It is not a city. Falmouth is a town."

"We are people of Maine now. It is a city."

"I hate Maine."

"Perhaps one day you shall learn to love it, as I have."

"That is only because you would love my uncle."

"I do not . . ." said Sarah, slowly. "Love."

But there was nothing else to be said about that.

Vinny didn't want to look after anyone except herself. She missed Sarah dreadfully. She decided that when Benedict Arnold and his men came into view on the river, she would not look; she would keep spinning and spinning, and see only a world of colored, bright blurs.

Sarah would want to be told what the *spectacle* was like, and had said so—"watch everything carefully, for it shall be a most amazing procession. You are such a clever girl, I shall look forward to your story! You must behave as though you are my eyes while I am gone, and perhaps from what you tell me, I shall make a drawing of it."

But she would not, *would not* look, not even for one instant.

She didn't care about drawings. She cared about what it was like to keep asking for things that people kept saying no to.

It wasn't just her parents and Sarah. It was Mr. Firth, who would not allow her in the foundry. Even Jacques! He would not let her inside the smithy, not even in the doorway to just *look*. And Naomi, too.

And the last time they all went down to Winnegance to look at the baby and remind him they were his family, she had asked please, could she go out to the clam flats and see what it was like to hunt clams?

Absolutely not! Lavinia Avens! Your new frock! There is mud out there! Digging clams is for other people!

Meanwhile, while those words were being said, her brother was out there to his shins in low tide, with so much mud on his breeches, you couldn't see the cloth. And *no one minded*.

"Papa," she had said just that morning, in the carriage on the way up to Augusta. "How old must I be when I shall learn to fire a musket?"

"One hundred forty," he had answered.

"How old before I fire a rifle?"

"The same."

"How old before I fire a pistol?"

"The same."

"How old before I fire a cannon?"

"The same," and she took some comfort in that, because it was not exactly a "no."

Behind the carriage they were riding were the wagons carrying the gun balls to the fort. She knew something about them. She knew something no one else knew. She had made up her mind to say nothing about it, except to Jesus.

"Lavinia Avens! If you insist on spinning about, you shall puke up your dinner!"

"I already did, Mama." (She was lying.)

She was slowing down now; the dizziness was getting the best of her. She was worried that, if she became too giddy, she might spill out her secret of the gun balls.

She wondered instead if she might have the chance to go over to the wagons, which were just inside the gates of the fort, and play her game one more time. She had not brought her dolls, but she could improvise.

Sometimes in her game it took her ten or twelve attempts to knock down just one doll, so she had attached them to each other with ties she had fashioned from strips of dried corn husks, which were as good as ropes. With a whole chain of dolls, all she needed to do was hit one. Most of the time, the one doll she'd hit would represent her brother, who was horrid to begin with, and always smelled bad. He hated to bathe, and no one cared if he stank. Worse than that, worst of all, her brother was going to be allowed to go to Harvard College if he wanted to, which he did not want to do: he was going to go to sea, or the war, or both, while she was *not to be allowed*, even though she had begged.

John had smiled at her, shaking his head; he had never denied her anything she wanted before. She could not understand how he could have denied Harvard College to her.

"Papa, I am going to be a preacher, to take your place because you had quit."

He had patted her on the head, and he said, "No, that can never happen," but he did not say why.

Sometimes the doll that was knocked over represented her father, and sometimes it was Jossey. It was never the baby. You don't bomb a helpless infant.

"Perhaps you shall marry a preacher like Papa," Jossey had told her.

"He is not one any longer. Papa hates God."

"You must not speak so!"

"All right, but I am going to go to Harvard College."

Her mother had explained it. "It is only for men."

"Then I shall grow up to be a man."

"But God had already made you a girl. It cannot be changed."

"But my name was changed."

"That was different."

"Then I shall put on Papa's clothes, and no one will know."

"But they shall see your beautiful hair."

"I shall wear it in a cap, Mama."

But all the same, every time she mentioned Harvard, they only shook their heads. She had the feeling that, should she tell them she had changed her mind, and would go to sea or the war like her brother, they would not allow her to do that, either.

She spent a great deal of time in the cornfield. Her arms were stronger already: she could lift a gun ball in her own hands. Each time she sent one careening down the slope on its mission, it went a little bit faster, she had noticed, with a little more power, which felt thrilling.

Down would go the chain of dolls, all together.

"Dead!" she would scream, with joy. Then she would rush to the fallen dolls and soothe them, and tell them, "You must all come back to life now, like Jesus." She'd set them up again, to be killed all over.

"We shall make more," her father had promised, when they came and took the gun balls away from her.

There was no sign yet of Benedict Arnold. She peeked down the river through her fingers. There would surely be time for one game of Knock Everyone Down To Be Dead, before the gun balls were unloaded from the wagons into the boats.

How could her father—and Mr. Firth, who knew everything about iron, and Jacques, who knew everything about everything— have been so completely mistaken about the size of the cannons that belonged to Benedict Arnold?

They were giving him six-pounders. Two wagons of six-pounders. But right there on the letter from Cambridge, it said that the cannons of Benedict Arnold required the size of four-pounders.

Four! Not six, four! The letter was from someone who was a clerk to George Washington *himself*. General Washington, in Vinny's estimation, was only slightly lesser than God, as he had gone to save Boston. Just because she didn't live there any longer, she very much did not wish Boston to be destroyed, or *owned* by the *enemy*.

She wanted Boston to be there, intact, free, and American, for the day when she would go back and take over her father's congregation. She loved to imagine herself on the pulpit. She loved to picture herself in a minister's coat and collar, but she would want to have hers dyed with a color, perhaps blue—anything would be all right, as long as it was not black.

Black was for when someone died. No one else was going to die!

You did not have to go to Harvard to take over your father's congregation, and go into the pulpit yourself, she had reasoned. You could simply just grow up and go there and take it.

She had noticed the letter from Washington's clerk on the wall of the foundry, by the door. It was a letter of command. Someone had speared it at the top with a small stick, and had hung it in a chink between stones.

Everyone in the foundry must have passed by it a hundred times. They hadn't looked at the numbers.

No one said, "Have we the correct size?" They were perhaps too excited with the production to note details. If they had allowed her into the foundry, she would *not*, she reasoned, feel the need to keep what she had learned a secret, which she was very much committed to doing.

Only she and God could know that the expedition to conquer Canada would be carrying a load of gun balls which no one would be able to use. The gun balls would be dumped on a bank higher up the Kennebec, abandoned with the green-wood batteaux.

The difference in size between a six-pound and a four-pound gun ball is only a matter of several fractions of an inch. The diameter of a four is a little over three inches. The diameter of a six-pounder is almost four. It wasn't much, in terms of width, unless you were attempting to load the muzzle of your cannon.

Trying to load a six-pound ball into the mouth of a cannon that was built for a four, Vinny imagined, would be almost the same thing as picking up a pumpkin, with the plan to put the whole thing into your mouth.

How could they have confused the sizes? It was such a remarkable thing, she hardly knew how to begin comprehending it. It wasn't as though that order-letter on the stone wall of the foundry was out of the line of sight for every grownup who passed it. She herself had had to drag over a crate to stand on, just to read it. And there had been the added element of danger of being caught inside a place that was forbidden to a *girl*.

She did not feel sorry for what Benedict Arnold and his men were in for, but she would have felt differently had she known that day at Fort Western that the expedition was doomed anyway and, in the first engagement of the Americans against the English at Quebec—that is, with what Americans had survived the ordeal of the journey—Benedict Arnold would be shot at once and badly wounded.

Most of the American soldiers who died on the way to Canada would die of exposure or starvation, or a combination of the two.

"Prissy! Prissy!" called her father. He had been talking with strangers, talking about the foundry, the war, men things, he would call them; and now he was pointing to the river.

She didn't answer him, because he had used her old name. Everyone was running toward the cliffs. People up on the walls of the fort were shouting and cheering. She saw her brother with his cap in his hands, tossing it into the air, with a look of rapture. Boats! Boats!

"Lavinia! Come see! Lavinia Avens! It's marvelous!" cried Jossey.

It would take a few hours before all the boats were all the way up to the fort. Then everyone would have to talk. There would probably be speeches. The men in the boats would want to eat. There would be plenty of time to slip in through the gate and climb into one of the wagons and borrow a gun ball.

Vinny looked around for a couple of sticks, which could be stuck in the dirt, and would do very nicely as dolls. Someone had thrown a few apple cores on the ground, which could be placed on the sticks, as heads. While everyone watched Benedict Arnold lead his procession, she would have a *much* better time. And when it was time to turn over the gun balls, she would make sure she was not close by. The plan for the presentation was not elaborate, although Mr. Wabanaki, being fond of speeches and ceremonies, had wanted her father to say a few words, formally, as he had done on the day on the funeral of the Mowlans, and again for the funeral of the man from Lexington—words like *freedom from tyranny* and *God grant us liberty.* She had no need, herself, of such words. She would take all the liberty she could, on her own; and freedom from tyranny, too.

The men at the foundry had not made the gun balls for a girl to use as toys. She knew this. They had a purpose. Gun balls were for killing.

She wondered what it looked like when a gun ball struck a person. Once, back in the corn field, she had tried to use a pumpkin: she had set it in place to roll a ball at it, really hard, but her mother had caught her at it: the pumpkin was meant for supper that night. Probably, Vinny reasoned, a gun ball hitting an actual human head would cause a great deal more damage than it would cause to a pumpkin, which was harder. This would especially be true if the gun ball hit someone in the face. She thought about that. She thought, "My father and his friends are making things to use for killing people."

There was *not* to be any more killing.

When the time came to hand over the gun balls, no one would think to take their measure. Vinny would not be tempted to tell her secret. She would play in the fort, then go back to the grass by herself, unrestrictedly, with the sun in her eyes and the river rushing below her. She would fling out her arms, and make further plans about her future, and spin and spin and spin.

CHAPTER XXII

FALMOUTH

O N THE SAME DAY the warships arrived, Sarah Dudley arrived in Falmouth to visit the other Sarah, her former maid,
and the other Sarah's mother, who had been ailing, and was kept
in bed with a suspicion of pneumonia.

Mrs. Pease and her daughter, Sarah, were in a comfortable small
house not far from the harbor. The two Sarahs fell upon each other
with cries of joy; it had been a long time since they had been together in Salem; it felt like a lifetime ago. The women barely took
notice of the warships, at first.

October 16. A clear autumn day, brisk, sparkling, with that keen
solemnity that comes into the air when the days are about to be
shorter.

It was ripe-apple weather. Harvest weather. Fill-the-fish-sheds
weather. Smoke-the-meats-for-winter weather. The leaves were
bronze, burnished red, and many shades of orange, yellow, gold.
On vines in gardens, there were acres and acres of squashes and
pumpkins, bursting with ripeness, and never picked.

On the morning of October 16, the British warships that entered the Falmouth harbor appeared to have arrived for the purpose of gathering provisions for a journey down the coast.

The commander of the fleet sent word into the town that it
ought to be evacuated. It took almost two full days for people to
believe that this was no jest, or idle threat.

Even when the bombing was commencing, there were those
who had lived all their lives in the town, and clung to incredulity.
They looked at the warships out their windows as if the ships were

paintings in frames, and said, like ailing Mrs. Pease, who objected to being taken from her sickbed and put into a cart, "I do believe that the terrible rumbling we hear is only thunder, although the sky is clear blue, and things seem placid."

Sarah Dudley—before the terror of what was about to happen fully set into her—wanted only to talk to her friends about Patrick. "I love a man named Patrick Rouse," she wanted to say. "Although for many hours of each day, I have the wish I never had met him."

But she kept silent. She never had the chance to mention him.

Bomb Falmouth? How could that happen?

Sarah had no love of the town, understandable in a girl who grew up in Salem and Boston. When the bombing began, she thought of it as simply a place with no meaning, a place to flee, a doomed, wretched town she'd had the bad luck to happen into. It was only later, on the road back north to Tibbetston, that she broke down and wept for the horror of it, and she would get on her knees to thank God that she had been in the Pease house, for Sarah Pease and her mother would not have managed to escape without her.

Falmouth. Sarah Dudley would never be able to hear that word again without the sound in her ears of horses and cartwheels on cobblestones: that would be the thing that stayed with her the most. The terrible slowness of horses and wheels, going more and more slowly away from the burning town, with a creaking, tapping sort of torture, and often stopping cold, in the press of hundreds of others.

Of the hundreds of people who died at Falmouth, most did not die in the fires or topplings or smashings. Most died in the roads, or on ships, in the act of escaping.

There were nineteen Maine ships of different designs and sizes harbored at Falmouth. The British captured a few of them for their own use—having first shot Americans aboard them—and sank the rest. Smoke and fire rose up from the Falmouth water, as if the bay itself was enflamed.

Falmouth, hub of Maine, one of the biggest ports in America. Patrick had loved it as a child. Up at the farm, in those hours they'd had together, he'd spoken of it to Sarah with an abiding fondness. He'd described what he remembered of being brought there from sleepy little well-behaved York. To go into the shops, to look at the docks, to see so many people, so much activity, were thrills and terrors combined. He had loved it.

Big, dirty, self-centered Falmouth: darkly bright, brightly dank. Character-rich, fortune-wise, fortune-foolish. Crowded, unpredictable, unreputable, virtuous.

Wonderful, dowdy, watery Falmouth. Rot-smelling, salt-smelling, sweaty Falmouth, a stepsister to Boston, some called it: a messy, unwashed, perfumey, come-as-you-are, up-and-down-on-her-luck, indulged, beloved sister, fronted by the bay and then the ocean, with its islands in the distance like giant, grass-banked, tree-studded whales.

Teeming, steamy Falmouth with its wooden houses, warehouses, rats, robbers, clerks, lawyers, weavers, builders. With its ships, docks, shipyards, noise, squalor. With its taverns, gambling, vices, filth, exuberance. The big city.

They would bomb it until it was bones of itself, bones and sticks and smoldering dust.

A new level of rage had been reached. What the English had in mind, after losing the naval battle at Machias, plus the terrible wreckage and losses of Bunker and Breed in Charlestown, was the destruction of every harbor town, including ships, wharves, buildings, and streets, along the whole of the northeastern coast, from the easternmost edge of Maine to Boston, then past it to Rhode Island, and toward New York.

They had imagined themselves possessing the might of a tornado. Such was their rage. But they succeeded only with Falmouth, which no one who lived there, or loved it, was counting as a blessing.

Destroy Falmouth? It had seemed as likely as a tidal wave rearing up in a quiet Maine pond. No one had believed the punishment would take place as it did, in spite of warnings.

"Have you noticed those frigates of ours, four of them, warships, in your harbor, like pictures framed by the windows of your waterfront houses and shops? Have you noticed the pointing of the cannons on their decks? Had you thought we placed them as decorations? Do you believe us when we tell you we are going to eliminate your big, important city?"

All day on October 16, dories containing officers had been freely leaving the warships and coming ashore. The officers dined and drank in Falmouth taverns, bathed and rested in Falmouth inns, strolled about the streets taking stock of the buildings that would soon not be standing.

"We do not want to kill you. We want merely to obliterate your town," they kept saying. "Please be kind enough to remove yourselves from these buildings."

On October 18, early in the morning, the evacuation was begun. The stubborn will to not believe that something unbelievable was at hand—all at once—gave way to desperate panic. People poured out of houses with everything they could carry; it was the same as a scene of people fleeing hell, and that was before the bombing started.

The cannons began their fusillade on October 18 at 9:00 in the morning. The bombing continued without stopping until evening, at 6:00.

It was not the setting of the sun that had ceased them, but the fact that they had run out of gun balls.

The walls which did not go down at once from the assault of the gun balls soon went down in flames. It would take almost a month before the fires of Falmouth were gone out completely, in spite of a heavy, wet fog that descended that autumn night, and remained for many days after. It was hard to tell fog from the smoke, except by the condition of the grayness. The fog was slightly whiter in hue.

Safe with her friends in the slow, slow cart, Sarah Dudley looked back on the burning town, her eyes stinging, her throat barely able to allow for the passage of air. Sarah Pease and her mother lost everything they owned, except for the clothes they were wearing, a few blankets, some coins in a purse, and the cart and pair of horses they had escaped with.

It was just as well Sarah Dudley had not had the opportunity to convey to the Peases the feelings she had for Patrick. It was not very difficult for her, now, to believe that those feelings were as removed from life as Mrs. Pease's handsome little water-side house, along with every other house that stood near it.

She had not had a letter from Patrick for weeks, but she knew his two men had been killed, and she knew that Patrick himself had walked away from Charlestown, intact, upright, spared. Like she was.

Spared. "We are spared," said Sarah Pease's mother, trembling, feverish, in shock. She said it as though it were something they ought to be pleased with.

Sarah Dudley watched the sky turn into a maelstrom of dense, ugly vapors, and when the fog rose everywhere, she had the sense that God must have sent it, to obscure from the view of heaven these things that transpired on earth. The thought occurred to her, as she had turned around in her seat, that if she dared to look back on the destruction, she might be turned to a pillar of salt, like the wife of Lot.

She almost wished she was, to be spared for the rest of her life the memory of what she had seen, and the knowledge that now was hers. The knowledge of what men are capable of doing.

It had always seemed to Sarah that "war" was something to be carried out away from view, in a field somewhere, with lines of opposing soldiers clashing, like boys at rough play, but with the weapons of men. It was not supposed to be something one actually was *in*.

"So this is war," thought Sarah. "So this is war."

She felt herself harden, as if a smooth, tough, new layer of cartilage was slowly being formed along the center of her body, as a lobster grows a shell.

She was not thinking about Patrick. For the first time since Patrick had left Tibbetston, his name was not in her mind, was not at the tip of her tongue. She was not being tormented by the formerly constant, nagging, dreadful worry that he was in danger, he was wounded, he was sick, he was lost. (Anything worse than that, she did not allow herself.) She thought instead of practical matters, such as getting Mrs. Pease attended to, and finding a place in the village for the two Peases to live.

But mostly, one thing was on her mind. She thought about how good it would feel to be back in Tibbetston on the farm, where heat and smoke and flames were coming from an American foundry, not from warships with British flags.

The part of her mind that had played to her, over and over, the memory of Patrick's face—and what it felt like for her to be near him, to touch him—had shut down as if it would never return. In its place was a new sensation.

"How I wish this old cart would go faster!" She could hardly bear the waiting until she was back. Soon, she remembered, the foundry would be able to begin the production of cannons.

She wondered if it ought to feel strange to her that the manufacturing of giant guns—for backs of carts, for ships, and independent ones as well, with their own set of wheels—was something she felt thrilled to look forward to. But it did not feel strange. It felt normal. It felt necessary.

She pictured herself walking into the foundry, the smithy. She closed her eyes and imagined the roar of the furnace, the sound of the hammers, the bellows. She pictured Jacques and the rest of the men. She pictured the moldings, the ashes, and the astonishing brightness of molten ore, as if part of the sun itself had descended to earth, and was poured into the troughs, in liquidy thickness, and hot beyond words.

She pictured the four-pounders, the sixes. She felt that she had never desired anything—or anyone—with half as much force as she now desired the feel of a just-cooled new gun ball in her hands: hard, solid, invincible.

ſON OF ƳORK

"Ꮪo THIS IS WAR," said Patrick, at the top of his lungs, to the two crew men he still had, who watched him closely, with anxious expressions.

"This is war," he cried, over and over.

He said it for all his memories of his sister, of William, of their children. He said it for the memory of the friend he had made in Lexington. He said it for his two boys who went down at Charlestown. He said it for the girl he had met at his crewman's uncle's house in Charlestown: the girl who'd come from Hingham on a pleasure trip with her girlfriends to watch a battle. She had not turned her eyes away, not even from the worst of it. Then she went home to her parents to write a farewell, explanatory poem; and then she hanged herself.

They printed her poem in the newspaper. What were the words? "My eyes that saw war are eyes that may never again look at life."

Something like that. As if war was a type of blinding. Patrick had considered tearing the poem out of the paper and sending it to Sarah, with a note saying, maybe not in these words exactly, "This girl's words express the way I feel." But he would never do that.

He didn't feel he was blinded. He felt that his eyes were wide open.

"This is war!" he said, and he said it for all the souls that had quit this world already in battles of this wretched, hellish business. And he said it to the not-yet memories of all to come.

"This is war, this is war, this is war."

He shouted it out to the clouds, to the wind, to the waves, to the depths beneath him, and to the cold, salty sprays of ocean that kept his hair and face and clothes always wet. His hair was matted with salt; his belly was rumbling with hunger.

"We shall not allow him to go mad," his crewmen said secretly, to each other. "Although he is exactly the type of man who just might."

They made the effort to be light about it. Jocularity at times of duress had served them well in the past. Patrick had been regaling them for years with stories he'd learned in his youth, and now they teased him by reminding him of the Greek seaman-hero Odysseus, who fought on the side of victors, and had to be lashed to his mast out at sea, so he wouldn't (the crewmen remembered) become beguiled by phantom ocean-demons, and have his sanity gone completely.

Somewhere in the fog were three more enemy ships, which comprised three-fourths of the fleet that was coming down from Maine. It would not have been a good idea to continue allowing a man's voice booming out from the much smaller sloop. Patrick would have screamed himself hoarse, like a lunatic, "this is war, this is war, this is war!" But he was taken in hand by the crewmen. He was ordered into silence.

"Should you want to keep shouting, we shall fear for the wreck of your wits, and find need to fix you with ropes to the mainsail, like that Greek which was nearly bewitched, Sir," they threatened.

They were hoping that Patrick would show some pleasure at being offered the comparison of himself to a hero. He did not.

He fell silent. The sound of his own voice had hurt his ears anyway. But it was better to raise his own voice than to listen to the cries of the enemy men, who were somewhere nearby in the water. They were unseen in the fog, and begging to not be left there. Their cries had not lasted long.

The autumn air felt like winter. There was no feel of victory in Patrick's heart, even though he had just won a victory. He could find no way to be warmed, even though the blood in his skin was steaming. He could not conjure up in the back of his mind a picture of Sarah Dudley, not even one small bit of her. He tried to imagine a space beside him, in which a phantom Sarah Dudley was standing with her arms out, like an angel from a childhood story.

The space was only empty. He could not remember what color her hair was, or how it framed her face, or what the feel of her bosom against his chest was like, or how she smelled. His memory felt the same as the fog.

Fog lifted. That was another thing he kept telling himself. It was the first thing you learned about a boat, after you learned a few things about wind. Fog lifted.

The *York Sawyer* was well south of Falmouth, near rocky islands off the coast of New Hampshire. Patrick and his crewmen knew what happened to Falmouth. It was the lead frigate of the enemy coming down the coast from Maine that they were after.

The wind was with them. They knew how to fight at sea, as the best of the militia men knew how to fight on land, like Indians.

Hide. Emerge. Aim. Fire. Strike. Hit. Flee.

Thick white pouches of fog had shrouded the sunlight and stretched down from the sky to the iron-colored sea. It had been like this for days, but now the fog was mingled with dark-gray smoke.

Patrick and his crewmen, having hidden under the fog, had crept up on the lead frigate like a ghost ship. They had sent six gun balls in a thunderous volley into its ribs. The deck of the sloop still trembled with the force of its guns. If the wind had changed direction even a little, burning wood or burning canvas, or burning clothes off enemy men, all borne in the air as lightly as thistles, might have landed on the American vessel and set it ablaze.

As chance would have it, the English frigate that was now keeling up and going under had this for a name: *Son of York*.

So there were two ships, one large and one smaller, from two warring countries, with names that were almost exactly the same. The name of the enemy ship could have been applied to his own. In the town of York that was English, he thought, there'd be saw mills, there'd be sawyers.

Perhaps there were sawyers who looked like his father. Perhaps there were sons of those sawyers who looked like himself. Perhaps there were daughters who looked like his sisters. Perhaps if he'd gone there, peaceably, he might have found kin.

What was it Lavinia said once, around the time when the English had taken William? "If only we spoke a different language." He could hear his sister's voice as if it rose up to him from the waves.

It occurred to Patrick that in going to war with this enemy, he was going to war with himself. So be it, he decided.

There would be no survivors from the stricken, sunk English ship. Twenty-nine men had been on board. It would not have been impossible for Patrick and his men to take onto the American *York* at least some of the men who did not die at once from the gun balls, and who clung for as long as they could to some pieces of wood in the sea.

"Oh, we were overly busy with the sails, with our escape in the fog from the rest of the enemy fleet, which would have destroyed us," they would tell themselves. "There had not been time to take enemy prisoners on board."

They would also tell themselves that surely, the cries they heard when the bombing was finished were only from gulls; they fooled themselves into believing that gulls would really fly in that fog, and not rush to flee that smoke.

"It's only the damned noise of birds. Pay no mind. It's only birds."

The other ships of the enemy fleet never saw the sloop. They only saw in their distance the brief fire, laying waste what was left of the frigate. It was the same as if the American *York* was cloaked with invisibility.

"This is war," Patrick said, inside himself.

This time, he was speaking to his sister. "Lavinia," he said. "Lavinia, can you hear me?" He sounded a lot like Jossey. He sounded like a small boy, too, except that the hardness and fierceness in his heart were no boy's.

He tried to remember what everyone used to be like when all they knew of war was the desire for it. It seemed now that they had all been as simple-minded as seagulls. How easy it was, when it was only desire.

The blood would rise, the spirit would soar. Then came the glee of that rough, huge, fierce instinct to defend and persevere. And strike back.

He remembered Lavinia reading to him. He had loved as a boy to hear of Troy, Greece, Rome, old Britain: warriors, knights, castles, valor, heroes. And here, close to home, the Indian wars: the fires, the tortures, the killings, the terror, the tales of whites stolen from their beds, the tales of Indians destroyed with gun shot, destroyed by white diseases, destroyed by any means at hand. He remembered all over again what it was like to imagine *scalping*.

But those were stories, told by someone else, and entered into only through the force of his big imagination. He thought, "What a fool I was!"

It was something else when war was happening. A boy hearing stories, he thought, was as ignorant as a doorknob. He knew what he had not known before: that there was no such thing as a desire for war when war was happening. There was only the desire to have it over with. Anyone who thought otherwise was a madman.

There was one other thing he kept telling himself. Over and over and over. "There is only one way I shall be able to manage what I know, what I have seen, what I have done. And that would be, with this war, we are going to win."

The older one of his two crewmen was standing close by, as a good father would stand close to his child.

"I'm not going mad," said Patrick.

"Aye. We know that. We're missing the two killed boys as much as yourself."

"I should not have brought them to Charlestown."

"Many things should not have happened. But, Captain, it won't go well for us to linger in these parts. In which direction shall we proceed?"

"In which direction did the English go?"

"South."

"Then so will we, unless the two of you would mutiny, and turn us back to home."

"And if we did, what would be your reaction?"

"I should outwit you. I should throw you both overboard, and proceed to the south on my own."

"That would be, Sir, what I had hoped you would say."

Then Patrick ducked his head in the force of the watery wind, as if praying. No sound could be heard that was not from the sea. The sloop took the wind in its sails like a good, mighty breath, and moved on through the night and the waves, as fast and sleek as a shark.

"Lavinia," said Patrick. "Tell Jesus I am sorry for what I have done, and for what I shall do, perhaps worse, in days ahead. I shall seek no redemption. But we shall have our freedom. We shall win." Then he said, "Please have Jacques and the Iron Man hurry with the load of six-pounders they are making for me. And tell my sister and Sarah Dudley, I shall be well. These things shall be lifted."

CHAPTER XXIV

GLORY

G ENERAL WASHINGTON WAS establishing a headquarters in Cambridge. The English were leaving New England. They were heading down to New York, and to the South.

They would say they had mastered Boston and all of the North and Northeast, leaving behind a subdued, subjugated population. But everyone knew exactly what they were leaving. They were leaving winter, and they were leaving people—former colonists— who hated them more fiercely than ever.

Jossey found herself looking at the recruiting posters for General Washington's Continental Army with a strange, new, unexpected aversion. She thought them alluring, attractive things, designed by thinking, cunning men in Boston to entice young men—and boys—out of their farms and fields and harbors, to experience the glories of battle.

Jossey wondered, what glory? The thrill of those first gun balls to have hardened in their molds was gone. The push inside her to want someone to answer for the Mowlans was gone, too, and so was the hot-blooded, heady joy of joining her voice with everyone else, saying, "We want war! We want war! We want war!"

The signs went up everywhere, spreading up the coast of Maine. They hung in every tavern, every shop, even on fence posts. Engravings were in the corners: pictures of pleased-looking, clean-faced, handsome men with muskets in their hands and powder-and-shot pouches looped over their shoulders, with eyes turned happily, boldly, toward a future of victories, victories, and more victories.

It would seem from the posters that the war would be the best thing that could ever happen to an American man, as though none of them would scream with pain at a British mortar put into their bellies, or a bayonet put into their ribs, or a gun ball that took off their legs, their arms, or parts of their faces. As though no one would suffer from dysentery or bad, spoiled food, or pure and horrible hunger.

Jossey knew about Lexington, she knew about Charlestown, and now she knew about Falmouth. And she knew that people were lying about the troops amassing with the General on the Common in Cambridge. They were not fit, they were not well-fed, they were not well-housed, and they were not well-equipped. They were sleeping in tattered tents and wearing clothes of their own, with no idea if, when the next day came, there would be any food to be had, at all.

The words on the signs went like this:

TO ALL BRAVE, HEALTHY, ABLE-BODIED, WELL-DISPOSED
YOUNG MEN,
IN THIS NEIGHBOURHOOD, WHO HAVE ANY INCLINATION TO
JOIN THE TROOPS NOW RAISING UNDER
GENERAL WASHINGTON
FOR THE DEFENSE OF THE LIBERTIES OF INDEPENDENCE
OF THESE UNITED STATES
AGAINST HOSTILE DESIGNS OF FOREIGN ENEMIES
TAKE NOTICE!

At the bottom of the posters were particulars, in smaller print.

"$12 Bounty to join, $60 a year pay, & the opportunity of spending a few happy years in viewing the different parts of this beautiful continent, returning home with pockets FULL of Money, & a Head COVERED with Laurels."

What laurels?

No laurel was on the head of the good Mr. Prout from Lexington, whose body was in the ground beneath the foundry. No laurel was on the heads of the two older Wabanaki sons who had already left for the army, and whose welfare was a constant source of agony to Jacques and Naomi and their brother Fleep, who had stayed to haul down ore from up country. No laurels were on her

Patrick's two dead crew-boys, or on anyone at Charlestown, or Concord, or Lexington, or Falmouth, or on the head of her brother at sea.

There had just been a letter from Patrick, that morning, addressed to all of them, brought by a fisherman who had gone out for lobsters and crabs, and having ventured further off-shore than he had planned, he had happened upon the *Sawyer.*

The fisherman had found guns pointed at his head, and was forced to find a means to identify himself as an American.

"Identify yourself," boomed out the voice of one of the crew, "or we shall send you to hell with a hole in your chest the devil himself can abide in!"

To which the fisherman calmly responded, "You shall do me a favor. My traps have come up empty all day and my wife shall do worse if I return with no supper." He was given a bucket of crabs from the sloop and made to wait while Patrick wrote hastily on a bit of paper addressed simply, "To My Family at Gun Ball Hill, Tibbetston, Maine."

"I am well. We must do as we must. I shall return as soon as I am able. Would God have chosen to take my life in this war, it would have happened already. I am spared to continue, and continue I shall. Know of my devotion. Speak of me to the children. Keep my name in your prayers. I live for the day I may thank God for having brought me safely home."

That was all. Patrick was establishing himself as the tersest, most strictly formal of letter writers. Jossey didn't care. She was only glad he wasn't dead. It was something to cling to: Patrick, not dead.

"Lavinia, you must continue to keep Patrick safe," she said. "Make sure he meets no harm. This is your job. I trust you to keep on doing it. You must bring him back to Sarah, and to me. Or else I shall truly never have words with you again, and I shall not visit your grave."

The Maine wind with its watery bite took hold of her words and flung them about, like icy little crystals.

They'd built a lean-to behind the foundry with nothing in it but a long, low, rough-hewn, hastily constructed wooden platform, on which were placed piles of packed-down hay, and this became the sleeping quarters of the men who were working in shifts around the clock.

Down from the north came cartloads of ore. Everyone worked like beasts, possessed of an inhuman passion.

Winter was coming. Unlike the last one, it would be fierce, long, and relentless. But it would never be cold in the foundry. Sometimes it seemed that its principal purpose was not for the making of iron war balls—and cannons—but to generate heat and brightness in the dark days and nights.

The foundry prospered. It didn't take long for it to hold the place of center for everyone who lived along this part of the river.

They built a small log cabin—quickly, with just one room—for the weak and ailing Mrs. Pease (who was carefully nursed) and her daughter Sarah, who was a maid no longer. As if that were something beneficial that came from war. A servant was freed from the domestic tyranny of a rich man's house in Salem, and granted the boon of a new life in Maine.

"I'm looking for things to be thankful about," Jossey said. "I sound like William. Remember how he'd always find something to say he was lucky about, no matter what happened?"

Jossey remembered that once, back in York, when she was a child, she and her brother and sister were told about martyrs in the Roman Catholic faith by a Frenchman whose name she didn't recall, who had stopped in York for a rest and much-needed provisions, as he was on his way into Canada. He had thrilled his Maine audience with tale after tale of followers of Jesus being tossed into pits of hungry lions, and speared through the hearts by gladiators, and left to starve in underground prisons.

Jossey's eyes had opened wide with the knowledge of suffering done splendidly, willfully. She remembered Patrick and Lavinia and herself—motherless children—leaping about at play, taking turns with each other as pagans and Catholics, each joyfully exotic. She remembered being tied by her brother and sister to an elm tree, to wait captively while they searched through some woods for lions to come and eat her.

She recalled that blissful, sweet surrender, imagining that her life was given over to God, as though martyrdom were the highest of callings, as though there were something magnificent in dying for a reason. For a right. For a cause. For something that was larger than one's self.

For glory.

But weren't those just the sentiments of a child?

She thought of Lavinia more keenly than ever before. She was supposed to have written for the newspaper as "A Mouth of the Province of Maine."

Would she have saved herself and her husband and children by keeping silent? Why had she been compelled to take that role? Well, because John had wanted her to, that was why.

But it wasn't because of John. It was no good trying to put the blame where it didn't belong. Had Lavinia been vain? Had she sought a certain fame, or a place in the world outside Maine?

Why hadn't she kept silent?

Everyone for miles about had known that she was sitting at the table in the farmhouse dipping her pen into ink, probably (Jossey imagined), composing rhetoric as inflammatory to the sensibility of the English as if she had thrown hot tar in their very faces, then rained down on them the pourings from a bucket of chicken feathers.

Had Lavinia been unschooled, had she never known to read and write, such need to pen words would never have come to her. "It is all Father's fault, for giving my sister so many books," thought Jossey. But that wasn't right, either.

Had Lavinia been looking for laurels and glory, when those things were no more than bits of ice, or dead leaves in the wind?

Now on the farm, look what they had created. Fire, and out of the fire came molten streams of liquid iron. Into the troughs went the streams. Into the smithy went the hard, cold steel, to be fashioned into objects with one purpose only: for the killing of those who were enemies.

How many household things could have been made, in other circumstances, with that metal? Before the start of the foundry, hardly anyone imagined that there was ore in Maine!

And now it would happen that it would all be exhausted in the making of war.

There could have been enough iron objects—spoons, pots, fire irons, plates, implements for the farm, for wagons, for everything— to supply the whole of coastal Kennebec, with plenty left over to trade or sell outright. Instead of cannons on Patrick's sloop, there could have been shipments of Maine products down to Boston and outward, to the world.

Jossey imagined her brother in commerce. She imagined the cooking pots that were not being created on the land she loved, peacefully. She thought of the spoons that were not being made, and the knives, the axles, the tongs, the nails, the tools.

"Lavinia," said Jossey. "War is not as I had thought it would be."

It was late afternoon. Someone was calling. Jossey was in the doorway of the foundry, and turned around. In the shadows of early, foggy twilight, with winter at the back of the wind, just now snarling and starting to bite, Winnie Goodridge was on her way, walking slowly, with a still-steaming pot of beans, just taken off the hearth in the farmhouse.

"Supper!" she cried out.

Jossey had cooked those beans. She was the one who was supposed to have carried the pot to the men. She had left the farmhouse empty handed, having forgotten it. "I fear I had been distracted," she said.

Winnie laughed at her. "I would not be surprised should you forget the head on your own shoulders, considering how things are."

"And what would you imply?"

"Only that there would be things to distract you."

Sarah Dudley was just behind Winnie, with a pot of stewed cod. Naomi was just behind Jossey, with a platter of bread and a bucket of cider. This would be the only meal of the day for them all. It had become a necessity to carefully ration all food. It had not been a bountiful harvest, or a bountiful season for fish, not with the activity of war.

The women changed their expressions, so that the men saw them smiling, as though their backs were not aching horribly, as though fatigue were not bending them down.

When they entered the foundry with supper, the men greeted them with as much enthusiasm as they could muster. They were weary to the bone—John was there, and Jacques, and Tobe Firth, who smiled at Winnie energetically.

Like the rest of the men inside, they were stripped to the waist. Their breeches were soaked with sweat. Their skin glistened, and Naomi Wabanaki threw back her head to laugh with the pleasure of so much male flesh.

She told them, "Gentlemen, I have been a married woman more years than I would care to keep track of, but I must admit to you, this war has furnished me with the sight of such physical delights, I would blush at myself, were I modest."

Jossey joined in. "So would I!" she cried out. She couldn't just stand there letting everyone think she was "distracted."

Sarah Dudley really did blush, and Winnie said, putting down the kettle of beans by the side of a molten trough, to keep it warm, "Your husbands have the bare strong chests of Atlas, Hercules, Zeus, and George Washington, all combined together, in each of them."

Tobe Firth cried out, "Mine is strongest, Mrs. Goodridge," and Winnie nodded solemnly.

"So it is, Mr. Firth, so it is."

"You are a brave, remarkable person, Winnie," Jossey suddenly said.

"You only say so because I carried your bean pot."

"I do not. I said it because I mean it."

She really did. She looked at Winnie, brave, good Winnie, who had thought of the foundry in the first place. It was the same as if Winnie carried about the ghost of her husband. You could almost see him, just behind her: a man who was robbed by the English of the right to do his own work, his own craft. Had not that happened?

Winnie had waited all those years for a means to strike back at English law. The man she'd been married to was put into a nightmare, when the English decreed no colonist could craft goods, but must only produce rough iron bars, to be surrendered to the office of the Crown. Jossey thought about that.

That was exactly what had happened. Colonists who operated iron-works were to furnish the raw materials to be sailed across the ocean, crafted into goods by English hands, then sailed back to America to be sold, at high cost, to the very colonists who could have made the goods themselves—and made the goods *better* (one would naturally suppose).

So American things and American money were to always be kept flowing to the Crown. That had been the plan. So American people were to always be kept in harness, no better off than oxen or field-horses, fearing the English whip.

So American people were to always be kept enslaved. So there would only be colonies. What would have become of American people, were there not this war?

There was no getting around it. There would be colonists only. There would be no American people. Jossey wondered, "Would I and John and our children, and Winnie, and Sarah, and Jacques and Naomi and all of us, and Patrick too, and Tobe—would we all sit down on the ground and say to the English that we shall be happy to remain as their colonists, in exchange for the lives of the Mowlans?"

Jossey gave herself a shake. What exchange?

"Lavinia," she whispered inside herself. "Just because I would hate what war is, is not a reason not to have it."

Jossey heard the children calling to her from the house. They were banished from outdoors—for the moment—for having been discovered, earlier that day, marching down the road side by side.

They'd had one change of clothing apiece, each tied up in a blanket they had taken off their beds. They had been off to join General Washington in Cambridge—Little John to fight his way to wherever his uncle Patrick was, and Vinny to make sure that the Commander was doing things *right*. Lavinia Avens had decided that her part in the war would be to supervise it.

Naomi had spotted them, and then Jossey, who would never have believed herself able to move so quickly, ran after them. They would not be trying anything like that again.

Tomorrow, Jossey will go down to Naomi's family in Winnegance to fetch her baby, who was now called Mowlan, back home.

"Mama, Mama, we shall *die* if we stay here locked up!"

"Mama, Mama, why must we be *prisoners?*"

"Rebels. They have turned into rebels," said Jossey. But before she went to them, she had something to confess about the supper.

"I was the one who made the beans, and I had learned to make them this way, with mustard and syrup, Maine-style, from my sister Lavinia," Jossey said. "In Boston we had used only a small bit of salt in the water, and perhaps a bit of ham."

She was lying about the part of her statement concerning her sister. Every time Lavinia Mowlan had attempted to teach Jossey anything at all about cooking, she would have none of it; she would rather go out playing in the fields with her children.

She was a terrible, inattentive, impatient cook, and she knew those beans would taste dreadful. She knew she had misjudged how much water to put into the cooking pot, and so the bottom layer was scorched, with a taste of burned-ness permeating every bean, and she had added too much mustard. There had not been sufficient syrup to balance it. And she had not soaked the beans properly in the first place.

So she would say it was all her sister's fault. "I am sorry, Lavinia," she whispered. "But I shall have the right forever to blame you for each wrong thing I ever do. It is a small compensation."

Jossey's hands went to her belly. She patted herself lightly, as though she had tasted the supper herself, and felt the pangs of indigestion. She was with child. She had only told John about it that morning, and she had told him that she wanted to keep it a secret, at least for a while, but she realized, by the way he wasn't meeting her eyes, and the way he was standing over the pot of beans, grinning at it, *grinning,* he'd told everyone.

Distracted, indeed.

"Mama! Mama! Let us come out of the house!" came the voice of Little John.

"Mama! We shall never march away again!" cried Vinny.

"Even though the militia is with the General in Cambridge, without us!"

"Even though!"

"I shall go and fetch them," said Jossey.

They were waving from the doorway of the farmhouse, and ducked quickly back inside as they saw their mother coming toward them. Behind Jossey, there was a nimbus of heat; there was the sound of the foundry furnace. Perhaps from a distance, as if an angel of God, or some unearthly, ethereal being, with an intelligence far better than a human's, could peer through the clouds at Tibbetston, Maine, it might seem to be a festive, lovely thing. Above the roaring great Kennebec, in the wintry cold, with an awful wind lashing the air, it would seem that there were brave, clever, peaceful, resilient people, warming themselves with a furnace that never stopped burning, as if they'd created a wonderful sun-on-earth for themselves.

As if there were no such thing as war. As if there were only life.

Reading Group Guide

Questions for Discussion

1.   What expectations do you bring to a novel set in the Revolutionary War period? How did this book meet or challenge those expectations? How does this book compare/contrast with your memories of school-day history classes on the Revolution?

2.   Though the novel is set at the outbreak of the American Revolution, it opens with the story of William Mowlan's capture by the English fourteen years before. How does this episode shape your expectations for the rest of the novel? How do you respond to his comment, "the English have a genius for prisons"?

3.   The opening chapter ends with a horrific event. How does this shape your experience of the story? The author devotes time to developing characters who will not survive the first chapter. Why might she make this choice? How does it affect your response to the chapter's conclusion?

4.   How would you have felt about the Mowlans if you had learned of their deaths second-hand, through other characters, or through a newspaper report?

5.   The novel features a number of point-of-view characters. How do the multiple viewpoints shape your experience of the story? What does this strategy contribute to the novel?

6.   How do you respond to the varieties of grief expressed by the characters? In what ways are the characters both united and separated by their grief? How are they differentiated by their responses to the tragedy?

7.   Winnie Goodridge believes that "revenge" belongs "in the category of things that constitute angels." How do you respond to

this? How does this description shape your understanding of the character? Of the novel?

8. Though the characters are spurred to action by the attack on the Mowlans, most already favored a war for independence from England. How does the author suggest some of the circumstances that brought these characters to this position? How do their attitudes change after the attack?

9. Although the province of Maine is part of the colony of Massachusetts, the characters often insist on the differences between the two. How do those differences shape the characters and the narrative? How do the characters respond in different ways to Maine as a place?

10. In her author's note, Cooney cites the advice she received to "make it real." Does she succeed? In what particulars, in your opinion, does this "realness" reside?

11. How does the author convey the uncertainty and fear of people on the verge of war?

Author's Note

I've always lived near a river. As a kid I had the Nashua of central
Massachusetts; from my twenties to forties, the Charles of Boston
and Cambridge; and now it's the Kennebec of Maine, and of *Gun
Ball Hill*. In my little low-engine outboard I've ventured to the
point where the mighty Kennebec changes into the ocean. There's
an astonishing, wonderful force of elemental powers, and even if
you close your eyes you can tell when you're not on the river anymore. The engine gives a little gasp of surprise, like "The Little
Engine That Could" when it meets the first incline of that hill.
The boat starts to struggle; the currents beneath you change over
to something a whole lot stronger and deeper than what you were
used to. The air opens up. The land is ending. The whole world
turns to water, tides, pure gravity, salt, pushes and pulls, waves,
waves, waves. "Uh-oh," you say, because you know you're messing
with forces a whole lot bigger than you. And it's terribly fright-
ening, and it's grand. And you grip the wheel a little tighter, and
hang on.

That was how I felt the whole time I was writing this novel. I
hadn't asked for it. I started with an idea for a farm on the Kennebec: I'd wanted to do a novel much bigger in scope than anything I'd tried before. The farm was to be begun in the 1770s, and
I'd follow the different families who lived there through, oh, two
centuries or so. But then I happened to read a real-life account of
a Kennebec farmer who was kidnapped by the British to pilot river
boats, and another account, from someone's diary, about what it
felt like to have the British around as an occupying army. And
there came flooding back to me all those stories of the Revolution,
and how my first-ever trip out of my little mill town was to
Boston, on a bus with other fourth-graders, for the Freedom Trail,
and how my first Boston apartment looked out on the U.S.S. *Con-
stitution*, and how I'd thrilled as a kid to all those books about
Concord, Lexington, the Sons of Liberty, the Tea Party. I realized
that the stuff about how New Englanders were the true elemental

force behind the forming of this country as an independent democracy was at the very foundation of who I am as a writer. This book came to me the way the tides come and I never felt so humbled as I felt when I took it on.

I'm no scholar. I'm a fiction writer. I didn't want to do a novel to illustrate an historical period. I wanted to write about characters at an extraordinary time. Real people in places I know, places I am bound to, and defined by: Maine and Massachusetts. I had to work my imagination the way the engine of my boat has to grind and groan when I'm crossing that line to the ocean.

I made rules about research. I knew early I'd do two years, 1774 and 1775, because you have to have some parameters. I read newspapers of the time and every book I could get my hands on, in some five libraries and as many historical societies. I went to all sorts of historical places, including an iron foundry, a bunch of old farms, and all the battle sites. I took no notes beyond a time line and major dates of things. Every time I read something that went beyond the year 1775 I closed the book. My sense of the future became my characters'. So did my sense of the past. There was definitely something very *Twilight Zone* about it, and I loved it. I asked, what did people wear? What did they eat? What did it feel like to be an Indian?

For some four months I crash-coursed this time period, like taking a language-immersion course. Along the way my characters presented themselves: I hadn't planned on so many but they just kept coming in. Two things happened that affected everything.

At one of the historical societies a wonderful woman librarian-archivist, who got me all sorts of diaries and listened to my ideas, gave me one piece of advice: Make it Real. The American Revolution was violent, it was harsh, it was grim, and there were atrocities, and the people who lived through it were not much different from you or me. I got that.

Then one day at Fort Western in Augusta, Maine, where I spent many hours walking around and pretending I lived there in 1774, I talked about my book with a guy who worked there. I told him I was going to build an iron foundry near the Kennebec and have my characters make ammunition for the War. Now, in everything I'd read, ammunition was a big problem, a big lack. It was my own War effort to help out with this. The guy at Fort Western gave me a big thumbs up, and just before I left that day, he came over and presented me with a tiny—about the size of a small marble—dull-gray ball. A gun ball. He said, "I'd give you one that's sized for a cannon but it would probably get me in trouble."

And that was the moment when I got the title for this book, and that night was the night I started writing it. It transported me. If I could have had any wish granted, it would have been this: I would have given a lot to physically be able to time-travel, and the place I'd go first would be Winnie's tavern, then Jacques's smithy, then the Mowlans' farm and the foundry, and then a ride in Patrick's boat. If only.

An Interview with Ellen Cooney

❁   *You have published four previous novels, but this is your first his-*
        torical work. How did you come to write a historical novel? How did
        the experience of writing it differ from your earlier books? What were
        the particular challenges and satisfactions of writing historical fic-
        tion?

On a superficial level, I was reacting to life in the Computer Age, where
everything's electronic and e-mail seems to be the force taking over written communication. A novel's a form of communication. I wanted no
computers, then no electricity, then no anything. And I wanted to do
something to draw from my experience leaving urban life and being part
of building a new house in a rural, wooded area of mid-coast Maine. You
learn a lot about life, and yourself, when you do things like live without
running water—it was temporary, but it changed me. One day when I
was melting snow to wash dishes, it came to me to do something historical. The writing was the same as my other stuff in that it's my same old
way of putting together sentences and paragraphs; like all writers I have
patterns in how I work. But this was a whole new thing because I had to
rely on my imagination so much more. I had to imagine the past, then try
to make it alive. It was a constant challenge to make sure I wasn't just taking a historical event and using characters to illustrate it; I was hugely
conscious of that. I wanted to use the past to make my characters real,
and not sound like a history lesson. It was a joy to feel part of the past, to
sort of feel I had time-traveled. I loved that.

❁   *In your author's note, you say that you began with the desire to write*
        a novel that was larger in scope than your earlier ones. Although this
        book does not span two centuries, how does its scope compare to your
        earlier books?

My earlier books tend to be more introspective. Previously, verbs like
"think" and "feel" and "is" were major action words for me. I've written a
lot about people's inner lives—their hopes, their thoughts, their emotions, and I've also been focused on writing about people's inner drives to
be creative and use their minds. This novel has an actual plot because lots
of external stuff happens—in fact, the external stuff forces the inner ac-

tion of the characters, which is completely the reverse of what I usually do. There is a great deal in the novel of what the characters are experiencing inside themselves, but the events around them are quite large and dramatic.

🌼 *The opening chapter ends with a horrific event. Why make this narrative choice? Was it difficult to create sympathetic characters who would not survive the opening of the novel?*

It's not a choice I actively made. When I first began sketching the Mowlan family, I had no idea what was going to happen to them. But then I began to turn myself over to researching the period, and the thing that struck me was that the American Revolution was a war. People get killed in wars. That is what wars are about. And I began to investigate the fact of the British being here as an occupation army. Those guys weren't like a benign security force, or even a governing power. They were an army. And after the Boston Tea Party, and other early forms of rebellion on the part of the colonists, those guys were mad. If a reader feels one-tenth of the horror I felt when I realized the whole Mowlan family was destroyed, then I did my job. And I loved Lavinia especially. The British knew that she was on her way to becoming a newspaper writer, urging for independence, and I think it turned out to be an interesting, effective thing that the writer would be seen to be dangerous, and would be targeted. It was difficult to keep the careful descriptions of the Mowlans, once I knew what was going to happen. I had an urge to delete the whole chapter and only handle the murders from other characters' viewpoints, but that would have been cowardly of me.

🌼 *The characters are united by their connections to the Mowlans, but the novel pursues their several stories. What were the challenges in keeping the different storylines and perspectives balanced? Why did you chose to include so many point-of-view characters?*

I always have lots of viewpoints; I can't help it. I love working with point of view, because everyone has one. It's what makes us human. It's what makes us unique. In one of my earlier novels I have over thirty chapters and almost every one is a different point of view. It's a way to stretch the possibilities of narrative, and a way to tell a story in which the reader is more actively involved. I don't have trouble keeping the various viewpoints and perspectives in line; in fact, I have to force myself to limit the number of characters. I grew up in a large family, so it's natural to me to have lots of people around. And in a novel, when you have a lot of points of view, you get a much wider, much deeper sense of the world of the novel. And you get to know more people.

🌼 *Late in the novel, you write from the viewpoints of some of the children. What drove this choice? How did their perspectives differ from those of the adults?*

Those kids kept popping up in my mind. I saved their points of view for late in the novel because they needed to have time to actually develop a point of view. And I was compelled to let them speak up, to let them have their say, and to let the reader (and myself, too) look at things, for a minute, from their eyes, and find out what's in their minds. Plus, they're great kids; I feel lucky they turned up at all.

🌼 *In your author's note, you say "My sense of the future became my characters'. So did my sense of the past." Can you say more about the experience of this dynamic and why it was important to the novel? What strategies did you use to keep contemporary attitudes or modes of thinking from slipping into the novel?*

When I was researching the novel, I was careful not to read about anything that happened after 1775, the second of the two years the novel covers. I read newspapers, journals, lots of first-hand stuff. I began to think about events that would have been in the past for my characters, and I absorbed that very deeply. I'd say to myself, "From the point of view of Winnie, or Patrick, or John, or Sarah, I don't exist because I won't be born for a long, long time." And, "Maine doesn't exist as a state." Stuff like that. It was a humbling experience, and also very wonderful, because I had to think about time itself. I am the kind of writer who uses metaphor a lot, and in creating characters, I work with their memories. I had to only use metaphors that would come from the characters' present—in the 1770s—and from the past, which would be their own past years. It was extremely tricky. This is where I had to push my own imagination more than ever. And in way, as I wrote it, I had to not be myself: I really had to not exist as a woman at the beginning of the twenty-first century. I had to be part of the time period myself, fully. I had no conscious strategy about keeping contemporary stuff out of it. I monitored my sentences and phrases as I went along, at first, then it just sort of became natural. I remember one moment when I was comparing something to something, for a metaphor, and my modern brain kicked in with "plastic." Whatever the metaphor was, and I don't remember the specific instance, it would have been perfect to use plastic as a point of explanation or detail, and it pained me to have to think of something else. But it wasn't a restriction. It was quite the opposite. I felt incredibly free in the world of the novel, once I'd got the hang of it.

    What were the special challenges with the language in this book? How did you maintain a balance between language that was appropriate to the period but that was also accessible to the modern reader?

It was like a thorn stuck in my finger, for the first few months of the writing, to work with language, especially in dialogue, and I got so fed up with how hard it was, I'd thought, "Oh, I'm going to write this whole thing without a single line of dialogue," which was nuts, because, besides handling point of view, dialogue is what I'm most competent with. I started with not using contractions because in the printed stuff of the time, there aren't a lot of them, and most historical fiction I've seen is done without them. But it was too weird to have lines with all those cannots and shall nots and would nots, etc. I ended up loosening up stuff that was way too tight, way too unreadable. I experimented with tones and patterns of speech to make the characters as alive as possible, and I realized I wasn't writing for them, but about them. I wanted a reader to be able to get as fully engrossed in their lives as possible. Somehow I figured out a way to strike a balance between then and now. I think I got lucky on that.

    In your author's note, you cite the advice you received to "make it real." Can you point to some places in the novel that were particularly governed by this injunction? Or to choices you made that were guided by it? In what particulars, for you, does this "realness" reside?

The "real" aspect is a big deal for me. The period of the Revolutionary War is so often looked at as a magical time, with heroes who are more like fantasy figures than real people. I tried looking at various Internet sites about the period, and I found a lot of really depressing so-called "patriotic" stuff: there's a tendency in our culture to look at people of the time as one-dimensional action figures, swathed in slogans. The whole novel is more or less "guided" by my desire to truly imagine real people in a real time, without making myths of them, or myths of the events that took place. Myths are great when it comes to things like how the world was created, or if you're talking about gods on a mountain. But history is about us, before. The realness of my novel resides in the daily lives of every character, even the minor ones. Living now, here in New England, we have no concept of what it's like to have an occupation army practicing maneuvers in our town squares, or shooting their guns at people walking around, or putting taxes on our purchases at the store or the post office, taxes that'll go back to their countries. What I tried to do was put myself in the shoes of the people who really had the stuff happen. They were just ordinary people, who had the chance to do great things. But "greatness" only comes when one truly deals with the reality at hand, and determines to try to make things better, even at great risk. I admire those people with all my heart. They didn't need songs to sing, or flags to wave, and they didn't make a big exhibition of proclaiming love for, and pride in, their country. The America they loved and felt proud of wasn't even a country yet. And it's a difference, too, in thinking about ways to approach and understand the past. So many Hollywood movies, for example, have a larger-than-life male action figure at the center of everything. Like that's the way it happened!

🏵   *Are any of these characters or incidents based on actual people or events that you uncovered in your research? If so, what made them suitable for transforming into fiction?*

No, I made everyone up, more or less. It's an old fiction-writing habit of mine. I based lots of the characters on composites of people I know, or knew, in real life. I have lots of siblings, lots of aunts and uncles, and bits of them turn up everywhere, along with neighbors living and dead, old classmates, colleagues, you name it.

🏵   *You lived much of your life in Massachusetts before moving to Maine. How has living in Maine affected your writing or inspired you?*

A reader of mine told me that after I moved to Maine, everything in my fiction started getting bigger in size—trees especially. And more sky, more clouds, more air. And everything has something of the ocean. I think my writing also got more direct, more close-to-the-bone. I'm sure my sentences reflect Maine accents I hear all the time, although personally, I still talk Massachusetts.

You are also a teacher of writing. How does your teaching inform your writing? What is your own writing practice? Do you write every day?

I've been teaching undergraduate creative writing for over twenty years. Every class, through all those years, ended up with me feeling like the student. I keep finding out new things about basic writing, and I've always been amazed and grateful for the students who surprise me with raw, honest, exciting experiments in putting words together. Right now I'm on leave from teaching, and I'm glad for the extra time and energy. I write every day, seven days a week, no matter what, at least for a couple of hours. But once I'm really into a novel, I tend to go flat out with it. I always love that point near the end when I take naps instead of actually going to bed, when I get to write around the clock.

More Hardscrabble fiction

The Old American
Ernest Hebert

"A brilliant work, destined to be one of the great American historical novels."
—*Kirkus Reviews*

"[A] deeply appealing novel . . . A painstakingly researched and beautifully developed reconstruction of life on the New England/Canadian frontier . . . Ernest Hebert somehow manages to capture both the strangeness and the universality of [Caucus-Meteor's] mind and heart . . . The novelist has found a perfect foundation on which to build a replica of a world long since lost to all of us newer Americans."   —Alan Cheuse, *All Things Considered,* National Public Radio

"Grounded in a fine historical sensibility and sympathetic imagination . . . [Caucus-Meteor] is magnificently alive—he is funny and brooding, by turns practical and maudlin . . . and he is slyly disrespectful of all received wisdom and the hypocrisies of European civilization in America."—*New York Times Book Review*

"[Hebert] makes a wonderful leap back in time in this new book—and a good leap forward in terms of craft and accomplishment . . . Caucus-Meteor seems an anomalous creation, as much a character out of Henry James as James Fenimore Cooper . . . [a] wonderful novel."   —*Chicago Tribune*

"Caucus-Meteor is a magnificent creation . . . *The Old American* is history, anthropology, adventure, comedy, and romance. It is a contrary-minded meditation on the pleasures of slavery and the burdens of kingship . . . the best work so far of one of New England's best writers."   —*Yankee*

"A great story, convincingly and colorfully told."   —*Boston Globe*

For more information visit: www.upne.com

More by Ernest Hebert

The Dogs of March

"The book rises or falls on the strength of Howard Elman, and this man could hold up a house. By turns tormented, funny, poignant and appalling, he lodges in the memory—and successfully launches the career of Ernest Hebert."
—*New York Times Book Review*

"The American dream goes belly-up in this brilliant, sensitive, and funny account of what it's like to be a disposable New England mill worker in the post-industrial economy."
—*Mother Jones*

"Hebert tells a story which is a triumph of spirit, skill, and imagination, a moving and oddly optimistic view of our times . . . not only a knowing picture of small-town life, but a human story in which each page offers some new insight into the human mind and heart."
—*Washington Post Book World*

"To the list of splendidly crusty New Englanders created by the likes of John Gardner and John Cheever, add the name of Howard Elman, the protagonist of Ernest Hebert's impressive first novel . . . extremely readable and well-crafted."
—*Philadelphia Inquirer*

Live Free or Die

"For more than a decade Ernest Hebert has been shaping with relatively scant fanfare one of the most interesting accomplishments of contemporary American fiction—a five-volume cycle about Darby, a southern New Hampshire hill town, into which the texture of class is as skillfully woven as it is in Faulkner's Yoknapatawpha County."
—*Boston Globe*

"The fifth and final novel in Hebert's masterful series . . . sure to send many readers all the way back to the first novel."
—*Entertainment Weekly*

For more information visit: www.upne.com

Two by Robert J. Begiebing

The Adventures of Allegra Fullerton

"The 'recovered' memoir is fascinating . . . Allegra describes her transformation
from 'mere traveling face maker' to sophisticated associate of Margaret Fuller and
John Ruskin . . . Allegra's insightful ruminations on the artistic life make up the
lively heart of this book."   —*New York Times Book Review*

"The green landscapes of nineteenth-century New England are beautifully
evoked, and Allegra Fullerton is as keen to catch the play of light in language as
she is in paint . . . the pleasure of the novel derives from its careful specificities of
time and place."   —*Times Literary Supplement*

"Art, philosophy, religion, slavery, sexual propriety, suffrage—all are addressed
with candid clarity. Although the language of the era is sometimes difficult for
modern readers, the effort it takes is ultimately rewarded. Highly recommended."
                                                                —*Library Journal*

"Begiebing has woven a seamless plot incorporating both fictitious and prominent figures of 19th century America to produce an outstanding work of historical fiction. It deserves a place in every public and school library and is a valuable
contribution to American and New England women's studies."
                                                        —*New Hampshire Sunday News*

Rebecca Wentworth's Distraction

"Arresting . . . A truly creepy tale."   —*Kirkus Reviews*

"With Rebecca Wentworth, [Begiebing] reveals a complex character with depth
and compassion . . . He explores the line between genius and madness with his
own brand of passion and brings another strange, strong New England woman
and her times to vibrant life on the page."   —*Concord (N.H.) Monitor*

"Robert Begiebing knows a great deal about 18th century artists . . . He catches
the spirit of that exciting age a century before photography, when people had
their children, their wives, themselves depicted, not to decorate their homes but
to perpetuate their images for prosperity."   —*Milford (N.H.) Cabinet*

For more information visit: www.upne.com

Two by Raymond Kennedy

The Romance of Eleanor Gray

"An atmospheric book, evoking a lost world and a powerful, erotic obsession . . . [the prose is] grave, almost ceremonial . . . Its restraint both suits the New England it describes and heightens the tension of the furious emotions it never quite names . . . a haunting book."   *—Boston Globe*

"A haunting tale from an established voice."   *—Kirkus Reviews*

Ride a Cockhorse

"Perhaps the funniest American novel since John Kennedy Toole's prize winner, *A Confederacy of Dunces.*"   *—Newsweek*

"[A] delicious and diabolical seriocomic novel . . . Kennedy is a wonderfully gifted stylist who in this, his sixth novel, shows all his gifts to best advantage . . . [T]he best comic novel to come my way in a long time."   —Jonathan Yardley, *Washington Post*

"A comic masterpiece . . . a work that has brought gladness to the heart of practically everyone I have known who has read it . . . It is impossible for me to imagine a person with even the most atrophied sense of humor reading the first three pages of *Ride a Cockhorse* and putting it down."—Katherine Powers, *Boston Globe*

"[A] wonderful comic novel . . . a ribald, risible and riveting read."   *—People Magazine*

"The hilarious manipulations of the press and [Frankie Fitzgibbons's] superiors give way to a Fascistic reign of terror over her inferiors, and Mr. Kennedy has us pinned at precisely the point where the comic turns nasty; what began as a madcap charade becomes a suspenseful and not unsatisfying meting out of consequences."   *—The New Yorker*

"Raymond Kennedy is a novelist of such diabolical artistry that he may be the most original American writer since Flannery O'Connor . . . Certainly nobody since O'Connor has so believably mixed farce with the fate of the soul and all-too-human psychology."   —Joseph Coates, *Chicago Tribune*

For more information visit: www.upne.com